LADY DRAMATIC

A Series of Senseless Complications
Book Four

Kate Archer

ARE YOU SIGNED UP FOR DRAGONBLADE'S BLOG?

You'll get the latest news and information on exclusive giveaways, exclusive excerpts, coming releases, sales, free books, cover reveals and more.

Check out our complete list of authors, too!

No spam, no junk. That's a promise!

Sign Up Here

www.dragonbladepublishing.com

Dearest Reader;

Thank you for your support of a small press. At Dragonblade Publishing, we strive to bring you the highest quality Historical Romance from some of the best authors in the business. Without your support, there is no 'us', so we sincerely hope you adore these stories and find some new favorite authors along the way.

Happy Reading!

CEO, Dragonblade Publishing

Additional Dragonblade books by Author Kate Archer

A Series of Senseless Complications
Lady Ferocity (Book 1)
Lady Graceless (Book 2)
Lady Impatience (Book 3)
Lady Dramatic (Book 4)

A Very Fine Muddle
Romance Me, Viscount (Book 1)
Be Daring, Duke (Book 2)
Stand With Me, Earl (Book 3)
Sweep Me Up, Baron (Book 4)
Write for Me, Marquess (Book 5)
Convince Me, Viscount (Book 6)

A Series of Worthy Young Ladies
The Meddler (Book 1)
The Sprinter (Book 2)
The Undaunted (Book 3)
The Champion (Book 4)
The Jilter (Book 5)
The Regal (Book 6)

The Dukes' Pact Series
The Viscount's Sinful Bargain (Book 1)
The Marquess' Daring Wager (Book 2)
The Lord's Desperate Pledge (Book 3)
The Baron's Dangerous Contract (Book 4)
The Peer's Roguish Word (Book 5)
The Earl's Iron Warrant (Book 6)

PROLOGUE

ROLAND NICOLET, THE Duke of Pelham, had not anticipated that one of the difficulties of unloading his endless supply of daughters was how exhausting it would be now that he found himself firmly entrenched in his middle years.

He supposed he had not considered his age because he'd not considered anything whatsoever. It had seemed to him that it must be the easiest thing in the world to locate seven foolish gentlemen to relieve him of his seven daughters. It had been his experience that London was forever drowning in foolish gentlemen. He did not require all of them, after all.

Upon reflection, it was proving more complicated than he'd imagined. His eldest, Felicity, had set a wild beast upon her promising young man and he was lucky to have survived it. Grace, not to be outdone by her sister, had pulled her preferred paramour off the side of a house and landed squarely on top of him. He also was lucky to be alive.

After those two near-misses in the fatalities department, he'd pointed out to his girls that if they were to go on threatening the lives of the gentlemen they were inclined toward, sooner or later they would positively kill one of them. This probably would not reflect well on the family. The duke was never over-concerned with society's views, but he would not wish to attract the attention of murderous relatives who were intent on avenging an accidently killed gentleman. Those sorts of people liked to pack their pistols and issue challenges arranged for daybreak on a lonely green. He was not even a morning person, much less a dawn person.

When it was Patience's turn, she had seemed to heed his advice. She'd not made any moves whatsoever that could have ended Lord Stanford's life. However, such were their relations that carriages and people raced one way and then another across half of England before there was any sense made between them. It might have been less fraught if she'd just shot him in the leg while they were both in Town.

He supposed he might congratulate himself that these things all seemed to come right in the end. He *had* unloaded three of his daughters, after all. Four more of them to get out the door and then his dream of a gloriously empty house was in reach!

That sanguine feeling he wished for did not wash over him, though. Serenity was to take her place in society next. That girl spent all her time either in the throes of ecstasy over a sunrise or the depths of despair over a dead bee in the garden. And *those* swoony highs and weepy lows were what he could expect in their quiet neighborhood in the Dales.

He was the smallest bit uncomfortable to anticipate what might come over her in London.

The duke could not be certain if there was a remedy, but he'd consulted his physician about Serenity's wildly fluctuating feelings. That good fellow had given him a flask of laudanum. He'd forgot to ask the man whether it was for himself or his daughter. He decided to assume it was for himself.

CHAPTER ONE

A Remote Estate in the Yorkshire Dales, 1805

SERENITY LOOKED TOWARD her father. It was the night before their departure from the Dales to Town and they had gathered in the dining room for dinner. She was feeling nostalgic already about the house she'd been raised in. The duke, on the other hand, was currently waving a sheet of paper with a look of consternation.

"You had better tell us, Papa," she said.

"I can guess already," Winsome said. "Nobody sends a letter that aggravates Papa more than our aunt."

"You are correct," the duke said to Winsome. "Lady Misery has taken her irritating impertinence to new heights this time!"

Valor laughed. "It's so funny when you call her Lady Misery. It's even funnier when she hears it, she gets so mad."

"Because it's so apt," Verity said. "A very common thing."

Serenity was used to Verity naming all and sundry a common thing when she in fact knew little about it. In this case, though, she might be right. An insult might be felt harder when the victim of it guessed it might be true. She still vividly remembered Winsome calling her the Queen of the Weeps a few years ago, even though she could not remember what she had been weeping about at the time.

Lady Misery was, of course, their aunt and known in the wider world as Lady Marchfield. While the lady meant well, at least they must suppose she did, she *was* rather miserable.

As it was the moment they were to travel to London for the

season, and as letters had arrived at such a moment in prior years, and as each of those letters had outlined the importance of employing a butler in Town, Serenity presumed that was the current subject of communication.

For three seasons, Lady Marchfield had been determined that a duke must have a butler and had so little faith in his hiring one that she'd installed one herself. For three seasons, their dear housekeeper, Mrs. Right, had driven those butlers out of the house. Mr. Sykes-Wycliff, Mr. Button, and Mr. Grimsby had all been shown the door, or run out the door, as the case might have been. The duke had no wish for a butler, as Mrs. Right ran his household to his liking and did not fan herself over his sometimes unusual habits.

"This time," the duke said, "she has somehow got in league with that vicar who depends on me for his living."

"Oh, Papa," Serenity said. "They must have planned it when our aunt was here for Patience's wedding." She paused. "What is it they planned, exactly?"

"She's determined to install another butler. He's a relative of that vicar's, Mr. Cremble is his name. Apparently, he was meant for the church but could not get a living. So now, *I* am supposed to give him a living? I already support one ridiculous churchman in that family."

Valor snorted. "Mrs. Right will make Mr. Cremble crumble. Or she will make Mr. Cremble tremble."

The duke laughed, "That's good, that's very good, Val. How about this—for however long he is in the house in Town, which I hope will not be long, I will call him Crumble or Bumble or Mumble or Tremble or Fumble—the possibilities are endless."

"Will he be unhappy all the time like the vicar is?" Verity asked. "It's understood to be a common thing among vicars."

Winsome looked as if she would like to challenge that statement, as she was always keen to challenge Verity's pronouncements. However, she said nothing. Serenity supposed she was forced to agree with the assessment.

"He'll be far worse, my girl. Lady Misery writes that she has been assured this fellow is as pious a man as ever lived. Pious, of all things. Pious people look down their nose at everything and everybody—nothing is ever dull enough for them. They should all be locked up together to frown at each other for eternity."

"If he looks down his nose at Nelson or even frowns at him," Serenity said, the notion suddenly presenting itself and making her eyes water, "I will be devastated."

The dog in question was currently under the dining table, making the rounds to see what might be dropped, or directly handed to him. They were all exceedingly sensitive to Nelson's effect on people. He had an unfortunate past, which had resulted in an unfortunate appearance. He was a three-legged dog, blind in one eye, with a rough coat that could not decide if it wished to be straight or curled. His tongue seemed rather long, and was known to drop out of his mouth as if he'd forgotten he had one. His eyes were rather bulgy, and Winsome speculated that they'd got that way because he only had one that worked. Serenity had spotted him outside of an inn and had prevailed upon the duke to have him.

"He will not dare look down on Nelson," Winsome said. "If he tries it, I will inform him of Nelson's tragic past, surviving on scraps at an inn. Nobody wanted him because he tragically lost a leg and is blind in one eye, even though he's the best dog living."

Valor nodded her head in full agreement. "We might even ask Mr. Cremble if *he's* ever tried to survive on scraps with only one working eye and three legs. Let him speak from experience, if he can claim to have it."

The duke roared with laughter. "If Mr. Cremble turns up with three legs, I will be very much interested to see it."

And so they went on, making various predictions on how long Mr. Cremble would last as the latest of Lady Marchfield's butlers and how superior a dog Nelson had proved to be, despite his outward deficiencies.

Serenity followed along the conversation, though her mind

was forever drifting elsewhere. On the morrow, she would begin her great journey. The journey every lady must take if she wished to settle herself well. She would go to Town and be seen by society. She would meet with gentlemen, and dance with them, and most likely wed one of them.

She might have done all of that last year, but she'd begged off using the excuse that Patience would make her too nervous with all the toe-tapping and hurrying she did. Though they were twins, they were not identical. From a temperament standpoint, they could not be more different. Patience had gone forward without her.

That had not really been the reason she did not wish to come out in society last season, though. Patience *was* always toe-tapping and trying to hurry everybody, but Serenity was well used to it. She did not avoid Town for a year because of Patience. She avoided it because of herself.

When she'd been younger, she supposed her wildly swinging feelings had been adorable. At least, that was what Mrs. Right said. Their dear housekeeper claimed there was nothing more entertaining than watching a five-year-old explain to the vicar that biscuits should be available at breakfast because their absence made her weep and God must be against her weeping. The vicar had counseled her not to be so dramatic and certainly not to drag God into her childish concerns, so she promptly gave him an example of her weeping fits.

Her lack of control over her feelings was no longer adorable. She had hoped that as she matured, her feelings would settle.

They had not settled, though! Her feelings were always climbing steep mountains of bliss and diving down to the depths of despair. She did not know why they did so when she did not wish them to. At least, she did not always want them to. Sometimes she enjoyed a good cry.

Serenity fully recognized that it was not rational, but she had difficulty in correcting it. So far, at least. She'd been hoping an extra year might do the trick and perhaps she had improved a little, but she still did not go through life with the calm and unruffled assurance that other people did. Serenity had not the first idea how they did it. Her papa said it was just her temperament and not to be condemned too much. She did condemn herself, though.

She was well-known in local circles for weeping over dead bees wherever she found them. Any insect who had lost its life in the gardens was upsetting, but bees particularly broke her heart. That nobody understood *why* she was so affected was neither here nor there.

Serenity had been stung once when she'd been very young. Mrs. Right had thought to console her by revealing the fate of the bee that had done it. It would die for its impertinence.

That had not consoled her at all. She'd felt responsible for the bee's demise. Why had she swatted at him? She had provoked him. What would his friends in the hive think when he did not come home? Did they know it was her that had killed him? Had his friends all loved him dearly, and now they were bereft? She would never know!

After Mrs. Right had run her stung arm under cold water, plucked out the stinger, and treated it with spirit of Minderus, Serenity had gone out to the garden to see if the housekeeper had been right about the fate of that poor bee.

After running back to the site of the encounter, Serenity had bent down and looked around for over a half hour. She'd eventually found him under a blade of grass. He was dead.

She had cried for quite a while and apologized to all his friends, though she did not know where they were. Then, she thought very hard on how she could honor his memory and his too-short life.

As she'd been only six, her ideas had not been very many or elaborate. At first she'd kept him by the fire in her bedchamber, tucked under a blanket of warm ash. She thought he'd be comfortable there while he made his trip to heaven. Now, of course, she realized she'd been drying out his poor little body so it did not mold. After she'd been confident he was with the angels, she'd ended by putting him in a small wood box. It was to be his crypt and she would keep him in her room so if his spirit chose to revisit the world he would see that he'd been interred with respect.

He had not rested in peace alone in that box, either. Every dead bee she found had made its journey through the warm ash, or in the height of summer a windowsill with full sun, and then been relocated into the bee crypt. After all, that first bee that she had murdered might be lonely. They might be his friends. It was just impossible to know.

She seemed to find more dead bees than one would have thought. Serenity suspected that when one was looking for a particular thing, one saw it everywhere.

Serenity was old enough now to know that the whole thing was absurd. She'd probably always known it, as she'd avoided telling anyone about her crypt of dead bees. She had to get over it, all of it! The dead bees were just an example of how her feelings were irrational and ran away with her in the stupidest manner possible.

Serenity Nicolet was to go to Town and pretend she was a grown lady and all along she had a wood box of dead bees in her bedchamber. From the outside, she did look grown. On the inside was another matter. What were the chances that nothing would occur to send her into fits of weeping when she was out in society? Not very good, she did not think.

She had come close to asking her father if she ought to see their family doctor about her high-strung emotions. Perhaps there was some sort of cure she could take. She'd not asked though, as the duke had joked that the doctor had given him something for *his* nerves.

Clearly, he was just as worried about how she would conduct herself as she was.

She burst into tears and covered her face with her napkin.

"Serenity, not a thing has happened. We are just sitting here talking—what's set you off?" Winsome asked.

"Nothing," she mumbled into the linen.

"And here we go," the duke said. "Hold on girls, the next months are likely to be the ride of our lives."

"Oh, Papa, do not make me laugh," Serenity said, laughing and weeping at the same time.

He was not wrong, though.

"Don't be sad, Serenity," Valor said. "Mrs. Right says we will do a lot of shopping and we can even go to Lackington & Allen, and buy as many books as we like."

"Books, ribbons, bonnets, shoes, and all the rest," the duke said. "At the end of it, we'll see what foolish gentleman is to remove my fourth daughter out of the house."

As was to be expected, this caused various laughing protestations from her sisters. At least, from Verity and Winsome. Valor had just dropped her fork.

"Wait a minute," she said. "Papa, you want Serenity to get married?"

"What else?" the duke asked. "That's what the season is for."

"I didn't know you were going to keep going on with it, though," Valor said. "You already miss Felicity, Grace, and Patience—why would you keep going? I thought we went to Town just for shopping this time!"

"Why would you think that, though, Valor?" Winsome asked.

Valor seemed to be searching her mind for why she thought that. Finally she said, "Because it makes sense. How many people have to get married? It makes no sense that Serenity does."

"Valor," Verity said, "everybody knows a lady has to be married. It is a long-established fact."

Valor gripped her fork. "Stop with all your facts!" she cried.

"Never mind it, girl," the duke said kindly. "You'll see the sense of it when it's your turn."

"*My* turn? I won't take a turn. Serenity," Valor said, clutching at her hand, "you should not take a turn either. You did not even want to go last season. You should stay here with us. You can't be forced to have some strange gentleman in your room all night, staring at you while you sleep. Mr. Stratton does that with Felicity and it's terrible."

Serenity squeezed her hand back. "I do not think our Felicity finds it so terrible. In any case, Val, it is the way of the world."

"Not my world," her youngest sister said darkly.

Goodness, Valor was taking the idea rather hard. Of course, Serenity was taking the idea hard too, if for different reasons.

CHAPTER TWO

ROLAND GARNER, MARQUESS of Thorpe and eldest son of the Duke of Mariton, had been in Town for several seasons. Had one gone round from drawing room to drawing room, inquiring into the *ton's* impressions of the gentleman, one would have heard the following:

"He is terribly reserved."

"Keeps things close."

"Reserved."

"Aloof."

"Reserved."

"Reticent."

"Very reserved."

He was well aware of the impression he made, and equally aware that the *ton* did not know why he made it. Under his tightlipped mien, he was a morass of conflicting feelings. He had learned, early on, that a marquess, or any man, should not be ruled by his feelings. Or, if he was to be ruled by them, they should probably not be so violent in their strength.

When he'd been younger, his brother Charles had informed him of it in a hundred humiliating ways once he'd spotted the weakness. Perhaps their duke would not have noticed that his eldest son was a rather feeling individual if Charles had not been always hanging about, pointing it out, and showing himself to be entirely the opposite in the temperament department.

How many times had his father counseled him to be more like Charles? That did not happen these days, but those occasions were burned into his memory. Of course, his father only saw one side of his second son. Charles kept his ugly side well-disguised when he was in view of anyone he considered of any import. To the wider world, Charles was a suave and jocular Corinthian with smooth manners.

Roland knew what he really was, though. He was spiteful. Charles was endlessly dissatisfied with finding himself the second son. Roland was certain Charles thought he ought to be the duke's heir and he was assiduous in trying to point that out to the duke. There was no particular point to it. It was not as if the duke could simply nod to who he wished to inherit the title. Rather, Charles satisfied himself with forever attempting to display his superiority. It soothed him somehow.

At least that unpleasant fellow was far away from him just now. Last he'd heard, Charles was carousing on the continent somewhere, likely gambling away vast amounts of the duke's money.

Havoc, Roland's rather lazy mastiff, sat at his feet and laid his heavy head on his lap. He occasionally glanced at the drawing room doors, hoping somebody would come in with a tea tray. At those moments when a tray did arrive, Havoc would put on a performance worthy of Drury Lane—longing looks, round eyes, and drool dripping to the carpet until he'd secured a biscuit or two.

His butler, Quinn, came in with the brandy. Of course, naming him the butler was slightly misleading. Quinn had begun as one of his tutors when he was very young. Then he'd acted as valet, and now he acted as butler. Really, though, he was a friend, a mentor of sorts, and the person who knew Roland best.

Pouring out two glasses, Quinn sat down and contemplated him. "You really ought to get married," he said.

Roland nodded, as it was no surprise he said so. He'd been saying so for the past two years.

"I fully intend on wedding soon," Roland said, "it is just the past seasons, well, the ladies, I have not found…"

"What is it, exactly, that you look for but have not found?"

That was a very good question. He hardly knew how to articulate it. He'd made such an effort to present himself as other than what he was. It had seemed necessary to present a mask of manly disinterest and stern looks, to appear as he imagined a marquess must look. It had worked all too well—society viewed him as the reserved heir to the duke. He could see very well that there were certain ladies who admired his reserve. He did not know what they saw in it, but they saw something.

The problem was, it was not him. It was all a charade. He was not the emotionless lord he pretended to be. If he wed one of those ladies, was he to continue the game for the rest of his life? It would be impossible. As it was, he sometimes rode into a lonely area of the park at dawn to shout at the sky, his pent-up feelings needing to be released.

"You ought to loosen up when you're out and about," Quinn said.

"Loosen up? How does one loosen?"

"I was not aware of how you were in society until you held that dinner here last season. That was a head scratcher, I can tell you. I kept thinking, who is this man who does not resemble the man I know?"

"Reserved, you mean."

"Wound tight."

"I do not see what else I am to do. I cannot very well go round being myself."

There was a quick knock on the door and a footman hurried in with a letter on a silver salver. "This just came, my lord. From the duke."

Roland nodded. His father sent letters monthly to inquire into the same matter Quinn was interested in—when was he getting married? The old soldier would be here in person, haranguing him about it, if he did not despise London so much.

"He'll want to know if you are getting married," Quinn said. "He always wants to know that."

Roland tore open the letter and perused its contents.

Thorpe—

How do you get on? Have you proposed yet? If not, get on with it. At this point, I'll welcome any lady with any sort of connection to a title at all. My ideas of shooting high have been knocked down by the ravages of time. I'll even take a baronet's daughter.

By the by, Charles has returned to our shores. He wishes to attend the London season. He writes that he is determined to wed so I have agreed to hand over Marshall Downs, as it is not entailed and he'll need something to support a family. Do not let him beat you to the altar, you've got the advantage there— you're to be a duke!

I told him he ought to go to the house, he's got rooms there, after all. However, he was determined to lease a set at The Albany. I've paid for it, so I presume that's where he's gone. At least have him for dinner. The two of you may not be fast friends, but he's your brother, after all.

I look forward to hearing you've contacted the archbishop for a special license!

Mariton

Roland laid down the letter. "Charles is here."

Quinn glanced around as if he might find Roland's brother hiding behind a sofa.

"Apparently, he wishes to wed and has come to Town to find his bride, so my father has promised him Marshall Downs," Roland said. "Oh, and he thinks we should have him to dinner."

Quinn downed his brandy. "If I know your brother, he looks at the marriage mart as some sort of competition between you. He'll wed the first lady who will have him to be able to say he beat you to it. It will be a pointless victory to everyone and only of relevance to whatever goes on in his mind."

Roland nodded. It was precisely what he thought himself. Charles was forever setting up competitions that Roland refused to participate in, and then proudly proclaiming himself the victor. He understood why Charles did so and he could not say what his own feelings would have been to go through life as the spare.

He sighed. He did not wish his brother ill. But he did not wish him in the same town either.

CHARLES SURVEYED HIS set at The Albany. He'd known his father would come through for him. Very predictably, His Grace had at first insisted that he could stay in the Grosvenor Square house—his brother would be happy to see him.

Of course, Thorpe would be anything but glad to see him. He felt just the same. It would put him in a very bad frame of mind if he were forced to view Thorpe lording it over the household and him being only of second importance. Thorpe was the marquess and he was only Lord Charles. To be the second to land on the sheets was a thorn in his side that could not be pulled out.

It would further annoy him to be always in the same house with Quinn. That butler had been around forever in one capacity or another. The fellow was fond of handing out his counsel when nobody had asked for it. Or at least, Charles never asked for it. Thorpe seemed a willing enough pupil, though he could not see why.

A second son's burden could not be remedied perhaps, but that did not mean he could not arrange things conveniently as he saw fit. The Albany would be very comfortable. From there, he could take his shots when the opportunity arose. He could be a thorn in *Thorpe's* side when he chose it. After all, his brother had all the luck—he ought to feel some heavy winds on occasion. He found it relieved his feelings to take the marquess down a peg.

He'd written the duke that while the offer to stay in the London house was very generous, he was afraid his presence in Grosvenor Square would make his brother too anxious. He would not like to fray the marquess' nerves in such a manner, as they were so delicate to begin.

He'd said something like it a hundred times before. He was the bold one and the duke's heir was…unfortunate.

A hundred ways to say he would have made an excellent duke, but there they all were, stuck with Thorpe. Thorpe, the boy who would weep for days after his horse had to be put down. The boy who was so upset over a house maid sent away after she was found to be with child that he'd gone into the duke's library and stolen fifty pounds and taken it to her. The boy who, even after he was caught and punished, fretted that he might not have stolen enough for the girl. The man he'd become was just the same and he was ridiculous.

Of course, these days, Thorpe covered it up well enough to those who did not know him intimately. He'd grown far taller than anybody would have imagined and he'd filled out. Despite his penchant for weeping over the misfortunes of all and sundry, he'd managed to become a sportsman of sorts. He was particularly known for his swordsmanship. But most of all, Thorpe had taken on the mien of stern and reserved marquess. Charles knew what was underneath that mask, though. A full-grown man who would take on all the world's tragedies and lament over them.

Charles intended to marry this season, not because he had a particular urge to do it, but because the duke had been pressuring Thorpe to do it for two seasons. It would be one more way to prove he was superior.

He gazed round the fine furnishings the duke had provided. He might not be the heir, but he was most definitely the favorite. He supposed Thorpe was made uneasy that he'd come to Town. He'd be uneasy that Charles could, at any moment, decide to relocate out of The Albany and into the house with him. The duke would have informed him of his younger brother's determination to wed, which would make him uneasier still.

He was a second son, all the power he'd got was to make his older brother uneasy.

THOUGH SERENITY HAD wished for time to slow down, it had gone by just as quickly as it always did. The morning of their departure had come sooner than was wanted, but it could not be made to go back to yesterday.

It had taken them hours and hours to get going, which she was not sorry about. Had Patience been on the scene, she would have lost her mind over it. Winsome hid Verity's pelisse twice and Nelson had been a bit too clever in hiding Mrs. Wendover. The stuffed rabbit had finally been found in Mrs. Right's sewing basket.

As they had left so much later than planned, they did not reach the inn they usually stayed in for their first night of the journey. Rather, they stopped at The Wolf and Lamb, and that innkeeper had at first been surprised to discover a duke and his party at his doors. Serenity was so attuned to the feelings of those around her that she could not have helped understanding his rapidly changing emotions. The innkeeper had been delighted to hear that they must have rooms and a private dining room. As the night wore on, that had changed—he had been chagrined. By the following morning, he had looked rather angry.

Serenity supposed the duke's brocabbage pie jest had not gone over very well. It was a Yorkshire staple, he said, and he must have it. After there had been much consultation in the kitchens, he'd informed them that it did not exist—he'd made the whole thing up.

Considering how they took it, her papa had been very naughty in changing his mind to Grassington Hambac, another nonexistent Yorkshire staple. They'd finally heard the cook shout, "You tell His Grace he'll be lucky if I don't serve him some deadly mushrooms and call it a local staple! I know where they are—I can walk into the wood and be back with them in a thrice."

Then of course, the footmen always took the journey to Town as a well-earned trip of merriment and relaxation. Their ideas of merriment began with copious amounts of wine and ale and ended with singing in the innyard in the early hours. They always looked very ill the following day, but that did not put them off it.

As Serenity tended to notice people's feelings more than the rest of her family, she could hardly be surprised that her father thought the inn well worth visiting again. The duke told the innkeeper as much, and somehow did not notice the man's downcast expression.

After several similar visits to various inns as they inexorably drew closer to Town, Serenity was beginning to get the idea that, as a general thing, innkeepers were not overfond of her father. The last one informed the duke that he was closing up and retiring and the building was to be remade into a private house and on no account should the duke attempt to disturb the new owners. Serenity was not certain she believed that.

Though she wished for one more night on the road, or one more year in the Dales, they did reach London. She had, of course, been there in other years. But it had not seemed so loud or busy or intimidating at those times. Those times, she had been one of the daughters not out, there had been nothing at all to fear, and she could safely stay at home and watch the goings-on of her older sisters. She'd even sat back and watched Patience, who was only older by minutes.

But now, all attention would be turned toward her and, she supposed, all fingers crossed behind their backs in the hopes that she would not make herself foolish.

As the carriage dodged traffic of all sorts coming from all directions, her eyes watered at the thoughts running through her mind.

Mrs. Right patted her hand. "There now, my girl, there is

nothing to fear from this godforsaken pit full of rogues and harpies. You are with your family and you have our full support."

"That's right," the duke said, "have you not witnessed the nonsense I have endured with your three sisters who have finally gone from the house? I stuck by them, though it was a trial, and I'll stick by you even though I am certain it will be a trial. What else can I do? Four more of you to get out of the house and my dream is within reach!"

Serenity mopped her eyes. "Do stop, Papa, you are making me laugh." He really was a sentimental father, though so few people could see it.

"Now, here we are and look at this, no Mr. Cremble in sight," the duke said as the carriage slowed in front of the house in Grosvenor Square.

Serenity peered out. It was true, there was no new butler at the doors, as there had been in other years.

"Perhaps Lady Marchfield told Mr. Cremble what he could expect from me," Mrs. Right said, "and he thought better of hanging around."

"Hah!" the duke said. "That would be something—got rid of him before we even arrived. Well now, let us go inside and find out."

As they had four carriages full of people and things, the getting out and going inside was like an army scattering under fire. Thomas raced to the doors and used the key he'd been given to open them. Serenity noticed he appeared delighted to do it. As the senior footman and no butler wanted round the place, he'd been given the keys years ago and had carried them carefully, though he'd yet to use them.

Serenity and her sisters all piled inside, and just then, a tall and thin man came hurrying down the corridor from the direction of the servants' stairs. "Your Grace, forgive me, I did not hear you arrive. I was deep in prayer just now."

The duke looked Mr. Cremble up and down and said, "Prayer? In my house? Who are you?"

Everybody snorted over that question, but for Mr. Cremble.

"Your Grace, Lady Marchfield, she did inform me that you might pretend to have no knowledge of me, however she assured me—"

"I see. You are one of *those*. Lady Misery is rather free with her assurances, whatever they were."

"One of *those*, Your Grace? Lady Misery?"

"The fourth of *those*, if my memory serves me. This is Mrs. Right, she runs the place."

At the mention of the housekeeper, Mr. Cremble did recoil just the smallest bit. Serenity supposed he'd been told something of the stalwartness of their dear Mrs. Right. And how no other butler had been able to overcome her so far.

"Come, girls," the duke said. "Let's get settled. Mrs. Right will explain to this fellow how things are."

They left Mr. Cremble looking as if he were very afraid to discover how things were.

MRS. RIGHT DIRECTED the footman and grooms to begin the onerous process of unloading the luggage carriage. The duke had very helpfully instructed her to explain to Mr. Cremble how things were. She planned to do just that. At least, how she wished them to appear to be at this moment in time.

"All right, Mr. Cremble, you heard the duke. We'd best take ourselves to the servants' hall and have a tea tray. Cook should have installed himself days ago and I suppose he's given you the lay of the land."

She charged forward into the house knowing very well that Cook would have told him nothing.

Mr. Cremble jogged behind her. "Actually, he has not, Mrs. Right. I asked him several questions, but all he would say was that I would find out for myself. He said it in a rather disturbing tone and then got rather surly the last time I asked."

"Disturbing? Surly?" Mrs. Right asked with an innocent lilt. "That does not sound like our beloved Cook at all."

"I can assure you of the truth of it. Last evening, I was served toast for dinner. That was all, just toast!"

"You must be mistaken, Mr. Cremble," Mrs. Right said, though she could not imagine how anybody could be mistaken over what they'd eaten for dinner.

They made their way down the stairs to the servants' quarters and Mrs. Right spotted something new on the wall. Mr. Cremble had found the temerity to hang a silver cross, just at the bottom of the stairwell. She supposed the would-be vicar wished to remind the servants, as they were coming and going, where their real duty lay.

As always with these unwanted butlers, they threw her clues on how to rid the house of them. Here was a delightful clue. If there was one thing a churchman-cum-butler would find terrifying, it was an ungodly housekeeper.

She came to a sudden stop and shielded her eyes. "Take down that cross at once, Mr. Cremble! It is too bright and burns my eyes!" She'd shouted it loud enough for Cook to hear it and then hurried past the cross as if it might incinerate her. She gave the cook a meaningful glance. He was a clever fellow and would catch on to it, even if he did not entirely understand what he was catching on to. They were long associated and he would trust her lead.

"The cross hurts your eyes, Mrs. Right?" Mr. Cremble said behind her. "The cross?"

She did not answer, as she might laugh if she did so. Rather, she hurried into the kitchens, rubbing her eyes. Hopefully, they would become as red as possible. "Cook, there you are, very good to see you, your kitchen maid will be down directly. Might we get a pot of tea?"

Cook nodded. "Already anticipated it, Mrs. Right. It's on the table. Goodness, your eyes, you look as if, well as if—"

"Yes, well, Mr. Cremble has hung a cross just inside the stairs."

"Mr. Cremble," the cook said in a condemning tone. "You ought not to have done it. You can see for yourself that it hurts her eyes."

"But why?" Mr. Cremble asked in a satisfyingly high-pitched tone.

Cook only shrugged, which was just as well. Why on earth would a cross hurt her eyes unless she was in league with the devil?

Mrs. Right went to the very shiny silver teapot on the servants' table and said, "It's the shine of the metal, you see, Mr. Cremble. It is too bright for my eyes and burns them."

Mr. Cremble's own eyes drifted to the shiny teapot that did not seem to burn her eyes.

Mrs. Right heard the familiar sound of boots coming down the stairs. The footmen had got the luggage into the great hall and would have a quick cup before hauling it all above stairs to its various destinations. She looked at Cook with her brows arched. The clever fellow raced to the bottom of the stairs and called up it.

"Charlie, Thomas, there is a cross on the wall. Dispose of it if you will—we all *know* how it burns Mrs. Right's eyes! You remember, boys, a cross will burn the lady's eyes something terrible. Mr. Cremble didn't know it and foolishly put one in the stairwell."

There was a moment's pause as the two footmen took in these clues as to what was going on in the servants' hall. Then Charlie answered. "A cross! Everybody knows a cross will burn Mrs. Right's eyes!"

Clever boy.

Charlie came in and said, "Do not worry, Mrs. Right, Thomas has taken it down and will put it away where it won't hurt your eyes."

"You boys are very good to see to it," Mrs. Right said, sipping her tea.

Mr. Cremble had gone rather pale, which was really saying something since he had been graced with a complexion like raw dough to begin. "I am a godly man, Mrs. Right. I must inquire more closely into this disturbing circumstance."

"What circumstance, Mr. Cremble?" Mrs. Right asked as if she could not imagine what he referred to.

"Why a religious cross would hurt your eyes."

"Oh that, well, it never used to," Mrs. Right said, prepared to spin a story of horrific happenings in the Dales, "but then there was the incident." She let the idea of a mysterious incident hang in the air.

"Incident! What sort of incident?"

"Oh, aye, I forget that you were not in the area at the time. You see, when I was a girl of fifteen, I was lost on the moors. Actually, I should not say lost—I was chased there by a ghostly figure. Gracious, what a cold night it was, moonless and the wind was whipping something fierce. Suddenly, I saw this fire. No, it was not precisely a fire, it was a towering, flaming fire in the shape of a man. It did not bend with the wind and it strode toward me. I was enveloped in the fire but did not burn. I cannot recall what it spoke of through the night but I was in the fire that long. As the dawn came, the fire collapsed into a heap of ashes. And what do you know, I survived the night and here I am today."

Mr. Cremble's teacup clattered on his saucer. If she was not mistaken, Mrs. Right felt confident she had planted the idea that she might have sold her soul to the devil that night on the moors.

"But the cross burning your eyes!" he cried. "Do you not wonder about it?"

Thomas had returned to the kitchens. "She don't have to wonder about it, Mr. Cremble—I took care of it. It won't bother her anymore."

"My brother has written me of the dangers of the moors, but he has never hinted at such ungodly goings-on as you describe,"

Mr. Cremble said, twisting his hands together.

Mrs. Right shrugged. "It's easily managed," she said, "I just stopped going to church. You can imagine, with all the crosses in there it really is painfully bright. The whole place is bright, even the doors. My parents, very naturally, were against my quitting my attendance, what a fuss they put up about it! I was steadfast, though, and not a day later my pa fell off a wagon and broke his neck, and the next day my ma suffered a deadly fever. Unexpected tragedies, one following the other, to be sure. But I reckon if you wished to look on the sunny side of things, you could say it all worked out in the end. Well! I'd better go above stairs and see how my girls are making out."

Mrs. Right rose and left Mr. Cremble to contemplate that he was just now up against one of the devil's handmaidens.

CHAPTER THREE

ROLAND WAS IN his bedchamber, sitting on the bench that ran along the long windows that overlooked Grosvenor Square. The sun was dipping below the rooftops, and a heavy, wet snow had begun to fall. He hoped it would go on long into the night. Snow was to London a balm of white silence, hushing the constant clip-clop of horses, covering over the dirt and grime of the town, and wiping clean the smell of the air. Snow was a velvety white cloak that made London beautiful.

If he had the ability to dictate the weather, he would direct snow through all the cold months and bright sunshine through the warm months. If there must be a heavy fog or a chill rain, then it could be done when all were sleeping.

As it was, English weather seemed determined to favor a heavy fog and a chill rain at every opportunity. Not at this moment, though. The square was quiet, as all the town would be, shops closed and people having hurried to their destinations to shut their doors against the weather.

Just then, an extraordinary sight came into view below him. Down on the street, a young lady accompanied by a matron and a distinctly odd-looking dog raised her face to the sky. She was positively lovely, her light brown hair escaping in soft waves from her bonnet. What a pretty smile she had. She seemed to be delighted to be out in the weather.

The lady laughed and caught at snowflakes to the delight of

her canine companion. He danced round her in a peculiar and awkward manner.

Upon having a closer look at the dog, it seemed the poor mite was missing a leg. That knowledge did give Roland the familiar pang, as visions of what must have happened to cause it raced through his mind, which prompted him to think of the long-ago pony he'd once had who'd broken a leg and had to be shot.

He forcefully stopped his racing thoughts from continuing in that direction and put his attention back on what was before him. Whatever the dog currently lacked in appendages, he made up for in enthusiasm. He was just as joyful as the lovely lady he accompanied.

Roland pushed the window open as the threesome passed underneath. The cold air rushed against his face and snowflakes drifted in.

"Mrs. Right, it is glorious! Has there ever been such a snow in all the world?"

"Aye, it's very nice. A bit chill, though, so we ought not stay out long. You should not like to catch cold before you've even set foot in Almack's."

"Not stay long?" the lady said, laughing. "I would stay out here all night. It is so different from the Dales—look how the lights of the houses show the snow to good effect."

"All very charming, I'm sure."

"And then look how it is covering the rooftops! It is like they've been transformed into marzipan."

"Serenity Nicolet, I understand your enthusiasm, but I must be firm about it," the matron said. "The duke would not thank me for bringing home a frozen daughter."

The lady laughed. "Very well. Come, Nelson, we will go inside and dry you off and give you your dinner, and then we will watch the snow out the windows. We would not like to miss nature's glory at such a moment."

Nelson, as that seemed to be the dog's name, seemed agreeable to whatever the plan was to be. He loped after his mistress, leaving three-legged prints in the snow.

The lady turned round, as if to take in one more view of the snowy scene. She looked all round her, then she looked up. Her gaze stopped at his window and he realized that with candles blazing in the room, he must be very visible. He held his hand up in a wave to see what she would do.

She laughed and waved back. The matron, seeing her charge waving at a strange man in a window, took her hand and hurried her to her house.

Roland quietly closed the window against the gathering dusk and blowing snow. The matron had named her Serenity Nicolet. She would be one of the Duke of Pelham's daughters, just two doors down. She would attend Almack's.

For once, he was anxious to meet a particular lady. He was interested to know this young woman who recognized the majesty of nature. Not everybody could see it. He supposed there were just now complaints all over London about the inconvenience of the snow. There would be speculation as to the messy roads come the morrow. The complainers could not perceive the wonder of the moment.

As well, she had a three-legged dog. He could not articulate why that said something well about her, but it seemed it must. He would have kept his pony as a three-legged horse all those years ago, had that been possible.

And then, when she'd seen that she was observed and he'd waved, she'd laughed and waved back. A small thing on its face, but it said a rather large thing. She had not pretended to be affronted over being stared at. There was no false modesty in the lady.

He attempted to think of knowing another lady who would take such joy in the snowfall or joy in a dog of such indifferent appearance or laugh over being stared at. He could not think of a single one. He guessed that there were in fact many, but they'd been trained out of displaying such things. They hid those inclinations so they might appear in a modest, *ton*-approved manner.

Roland was not so unaware of his own circumstances as to miss the irony of it. He had done precisely what all those ladies had done. He'd fallen to the same pressure to be regular or usual or expected. He'd put on a mask to appear acceptable to the *ton*.

This lady, Lady Serenity Nicolet, had seemed to leave her mask at home. Or perhaps she did not have one at all. The Duke of Pelham was well-known for his eccentricity, and while Roland did not know the daughters who were since married particularly well, there certainly had been stories.

Perhaps the duke did not go in for producing ladies like loaves of bread—all identical in their appearance and just as bland.

Roland suddenly laughed. He supposed he'd find out more about her at Almack's. He also would not forget that she lived so nearby and seemed in the habit of taking her dog to walk in the square. Perhaps his own dog, Havoc, would like to be introduced to Nelson one of these days. He'd been in the habit of letting out his lumbering canine into the small back garden, but perhaps Havoc would appreciate a change of view.

THE NIGHT PRIOR, Serenity had come tumbling into the house from the snow-covered pavement. What a scene it had been on the square! The snow coming down in fat flakes and Nelson prancing around and biting at the air. And then, just when Mrs. Right was making her come inside, she'd looked up. A glorious gentleman had been smiling down at her and he'd waved.

She'd waved back and seen him smile.

Very naturally, this encounter had been looked at backwards and forwards over dinner. Though her father was so very terrible about remembering who anybody was and claimed he had not the first idea of who it could be, it finally came to him.

"Wait a minute," he said, his brow clearing. "I suppose if I cannot recall the names of my fellow dukes that would be a rather sad case. You said two doors down?"

"Yes, Papa," Serenity said, leaning forward and willing him to remember.

"Mariton. The Duke of Mariton," the duke said. "I remember the fellow from my school days—he's always had the house two doors down and we've always been in this one. He's got two sons as far as I know it, maybe more. No telling which one it was. Family name is Garner."

Serenity did not give a toss for which son it was. "Do you suppose he will go to Almack's?"

"Of course he must go," Verity said. "It is such a usual thing for a duke's son to go."

"You do not know that," Winsome said, "though it is probably true."

Valor heaved a sigh. "Every year I get aloner and aloner and aloner. Soon it will be just me and Papa and Mrs. Right. Don't worry, Papa, I will never leave you."

The duke did not look particularly relieved to hear it, as it flew in the face of his claim that he wished them all gone. Though Valor had begun to grow out of her most childish habits, and Mrs. Wendover, her stuffed rabbit, spent more time left behind in her room, she'd seemed to cement her feelings about her sisters getting married. She did not wish for the family to do any more changing.

"Well, let us just hope you have not waived at a valet," the duke said. "It could have been anybody at that window."

Serenity had not considered that possibility, but she really did not think so. There had been something in the way he'd carried himself, though he was just sitting. She knew very well that was a ridiculous estimation and therefore kept it to herself.

Valor was still muttering, "Aloner, and aloner, and aloner."

"Valor," Serenity said, "It was only a wave from a window, not a proposal of marriage."

"But it always starts somewhere, doesn't it?" Valor said, pushing around her cake with a fork.

Serenity did not argue the point. It was true, things always did start somewhere.

Now, the carriage rattled along, getting ever closer to King Street. This was the moment she would be introduced to society. She felt nerves and excitement and dread and an urge to direct the carriage faster and at the same time make it turn back. It was every feeling all at once.

She took a deep breath.

The duke patted her hand. "Do not let your nerves get ahead of you. I make the same speech every year at this moment—you are a duke's daughter and need not impress anybody."

Serenity nodded, though she did not quite agree. She had a great wish to impress a certain person who had waved at her while she was out in the snow. She did not know who he was yet, but for him being one of the sons of the Duke of Mariton. At least she was fairly convinced of it. She could not believe that handsome face belonged to a valet. Her father's valet looked nothing like him. There had been something in his smile…She knew very well she should not be so nonsensical as to be bowled over by the first gentleman who'd smiled at her, and from a dark window no less, but there *had* been something in it.

The carriage came to a stop. It was time. She took another deep breath. Whatever was to come, Serenity Nicolet would use all her self-control to avoid weeping over something or other. It was the only thing that could spoil such an evening and she intended to keep her ever-careening feelings on a steady course.

A footman helped her to the pavement and her father led her inside. If she was not personally brimming with confidence, her dress was. It was a delicious dark blue silk the color of the midnight sky with a pale blue tulle overlay that had been embroidered with small paste sapphires in small diamond patterns. It shimmered with every step she took.

As all of her elder sisters had informed her, if one did not know where they had arrived, one would not be exactly overwhelmed with opulence. The hall they stepped into was not overlarge and everything from the carpets to the curtains appeared slightly worn and faded.

A stately lady in a rich silver satin dress glided up to her father. "Duke, very glad to see you. This is number four, I presume?"

The duke laughed and said, "That's right, Duchess. I'm heaving them out of my house as fast as is humanly possible."

Serenity's eyes widened just a bit. Though she understood her father was full of nonsense on the subject, she was not certain others knew it.

The duchess laughed in response, so Serenity supposed she, at least, did know it.

"Serenity, this is the Duchess of Devonshire. Do not bet at cards with her, she'll take every guinea out of your pocket."

Serenity curtsied low.

The duchess tapped the duke with her fan. "If only I *was* that lucky at cards, my duke would not complain so much about it. Lady Serenity, I will take the honor of filling your card and I must tell you, I have already been approached."

"Approached?" Serenity asked.

The duchess nodded. "A certain marquess has requested to be put down. Roland Garner, Marquess of Thorpe."

Garner. That was the family name of the man in the window. That was the man.

"Now," the duchess went on, "he would not reveal to me how he happens to know of you or know you would be here, but I am intrigued—this is certainly the first time he has ever made such a request. As a usual thing, the marquess is frowning at all the world and appears as if he were dragged here."

Serenity was surprised to hear of him frowning, as she'd only seen him smile. On the other hand, she could not help but feel the compliment of him seeking her out when he'd never sought out any lady before her.

"He saw me walking my dog in the snow," Serenity said.

"That's right," the duke said, "this girl is very affected by sunrise, sunset, and weather of all sorts. I expect she was shouting her compliments to nature."

"I was, rather," Serenity admitted.

"Who would have guessed that would spark an interest in the reserved and serious marquess," the duchess said. "Well now, he requested the dance before our modest little supper and I suppose I ought to comply."

The reserved and serious marquess? Goodness, she had not thought of anything like that. She wondered how he would view her own temperament, which was not precisely reserved or serious.

She pushed those thoughts aside. She had not even met the gentleman yet. Perhaps the duchess had it all wrong. She could not say how likely it was that the Duchess of Devonshire had got it all wrong, but she might have.

"We're calling this thing you put on a supper now, are we?" the duke said with a snort.

"Do not be naughty, Duke," the duchess said, "the eccentricities of Almack's are of long tradition and not likely to change. Consider it a bit of well-bred suffering."

The duke and the duchess further sparred on the merits, or demerits, of Almack's idea of a supper. Serenity paid little attention to it, though. The gentleman in the window was here and had sought her out. He was not a valet; he was a marquess and he had smiled at her out his window, and then he had sought her out.

She put aside the idea that he was thought serious and reserved.

ROLAND HAD KEPT a sharp eye on the ballroom doors, waiting for Lady Serenity to appear. The Duchess of Devonshire had sworn she would put him down for supper and he presumed she would do it. Of course, she'd been overcurious regarding his request, but he'd revealed nothing. What could he say? You see, Duchess, I saw a lovely lady with a three-legged dog shouting at the wonder of the snow and was enchanted by it.

Once the duchess was convinced she'd get nowhere with her questions, she'd changed course. She'd negotiated a deal by insisting on him escorting several other ladies who were expected to attend the night. One, in particular, a certain Lady Matilda, was one of her personal projects. The lady was cousin to her duke, and her lord was determined Lady Matilda make a good match. Lord Devonshire was to turn his irritated gaze away from his wife's current gambling debts if she could manage his cousin being well settled.

None of that was of any matter, as he had to do something with himself until the dance before supper. He'd rather not relocate to the card room, as it was always filled with smoke and gossip. One did not have the luxury of turning up late to Almack's, as the patronesses were delighted to bar the doors at eleven. Even if that had not been the case, he would not have risked strolling in late. Lady Serenity Nicolet would not be standing round with an unfilled dance card.

As he awaited Lady Serenity's arrival, he was attempting to ignore his brother Charles, who had annoyingly turned up. He supposed a younger son of a duke was always going to receive a voucher, though he wished it was not so. There seemed to be nowhere in Town where Roland could be assured of not encountering his brother, not even his club.

"The race is on, I suppose," Charles said.

"What race?"

"The race to the altar. I have vowed to our father that I will wed this season, and he has been disappointed by your lack of progress for two seasons running. I suppose you will not want to disappoint him again."

Roland did not respond. It was one of Charles' long-running

commentaries that he was a disappointment to the duke. He did not particularly believe it. Not these days, anyway. Though the duke had in the past often counseled him to be more like Charles, his father had seemed to slowly grow to have a healthy respect for Roland's horsemanship and his swordsmanship. Both of which were superior to Charles' own skill. As well, the duke was rather approving of the reserved mask he wore these days.

"Perhaps this recent habit of always looking frowning and serious," Charles said, "is not attractive to the ladies. Or, I should say, this mask you wear that has little to do with yourself."

"You might try a mask on someday," Roland said, "I expect it would be a vast improvement."

Charles laughed his brittle laugh that was not really a laugh. It was more a laugh emanating from being stung. His younger brother was expert and enthusiastic about handing round the insults, but not a very sanguine receiver of them.

"Has he told you? He's given me Marshall Downs in anticipation of my nuptials. He has great faith in my ability to accomplish my aim."

As his brother had nattered on, Roland had kept his eyes on the doors. Then, there she was. Lady Serenity Nicolet. She had been lovely in the snow on the square. Now, she was lovelier still.

She wore a dark blue dress encrusted with jewels that sparkled in the candlelight, and her hair, though more restrained than he'd first seen it, was a miraculous shade. It was the softest brown he'd ever seen and seemed perfectly matched to her eyes. Her lips were rather wonderful too, just full enough and turned up at the corners.

"Well," Charles said, "the marriage mart is booming just now. There certainly are enough ladies to choose from. It seems like a marquess could convince at least one of them to step into a church. But I suppose we will see if this season ends like the last two—in disappointment."

"Do shut up, Charles," Roland said, striding forward toward Lady Serenity. If Charles had an answer to that, he did not hear it.

Nor did he care.

"Your Grace," he said with a bow. "Roland Garner, Marquess of Thorpe. The Duchess of Devonshire has been so good as to put me down on your daughter's card."

He turned and bowed to Lady Serenity, who answered with a tidy little curtsy.

"Hah!" the duke said, "the window peerer. The peer who peers."

Roland hardly knew what to do with that assessment so merely nodded. "Lady Serenity, you seemed to be enjoying our unseasonably cold weather last evening."

"It was magnificent," Lady Serenity said.

"I warn you, Thorpe," the duke said, "my daughter weeps over anything and everything Mother Nature chooses to do."

"I certainly do not, Papa," Lady Serenity said. "My father likes to jest, Lord Thorpe."

"Helps keep me sane, you see," the duke said. "Seven daughters are enough to send anybody over a cliff and we live on the moors—all too many opportunities for it. Oh, what ho? Here's another of the fairer sex intent on sending me over a cliff."

Roland turned to see Lady Marchfield, a very respected matron. If he was not mistaken regarding family connections, she was the duke's sister.

"Lady Misery," the duke said, "who let you in? I thought this place congratulated itself on its standards."

Roland's eyes widened, though Lady Marchfield herself seemed to give little notice to it.

"Serenity, you look very well indeed," Lady Marchfield said. "Lord Thorpe, good to see you again."

Roland bowed. "Lady Marchfield," he said.

"Thorpe here has got himself down on Serenity's card," the duke said. "Saw her cavorting round in the snow last evening."

Lady Marchfield's brows raised ever so slightly over that information. She said, "Lord Thorpe, do not pay much mind to anything my brother has to say, and certainly do not hold it over his daughter. He thinks himself original, though the world finds him otherwise."

The duke nodded. "You see what I'm up against, Thorpe." He patted his coat and said, "I've brought a flask of brandy in case you need a nip—Lady Misery could make a Rechabite gulp down a whole bottle of the stuff."

Roland had never been involved in such an awkward exchange in his life. Clearly, the brother and sister were not admiring of one another. Further, the duke was his own brand of eccentric. It was not every gentleman who could work the mention of an ancient sect of Israelite teetotalers into a conversation.

"Do not be fooled by his pretensions of knowing the bible," Lady Marchfield sniffed. "He would be more likely to have a deal with the devil than God."

"You've gone wrong again!" the duke cried. "My housekeeper has a deal with the devil, or so she says."

"I would not at all doubt it," Lady Marchfield said.

Roland looked toward Lady Serenity to see what she would make of her father's and aunt's exchanges. He had imagined she'd be ready to sink through the floor at the insults hurled back and forth. As it happened, she did not look at all perturbed. She must think what was occurring was quite usual. Perhaps it was.

He supposed he ought not be too surprised. His relations with his brother were not much better. Perhaps all families had such disputes? If they did, they hid it better than the duke and Lady Marchfield.

"Your Grace, Lady Serenity, Lady Marchfield," a voice said behind his shoulder. It was a voice he knew all too well and had just left on the other side of the ballroom. Charles.

"Lord Charles," Lady Marchfield said.

"Lady Marchfield, the Duchess of Devonshire has very kindly put me down on your niece's card, if she does not object to it."

Lady Serenity said, "No, certainly I would not object."

"Lord Charles is Lord Thorpe's younger brother," Lady

Marchfield said, explaining the connection.

"Hah!" the duke said, "that is amusing, is it not? Two brothers take Serenity round the floor. Not at the same time, I hope."

"I have been given the honor of the first," Charles said.

Of course he would have run to the duchess and asked for it, Roland thought. As soon as he'd seen Roland approach the lady, he'd been determined to find out more. His brother would have seen that he'd taken the dance before supper and decided to make it into some sort of competition. There was nothing Charles could not make a competition out of.

"I will lead Lady Serenity into supper," Roland said.

"Ah," the duke said, pointing at Charles, "he's got you there, has he not? He got you on the title, and now he's got you out the gate at Almack's. Though, naming it a supper is very complimentary and entirely a fib. I wouldn't feed that nonsense to my dog, and he's only got three legs and one working eye."

Charles' back stiffened. The duke would not know he'd just hit a very sore spot by mentioning the title.

"Roland!" Lady Marchfield hissed.

Roland turned to her in alarm, but she was glaring at her brother. Then he recalled that they both carried the same given name.

"Papa, you know perfectly well that Nelson is the best dog in the wide world, despite what might look like deficiencies."

"So I've been told many times, my dear," the duke said. "I suppose that's why he gets the best of our meats for his dinner?"

"Just so," Lady Serenity said. She turned to Roland and Charles. "We discovered Nelson outside of an inn. He was surviving on scraps."

"Scraps?" Charles said. "How cruel!"

This pretending to be shocked seemed to strike Lady Serenity rather hard, though it was nonsense. Charles did not have a care for animals at all, and it had caused many a rift between them over the years.

The orchestra had been tuning for some time. Now couples

began to move to their places for the cotillion. "Lady Serenity," Charles said, holding out his arm.

His brother led the lady away. Roland suppressed a sigh and walked off to find Lady Matilda.

CHAPTER FOUR

CHARLES COULD SEE very well that Thorpe had an interest in Lady Serenity. He did not suppose it was surprising—the lady was very comely and she was a duke's daughter. As his brother *did* have some kind of interest, it amused him to walk off with her for the first.

As they waited for their turn at the steps, he said, "Lady Serenity, have you known my brother long?" He would like to get a feel for where, if anywhere, things might be going.

"Oh no, we were just formally introduced tonight. He, well, he did see me out his window last night. It was snowing and glorious, so I took my dog out for a walk."

"Ah, the three-legged dog?"

Lady Serenity nodded. "Nelson," she said.

Charles laughed. "Is he named after Lord Nelson?"

"Indeed, he is. My sisters and I felt it both honored his missing leg and distinguished him."

The whole idea of taking in a three-legged cur one found loitering outside of an inn was absurd. Naming it after the greatest naval man in the history of the world was worse. Particularly for a duke's daughter. She really should have some sort of rarified breed she could be proud of. However, she seemed to be quite enthusiastic over this Nelson. He suspected she was of the sentimental variety of lady and he was determined to test out the theory.

"I must admit," he said, "I was shocked to hear that Nelson had been surviving on scraps before you rescued him. That innkeeper ought to be ashamed of his neglect of the poor thing."

"Yes, just so! Actually, I do believe he was the littlest bit shamed when he saw how we all were so taken with Nelson. It was as if he saw the little dog who'd been living at his doors with new eyes."

New eyes, indeed. Charles deemed himself correct in his assessment regarding the lady's sentimentality. "Quite right he do so," he said. "Let us hope it causes that innkeeper to do better in future."

Lady Serenity nodded vigorously. It seemed he was hitting the right notes with her.

"Well, it's all come right now, has it not?" Charles asked. "Nelson finds himself in more luxurious circumstances than he could have dreamed of."

"My father says we spoil him, but he spoils him more than anybody. He always pretends to accidently drop bits of meat at table and Nelson is right there waiting for them. Do you have a dog, Lord Charles?" he asked.

Of course, he did not have a dog. His father maintained a pack for hunting, but he could hardly be expected to drag a dog hither and thither. That idea would not suit Lady Serenity though.

"I fear it will be some time before I have a dog again. I was too wrecked about losing my dear Nero to old age last year."

He worked to look suitably sad, though no such dog had ever existed.

"Oh, I am sorry. It is heartbreaking," Lady Serenity said.

If he was not mistaken, her eyes were teary. She was set to weep over a dog that had never existed. If there was anything that might fix her temperament in his mind, this was it.

Disturbingly, her temperament was very like Thorpe's own—weeping over the plight of animals every time one turned round. She might be admiring of such nonsense.

But that was only if she knew it. Thorpe kept his real nature very under wraps these days. Perhaps there was something to be done with that.

"Do you also live on Grosvenor Square with your brother?" Lady Serenity asked. "I assume it is a family house?"

"It is a family house," Charles said, "But at the present time, I am at The Albany." Charles paused. This was the moment he'd really have to paint a picture that was not at all the truth of the situation, but very much to his benefit. "Nero and I spent many good years in that house and made a lot of memories. I think you can imagine how that might pain me. Because of my loss."

"Goodness yes, I certainly can. I could not bear it. You are quite right not to put yourself through it."

He had guessed right. Good luck to the seemingly reserved marquess in besting him. "I thank you for the sentiment. It is the sort of thing my brother cannot understand. He finds it too sentimental, I suppose."

This seemed to give the lady pause.

"Oh, I see, yes, the Duchess of Devonshire mentioned he was very reserved."

Did she, now? Excellent. He need only reinforce that idea. If he had understood the situation sufficiently, Lady Serenity was a rather soft touch. She would not prefer a frowning and serious marquess. The marquess, however, did prefer her. Else, why would he make it a point to approach the duchess to get on the lady's card?

There was some mischief to be made here, and he was happy to make it.

SERENITY WORKED VERY hard to keep herself on an even keel. So many things were affecting her! When the marquess had approached, she'd felt her heart in her throat. He was positively glorious up close. He was tall and broad-shouldered and impeccably dressed. She noted his hair, which had seemed a darker shade as he sat at his window, was a charming dusky blond, the type that would lighten and darken with the seasons. His eyes, which she had presumed were brown, were in fact a very deep blue. Perhaps his most attractive aspect, though, was that his bone structure was so distinct and strong-looking. There did not seem to be an ounce of padding on him and it gave him a rarified and sophisticated presence.

The idea that a man such as that had sought her out specially had near overwhelmed her feelings.

Then, dancing with his brother, she'd come very close to weeping. Poor Nero! She could not bear to hear of any animal dying of old age. Why did there need to be such a thing? Poor Lord Charles was heartbroken over losing his beloved dog.

After that, she'd gone on to dance with several other gentlemen and it was speedily becoming apparent to her that she would have to guard her feelings very carefully indeed. One never knew when a gentleman would say something to set them off.

Lord Kilgard had mentioned a new horse he'd bought at Tattersall's and she'd inquired into the old horse. He'd just shrugged and said he did not know—he'd handed it over to the stablemaster. Anything might have happened to that poor horse, and Lord Kilgard did not know the first thing about it. Her eyes had stung as she imagined the worst.

Lord Metley had described sailing on his rather large lake. The description of setting off at sunrise and the breeze catching the sails as the light came over the hills was devastatingly beautiful, and she'd almost wept over that.

Lord Littleton remarked that he'd not been sure he would make it inside the ballroom before the doors closed. He and his brother had been all the day long resetting their old cook, as he'd begun to go a little funny in the head. He could not be trusted around lit fires anymore and so they'd hired several caretakers to watch over him. It was so kindly done that once more she felt her eyes water.

She began to wonder if her family avoided certain topics that might set her off, as this night it seemed every time she turned round there was something to send them shooting high or falling low. As always, her eyes did not seem to care which direction her feelings were going, as they liked to water whenever they were going somewhere.

Now she was to dance with the marquess and she was a bundle of feelings. He was so handsome that her heart beat faster at the sight of him. But then, his brother had described him as so different from himself. Lord Charles was genially sentimental, but claimed his brother would not understand his feelings over his dog?

First the Duchess of Devonshire and then Lord Charles had hinted that Lord Thorpe was rather…austere. It was hard to believe, considering the way he'd smiled out the window. He had not looked unsentimental or reserved then.

Who was he really? She could not be certain, but even so, she knew she liked him. She could not help but to like him. It had been an instantaneous thing. How funny that it would be—Patience had done just the same. She'd laid eyes on Lord Stanford and had been set on him. At the time, Serenity had really wondered at the wisdom of it. Here she was doing just the same.

She was determined to keep a tight control over herself while in the presence of Lord Thorpe, as it did not seem as if he were the sort of gentleman who would appreciate a weeping lady.

He had come to collect her and they had danced a lively Scotch reel. Between their turns, he'd asked her about the Dales. He said he'd always had an interest in traveling there but had not yet had the opportunity. Serenity described the sunrises over the moors, and then noticed she was getting a bit carried away with it and regained control over herself.

The dance had come to an end and Lord Thorpe held his arm out. She laid her hand gently upon it. It was thrilling to be led into the dining room on his arm.

They were seated at the far end of the table, though just as they sat down it seemed Lord Thorpe looked unhappy about their placement. She followed his eyes and found Lord Charles had hurriedly sat down across from them. It was a very wide and square table, so she did not suppose there would be any conversation across it. She could not work out why the two brothers stared at one another as they did.

Lord Thorpe wrenched his gaze from Lord Charles and turned to her. Tea was brought, along with dry cake, as Lord Thorpe warned her against the sour lemonade and barely buttered, very stale bread.

Serenity said, "My three sisters who came before me all warned me off the lemonade. Felicity said it was so sour it could curl your hair."

Lord Thorpe nodded. "That is an apt description of it. I believe the patronesses find a delight in promoting suffering at supper. I imagine they see it as their members proving they are willing to be inconvenienced by the institution."

Serenity could not care less what was on the patronesses' minds. She was determined to see if the marquess really was as unsympathetic as his brother made him out to be.

"Lord Charles told me of his tragedy," Serenity said.

"His tragedy?" Lord Thorpe asked. "Is he calling being a second son a tragedy now?"

"A second son? No, he did not speak of that at all. He spoke about the loss of Nero."

"Nero? Who is Nero?" Lord Thorpe asked.

Serenity took in a little breath. Could it be true that Lord Thorpe did not even remember the name of his brother's so dearly loved dog? It did not seem possible.

"His dog, Lord Thorpe."

"He has a dog?"

"Had a dog," she corrected. "Poor Nero sadly died of old age last year."

"Did he?" Lord Thorpe said in a rather dismissive tone.

She could hardly believe it. It seemed that Lord Thorpe re-called nothing about the beloved dog. She did not know what to make of it.

"Lady Serenity, though you do not know either of us particularly well, I will caution you that my brother may…exaggerate, I suppose would describe it politely. If he ever had such a dog, I know nothing about it."

This was disheartening indeed. What was she to do? As for looks, she was so drawn to him. But was his temperament suited to her? Could she love a man who'd forgotten all about a beloved dog? What did that say about how such a man would treat Nelson? Though Nelson lived as a family dog, he was very much her dog and would come with her when such time came to leave the house.

"Lord Thorpe, do you dislike dogs?" she asked. "I understand that not everybody is enamored with them."

"Dislike dogs? Certainly not. I am in possession of a great beast of a slobbering dog named Havoc. We get on very well."

That was encouraging, of course. But she had not seen him walking a dog. How did he treat him? Did he only have a great beast of a dog because a marquess ought to have one? Did he have him locked up somewhere?

"I have been thinking that Havoc might like a walk round the square. Do you often take Nelson out?"

"Indeed, yes," Serenity said. "My aunt does not like it, she thinks he should be hidden from view on account of his missing leg and his being not very showy."

Her father tapped her on the shoulder. "Guess whose brandy flask is empty?"

Serenity laughed. "I will guess it is yours, Papa, as you would be the only gentleman to have brought one."

"As far as we know. Now, Thorpe, your brother is a shame-less opportunist. He went out of his way to inform me that he would have me to dinner if he had the space for entertaining properly. Apparently, he is in an apartment somewhere or other.

Then he executed a long pause heavy with suggestion. I can ignore a hint as well as the next man, but then I thought it might be amusing to have both of you to dine. Thursday, if you can clear your calendar to attend us."

A look of consternation had flashed on the lord's features but he quickly recovered an appearance of equanimity. "Consider my calendar cleared, Your Grace."

Goodness, both brothers were to come to dine. Serenity was not at all certain her father realized how clever that was. It would be something to see them both in close quarters. She would receive clarity on who Lord Thorpe really was.

He must be as she hoped he was, despite not remembering anything about poor Nero. She was so drawn to him that she did not want to look away, she could not look away.

"Well, my girl? Can we be off from this den of dullness? Who knows what's happened at the house since we left it. With any luck, Mr. Cremble has run out of it to get away from my devil of a housekeeper!"

They left Lord Thorpe a bit wide-eyed and set off for home. As the carriage horses clip-clopped through the quiet streets of the early morning, the duke said, "I probably should not bother asking."

"Asking what, Papa?"

"Three times over three seasons I have looked at one of my daughters in this very carriage and said, 'So is this to be it? Have you settled on him?' Each time I am told no, certainly not, when in retrospect, I ought to have been told yes."

"Oh, I see, you mean in regard to Lord Thorpe."

"Of course in regard to Lord Thorpe."

"Well, then, I will not say no. I will say I hope so. I hope he proves to be everything I have imagined."

The duke snorted. "Nobody in the wide world could be everything *you* will have imagined."

Serenity ignored her father's teasing. "You see, it's just that, well…"

"Out with it, my girl."

"It's just that when I look at Lord Thorpe I cannot look away. He really is perfect, Papa. But then, it was Lord Charles who said things that I wish Lord Thorpe had said. Lord Charles lost a beloved dog and was devastated, but Lord Thorpe claimed he did not even remember the dog. Could a gentleman be right for me who does not remember a dog?"

"Not when you remember every dead bee you've ever hunted down in the garden."

Serenity nodded, though she did not mention that said bees were currently in her bedchamber in their crypt.

"So one looks right and the other one talks right," the duke said. "Is that the size of it?"

"That is the size of it."

"Well, no matter. These things have a way of clearing themselves up over time."

Serenity leaned back in her seat. She supposed her father was right. Though she'd really prefer if they would clear themselves up this instant.

CHAPTER FIVE

ROLAND HAD BEEN left sitting alone at the dining table at Almack's. Charles caught his eye and smiled at him, as if satisfied with the situation. He'd not stayed long after that, as there really was no point to it.

He had, at first, viewed Charles turning up at Almack's as a simple irritation. Now he'd begun to think differently. It was becoming clear that Charles had decided to compete with him for Lady Serenity's attention. Whatever Roland was interested in, Charles must have.

He'd not heard the whole story about the mystery dog Nero, but he suspected that Charles had noted Lady Serenity's sentimentality over her three-legged dog and had invented one of his own. He'd certainly never owned a dog and Roland was glad of it. Charles had so little care for anything but himself that he could not imagine another being having to depend upon him. Very typical of Charles to claim the dog was dead, as that would be the most convenient for him.

Roland wondered what Lady Serenity thought of it all. He dearly hoped she would not be taken in by his brother. What a lady! She was the most lovely lady living, of that he was certain. Then, there was something in her manner that was so charming. Her enthusiasm in speaking of her dog, or the Dales, or her sisters, or her father, had really been very touching. Her eyes, those beautiful brown eyes, fairly sparkled in the candlelight as if she was near overcome with the recollection. She really was perfect.

He smiled to himself as he thought of the duke. Had it been any other lady, he would be counting the duke's behavior as a strike against her. The conversation between His Grace and Lady Marchfield had been positively outrageous. And yet, he found he did not give a toss for whatever outrages might emanate from her father.

Quinn entered his bedchamber with two glasses of brandy. Roland sat on the windowsill, keeping an eye out on the square. It seemed vastly unlikely that Lady Serenity would appear out there with her dog at this late hour, but he was compelled to watch anyway.

Quinn handed him his glass and sat in his preferred leather chair by the fireside. Havoc struggled to his feet, having just woken from a doze, and ambled over to the chair. He unceremoniously threw his head on Quinn's lap for a scratch. "Was she everything you imagined?" he asked, looking down at the dog and petting his very large head.

"I did not imagine anything."

"I see."

Of course, Quinn knew him inside and out and knew perfectly well that he had been imagining. "She is," he said.

"Very good news, very good indeed. I suppose you will initiate a pursuit."

Roland was silent for a moment. Of course, he would pursue. Quinn was as yet unaware that Charles was making a game of it though. "Charles was there, and seemed to notice my interest."

Quinn issued a small groan, as his butler would well know what that meant.

"Charles finagled an invitation to dine from the duke, and I have been invited too."

"Here we go," Quinn said. "Your brother will be thinking night and day how to best you regarding the lady. You had better begin thinking the same. This is one competition he cannot win—

it is the first and only time you have showed positive interest in someone. He cannot be permitted to meddle with it."

Roland had been thinking along the same lines. Charles had already meddled with it in his own way. "He noted that Lady Serenity is very fond of her three-legged dog, and spun a story of having lost his own beloved dog. Nero was his name."

Quinn chuckled. "Charles having a beloved dog. It's preposterous."

"The lady will not know that, though," Roland pointed out. "I think I will arrange to have a special dog collar made for Nelson, just as I did for Havoc."

He'd harbored a lingering fear that Havoc would be lost, or even stolen. Especially when he'd been a puppy. He still worried about him becoming lost, but stolen was less of a risk these days. He could not imagine what person could wrestle that lug of a dog into a conveyance. In case he *was* lost, he wore a black leather collar with an inscription on the inside. The message read similar to the newspaper advertisements for lost dogs by offering either a reward for return or prison for failure to do so. "Havoc, of the Marquess of Thorpe's household. Reward or law."

Had he more room to expand the inscription, he'd have informed whoever had his dog that he'd better bring him back or he would be tracked down by the Marquess of Thorpe. If one hair on Havoc had been harmed, the perpetrator would be torn limb from limb. Or something along those lines.

"A collar. Very good thought," Quinn said. "Let Charles wax on about his invented dog while you do something tangible and practical for a real dog."

"I will arrange it on the morrow so it arrives before the dinner."

"And flowers. You ought to send flowers."

"The message must be careful," Roland said. "It must indicate interest but not be so forward as to startle the lady or annoy her father."

"Pink musk roses would say what needs to be said at these

early days."

Roland nodded. Pink for new beginnings, and musk roses for the lady's charm.

"You will likely have Charles on the backfoot with the effort; he never thinks much about doing anything for anybody. He will depend upon himself to turn up at that dinner and turn on his alleged charm as being quite sufficient."

"You are probably right," Roland said. Though, one never knew with Charles. If only his brother would find happiness in his situation in life. Nobody picked Roland to be the heir or denied Charles the opportunity. It was just the chances of birth order. As well, being the younger son of a duke carried quite a few advantages. Charles was afforded respect everywhere, he'd been gifted Marshall Downs, which was a large estate, he had access to all the funds he could wish for, he was not forced into the army or the church, and he would never have the headaches that came along with managing a dukedom.

"Now, to a stickier question," Quinn said. "Who, exactly, did Lady Serenity meet with at this first introduction? Was it you, or was it the reserved marquess you've been pretending to be?"

"The reserved marquess," Roland answered. "I do not wish to frighten her off with the true me."

"Until when? You cannot keep up the mask forever. Sooner or later, you'll see something that sets you off. You'll pass by a limping horse and think about your old pony and weep at the sight. If she does not understand your real temperament, she will presume you've gone insane."

"Perhaps I can change, though. Perhaps I can be what I only act now."

"People do not change who they are," Quinn said. "In any case, I would not wish you to. You are a good man who cares for your fellow beings on this earth, and there is not a thing wrong with it."

Roland did not suppose there was a thing wrong with it when it was described that way. It was another thing when his feelings entirely overtook him. He perfectly well knew what set him off. A person or animal powerless and being hurt—that set him off. He was relatively sure it all led back to his pony. He'd been riding Balthazar when he broke his leg by galloping right into a deep hole in a field. The horse had to be put down. His father had made him do it, he'd been forced to pull the trigger. The duke said that if a man were to own animals, that man must take responsibility for them right up to the end. Roland felt that to be true and he knew putting Balthazar out of his misery was a kindness. A horse could not survive on three legs, as much as he wished it were possible. That entire horrendous morning was burned into his memories. Anything at all remotely like it set him off.

He was not certain what to do about how he appeared to be the unfeeling marquess. Perhaps he could inch very slowly away from his alleged reserve but not all the way to who he really was. He might find a happy medium of some sort.

But not while Charles was sniffing around. He had to be got rid of first. Somehow.

Mrs. Right was just now engaged in a game of cat and mouse with Mr. Cremble. Or a game of ungodly housekeeper and pious butler, as the case was. She'd planted the idea that she might be in league with the devil and he'd been watching her carefully at every opportunity. Though she was tickled to pretend she did not see him peering round doorframes, she had, for some days, been stuck on what to do next. How did one confirm that one was in league with the devil? It was the sort of thing that did not come up in everyday conversation.

Then, as these butlers always seemed to do, he gave her a direction to follow. Cook had spied him slipping into the servants' hall and affixing a small cross underneath the table at her place.

Mr. Cremble meant to test her like their very own Spanish Inquisition! It was too convenient, really. His worst fears were about to be horrifyingly confirmed.

Some hours had passed and that time of day had arrived when all the servants would gather for tea. She noticed Mr. Cremble had hurried ahead of her, no doubt to be in place to view his test.

Mrs. Right took her time down the stairs. When she turned the corner into the servants' hall, she would launch the performance of a lifetime.

She suddenly shielded her eyes. "Why is it so bright down here? Oh, it burns my eyes. I can come no closer."

Mrs. Right heard the very recognizable sound of a chair scraping the stone floor. She peeked out between her fingers. Mr. Cremble had leapt from his place and was as white as the inside of a turnip.

Charlie, who was well aware of the game, looked around at the walls and said, "Mr. Cremble, you ain't gone and hung a cross somewhere again?"

Mr. Cremble pointed a shaking finger at the table. "It's underneath the table, out of view," he whispered, "how did she know?"

"Stand back, Mrs. Right," Charlie said, "I'll handle it."

She could see Charlie dive under the table and then come back up again with the offending cross. For good effect, she staggered back at that moment. She wished to give the impression that while she could not see it, she could feel it come closer.

"I'll get rid of it, Mrs. Right," Charlie said in a comfortable tone, as if he were chasing a fly out of the kitchens.

He put it under his livery coat and jogged past her. She fell back in a dramatic retreat.

Mr. Cremble cried, "Does nobody wonder about this?"

Cook, who'd been watching things unfold with his usual brand of equanimity, said, "We wonder about you, Mr. Cremble. If you know a cross hurts the lady's eyes, why did you go and hide one for?"

"*Why* does it hurt her eyes, though?" Mr. Cremble cried. "It was under the table, it was not in view, how could it have hurt anybody's eyes?"

Cook shrugged. "People got peculiarities, Mr. Cremble. It's my opinion that a sensible man just works round 'em."

"Works around a cross burning the housekeeper's eyes?" Mr. Cremble whispered as if he'd never heard of such an idea. Which, Mrs. Right supposed, nobody ever had.

She pressed her lips tightly together and worked to look exhausted from her recent encounter with a cross.

Charlie had jogged up the stairs and was now well away. Mrs. Right dropped her hand from her eyes and smiled. "There now, that's better. Well! Tea is on, is it?"

As Mrs. Right strolled to the table as if there were not a thing wrong, Mr. Cremble backed away from it. He turned on his heel and fled up the stairs. Mrs. Right presumed he would keep going all the way up to his quarters. He would take up his bible and search it for clues regarding what ought to be done to fight the devil. She hoped he found some passage that said: "Get out of the house, Mr. Cremble."

The only hole in her plan was that it must not go on for too long a time. She must get Mr. Cremble out of the house before he wrote to his relation, the duke's vicar in the Dales, about his current circumstances. It would all fall apart when the vicar wrote back that Mrs. Right was a regular attendee at church, had never complained about her eyes burning, and was in the habit of wearing a small gold cross under her fichu that she often mentioned as having been given to her by her parents. He might also mention that her father had not died falling off a cart, and her mother had not died of fever. That vicar knew too much about her!

There must be the final push to get Mr. Cremble out the door, though she did not yet know what that would be.

She satisfied herself that it would all come right in the end.

Mr. Cremble would be driven out of this house and Lady Marchfield would be forced to find him another place. Then the poor fellow would land in a house that actually wanted a butler.

Mr. Cremble could not know it, but she'd have done him a kindness.

SERENITY FELT AS if her life were speeding up in some manner. There had been so many days in the Dales where not a thing out of the ordinary happened. She and her sisters would wake, and if the weather was fine, take out their Dales ponies. Those surefooted horses would fly them across the countryside, nearly always annoying their neighboring farmer and his sheep. If the weather was raining, they would all cozy up in their father's library and read whatever took their fancy in front of a fire. Often, Winsome would read to them all, Verity having invariably talked her into it by claiming her sister had the best voice for it.

Here, in just one morning, the surprises had come rapid fire. First the musk roses from Lord Thorpe. They were so perfect in their meaning, it was just what it ought to be. His note had said: "To the most charming lady at Almack's." Even more perfect.

Then, a folded piece of paper had been delivered. It was from Lord Charles and it was a pencil drawing of his beloved dog, Nero. The dog was curled in front of a fire and the note said: "As we did speak of my dear departed Nero, I wished to give you an idea of what he looked like." It really was very kind of him to think of it!

That was not to be all, though. A package had just arrived for her. As Valor leaned over her shoulder to see what it was, she unwrapped it. It was a red leather dog collar. On the underside of the collar was an inscription burned into the leather: Nelson, of the Duke of Pelham's household. Reward or law.

Lord Thorpe had enclosed a note with it. "Lady Serenity, I

have often worried that Havoc would be lost or taken, and he wears a similar collar to hasten his return to my house."

That gift really had affected her the most. She *had* so often worried that someone might take Nelson. He was unique and wonderful and who could see him without feeling it? When she'd found him at the inn, she'd prayed he did not have an owner as she desperately wished him for herself. Might not another person come along feeling just the same, but without the scruples to find out if he was owned? Those early days had set the habit of him sleeping in her room under the guise that he would cry all night if he were left alone in the kitchens. The truth was, *she* would have cried all night, worrying over whether he was still there or not.

Valor looked it over. "Oh I see, if Nelson ever got lost, people would know where to bring him back to. What's the reward? I hope it is significant."

Serenity brushed tears off her cheeks. "It doesn't specify, but of course it must be handsome."

"Maybe I should get Mrs. Wendover a collar of red leather too," Valor said pensively. "Nelson keeps getting *her* lost—I have not seen her in days and he will not show me where he put her."

Serenity smiled. Nelson was indeed entranced with Valor's raggedy stuffed rabbit. He was forever making off with her.

Just then, Thomas opened the drawing room doors. "Lady Felicity and Lady Grace," he said.

Two of her elder sisters came into the room, followed by a lady in a starched uniform. Felicity carried her baby in her arms and Grace struggled to hold on to young Miles Delatore, who speedily got away from her. He ran to Serenity and Valor on the sofa, much changed and much steadier on his feet. "Aunts!" he said. "Which ones?"

Serenity laughed. It had been a year since they had seen the young man and he could not be expected to remember who was who. "I am your Aunt Serenity and this is your Aunt Valor."

"Grace sent me a note that we ought to surprise you and we all piled into the carriage together," Felicity said. She looked round the drawing room, noting the flowers and the brown paper strewn on the table. "Goodness, what's happened here?"

"I'm going to be all alone, is what's happened," Valor said.

Young Miles seemed struck by this. "I'll be your friend," he said, taking Valor's hand.

"Thank you," Valor said gravely. "I'll need all the friends I can get, as I will be very alone."

"Should we suspect the flowers are from a gentleman, then?" Felicity said, sitting down with her wriggly baby.

Serenity nodded, leaning over to have a look at Miss Isabelle Stratton. She was a pretty little thing and was just at that stage that could not be named. She was less a baby, but not yet a toddler. Eyes alert and taking everything in, not content to stay in her mother's arms, not yet ready to make experiments in walking, and not yet accomplished in talking. Isabelle grabbed at Serenity's finger and pulled it toward her mouth. That was another area that would change in time, but as of yet, everything might be food and should be tried out.

"Nurse Green," Felicity said, "Perhaps take Isabelle down to the servants' hall, as they will all wish to see her."

The nurse nodded and Isabelle was whisked away to entertain or harass the servants, however the case might turn out to be.

Winsome and Verity burst into the room. "Felicity! Grace!" they cried. "We've just seen Isabelle, she is grown. And here is Miles."

"More aunts?" Miles said, his brow wrinkling. It seemed he'd lost track of precisely how many aunts he had.

"Aunt Verity and Aunt Winsome," Grace said, for her son's elucidation. "Now I wonder, Miles does so like to see a stable."

"Horses!" Miles shouted to confirm the idea.

"And he has only ever seen my own Dales pony," Grace went on. "He's been so keen on seeing more."

"Ponies!" Miles shouted.

"Oh, let's do take him to see the stables," Winsome said.

"Come, Miles," Verity said.

"I'm coming too," Valor said. "If he gets scared, I can tell him of all the times I've been scared. It's less scary to know that other people are scared."

With that, the circus of young people left the drawing room to hinder the grooms in whatever work they were trying to get done.

Charlie brought in a tea tray. Serenity poured, as Felicity and Grace were guests now. "I did not know you had a nurse that followed you everywhere, Felicity. I supposed you had one at home, but does she come with you whenever you go out?"

Felicity laughed. "There are three of them, in fact. At first, I resisted such a setup. After all, how much trouble could one little baby be? Stratton was so insistent though, and I have come to the conclusion that he was right. With each passing day, she becomes a little bit more of an adorable trouble."

"Wait until she's up on her feet," Grace said. "Take the time now to remove everything you value and store it in the attics. Miles gets away from his nurse more than you might imagine, and instantly races to whatever is the most breakable in his reach."

Serenity laughed, as she'd seen young Miles at his worst the year before. If there were a thing to be broken, he would find it and break it. And then cry because he broke it.

"Enough about us two married ladies," Felicity said. "You've been to Almack's and flowers have arrived, and what else is here?"

"The flowers are from Lord Thorpe," Serenity said. "He lives two doors down and I saw him in the window the night it was snowing. Also, he's sent this collar for Nelson, which is really very thoughtful."

Just then, Nelson came bounding in with his usual three-legged lope. He came to a halt and looked round, wagging his tail. Then he turned round and ran out again.

"He will have been sleeping on my bed and has heard the

sounds of children in the house," Serenity said.

"This is from Lord Thorpe," Felicity said, admiring the collar. "The marquess?"

"The reserved marquess?" Grace asked.

"Goodness, everybody keeps saying he's reserved and, well, I suppose he might be. I do not really know. He is to come to dinner on the morrow with his brother, Lord Charles. Do come too."

"I would not miss it for the world," Grace said. "Dashlend will come along too, I am sure."

"And I will accept for Stratton. I imagine they both are acquainted with Lord Thorpe. If only Patience were in Town, but she and Lord Stanford have been delayed in Brighton. They oversee the renovation of his house there and it has gone on longer than they imagined. She does say she will be on her way as soon as she can."

Of course, Serenity did feel the absence of a sister. Though, she could not keep her mind on it for long. It kept drifting back to Lord Thorpe.

"He is really something to look at," Serenity said. "He said he planned to take his dog out walking in the square one day soon. I have looked out the windows sometimes, but I haven't seen him."

Felicity and Grace looked at one another. Both of them laughed. "No, you will probably not see him. At least, not until you have gone out to the square yourself," Felicity said.

"You see?" Grace said, "It was said to excuse the moment when he very coincidentally encounters you walking your own dog."

Serenity felt rather stupid to have failed to comprehend it, if it were true.

"What do we wait for?" Felicity said. "The children, and Nelson of course, require taking the air."

"Nelson can wear his lovely new collar," Grace said.

As they rose, Felicity said, "By the by, Winsome wrote me

that our aunt has installed another butler, but we have not seen hide nor hair of him."

Serenity nodded. "Mr. Cremble. He seems to be spending most of his time closeted in his room with a bible. He thinks Mrs. Right is in league with the devil."

Both of her sisters nodded, as they were both well-used to the dear housekeeper's interesting gambits with any incoming butler.

CHAPTER SIX

ROLAND HAD KEPT an eye out of the various windows of his house to see if he might catch Lady Serenity taking her dog for a walk. He'd confided in Quinn, who also kept an eye out, and who had a discreet word with the footmen, who also were keeping an eye out.

He was signing papers at his desk when he heard one of the footmen shout from the hall. "The lady with the three-legged dog is on the square!"

Roland jumped up and threw the doors to the library open. "Find Havoc and get a leash on him and tell my valet to bring my coat."

One footman ran down to the kitchens. It was well known in the house that if Havoc was not at Roland's feet, he was at the cook's feet waiting for accidents of the dropped variety. Another flew up the stairs to pass on the order for his coat. Roland straightened his neckcloth into better order as he left the library for the drawing room and a better view.

He did not know what he expected, he supposed it would be as it was the night it snowed. Lady Serenity, her dog, and the matron who accompanied her.

That was not what he saw this moment. It was a veritable crowd of people, all of them women but for a very young gentleman with them.

His valet ran in with his coat, hurried him into it and brushed it. One of the footmen brought Havoc, who was beside himself with excitement. He could not know what the cause of his excitement was, but dogs were very good at sensing something interesting was in the offing.

Roland took the leash. "Calm down and attempt to appear dignified," he pointlessly told the dog. Or perhaps he told himself too. It was hard to know.

Quinn had the front doors open and Roland strode out. The party had gone past his house and got ahead of him. They were just now turning into the gate that led into the square's garden.

He picked up his pace, Havoc joyfully keeping up. "Lady Serenity," he called.

En masse, the group of ladies stopped and turned to him. Lady Serenity said, "Lord Thorpe, how fortuitous we should unexpectedly encounter you here."

She was looking delightfully pretty, wearing a dark green velvet pelisse and matching bonnet. He reached the party and bowed. There were various expressions in response to unexpectedly encountering him. Two of the ladies, who he knew of in society, Lady Grace and Lady Felicity, looked amused. Two of the younger ladies looked him over suspiciously. One of the ladies, who seemed she must be the youngest of them, did not look at him at all. Rather, she stared in horror at Havoc and slowly backed up. The nursemaid that accompanied them appeared bored, as if she'd seen it all before.

The young gentleman said, "Does he bite?" hooking a thumb at Havoc.

"Of course he bites," the youngest lady shouted. "Look at how big his mouth is!"

"He does not bite," Roland said. "He only feels terrible that people are afraid of him because of his size. He does not mean to be so big."

"Really," the girl whispered.

As the young gentleman inched up to Havoc to test out the idea, Lady Serenity said, "Lord Thorpe, these are my sisters, the ladies Felicity, Grace, Winsome, Verity, and Valor. That is Grace's son, Miles, and Nurse carries Felicity's daughter, Isabelle. And Nelson, of course."

Just as young Miles was doing, Nelson edged ever closer to Havoc. Roland prayed Havoc would remain calm and not frighten anybody.

Seeing that he was approached, Havoc threw himself on the ground and rolled on his back. Good dog.

Nelson was particularly delighted by this turn of events, as Havoc had sent the clear message that he wished to be friends and would not attempt to boss about his new, and very much smaller, acquaintance.

Roland also noticed that Nelson wore the red leather collar he'd sent over.

At that moment, Lady Serenity seemed to notice it too. "It was very thoughtful to send a collar for Nelson," she said. "I had not thought to have engraved his home address on the collar he'd been wearing."

Roland did not say that he had sent it as a compliment to her, rather than Nelson.

"You would be surprised to know how often I have worried that somebody might take him," the lady went on. "My father jokes that nobody but us have any use for a three-legged dog."

"And half blind, too," Lady Winsome added. "As Thomas says, our Nelson has been through the wars."

"But I think he is just so charming, and of course there must be people who would think just the same. What if they could not resist their worst instincts and stole him?"

"I understand perfectly," Roland said. "I am not so worried about Havoc these days as he is so big, but when he first came to me I guarded him very carefully."

Havoc and Nelson took that moment to leap to their feet, knocking Miles off his own. He landed with a thud. Before Grace could run to him, exclaim, or otherwise assert her motherly role, he sat up. "I am all right, Mama."

Roland gave him a hand up. "Perhaps we'd better get these two dogs walking, else they trip up the whole party in their enthusiasm. Lady Serenity?"

The lady nodded prettily and they set off through the gate to the square's paths through the trees. The rest of the party followed behind, which Roland was beginning to see as awkward in the extreme. They were a silent following party, seeming to prefer listening to what might be said between him and Lady Serenity.

Aside from them occasionally stopping to sniff one another, Havoc and Nelson were relatively behaved and seemed to enjoy walking together.

"They like one another," Roland said.

Lady Serenity nodded. "I have not known how Nelson would be near another dog, as he has not had any friends. The only other dog we encounter here is Lady Maribel's bad-tempered Pekinese who hates everybody, even Lady Maribel, I believe."

Roland laughed. "I know the dog you speak of. Lady Maribel is rather terrified of the little beast—it has a habit of biting ankles and she's had several staff leave on account of it."

"Havoc is very well-behaved," Lady Serenity said.

"It is his temperament," Roland said. "He is an easygoing, small dog hoping to be approved of, walking round in a very large body."

"I believe you are right about temperament," Lady Serenity said. "We cannot know what happened to Nelson before we found him, but certainly many terrible things. He ought to be bitter over it, but he is not."

"He was surviving on scraps!" Lady Winsome said loudly behind them, a further reminder that their conversation was not at all private.

"And yet, he is such a darling, despite it all," Lady Serenity said. "I wonder if temperament is rather fixed, despite whatever might befall a person."

This of course did give Roland pause, considering he was

determined to modify his own temperament.

"Perhaps only *mostly* fixed," he ventured. "I do think one's circumstances and preferences can move inclinations a bit one way or the other."

Lady Serenity looked thoughtful over it.

"Serenity," Lady Valor called from behind, "did you thank Lord Thorpe for the roses, but tell him not to send any more, because you have decided not to ever leave the house?"

"Valor!" Lady Grace said.

"She doesn't have to leave if she does not want to. I'm not ever leaving my papa," Lady Valor said.

Lady Serenity's cheeks pinked. "My youngest sister is not approving that my three older sisters have married."

"No, I am not," Lady Valor confirmed.

Roland could hear Lady Felicity hushing the youngest of the Nicolet sisters. They had reached the other side of the gardens and followed the turn on the path that would take them back round to their own side of the square.

Havoc and Nelson were ahead of them, walking side by side in a surprisingly rational fashion. Nelson's head only came to Havoc's shoulder and he did not have the same stride, what with him being smaller and down a leg, but Havoc seemed to be making allowances. "As they have seemed to become fast friends," Roland said, "perhaps it would not be kind to forever separate them. Perhaps they would like going on further walks in the square."

"Oh, I think that must be right. I could not bear to disappoint Nelson and this is the first friend he's ever had. That I know of, anyway."

"I find eleven o'clock in the morning is a good time to walk a dog. Perhaps we ought to arrange it?"

"I am almost always free at eleven," Lady Serenity said.

"As am I."

"Excellent," Lady Felicity said behind them. "There will be dog walking at eleven each morning."

"If, of course, your father approves the plan," Roland said to Lady Serenity.

"I'll tell him not to," Lady Valor said. "This dog walking idea is terrible!"

"I am certain he will approve," Lady Serenity said, ignoring her youngest sister's opinions.

They had come to the gate leading out of the gardens. Roland would like to suggest going round a second time, though it would be rather preposterous. It would also likely send Lady Valor into fits, as she currently wished he'd disappear into a puff of smoke and never be seen again.

"I suppose I'd better take Havoc inside," he said, "he'll wish for water by now."

"As will Nelson, I'm sure."

Roland turned and bowed. "Ladies, and young sir," he said. Then he led Havoc away toward his house, attempting to ignore that he had an audience in doing so.

The audience was not all behind him either. As he approached the house, curtains dropped in all the front rooms.

There was something embarrassing in publicly courting. But no matter, there were to be dog walks at eleven each morning. Hopefully with less of a crowd.

It was the most natural thing in the world that all her sisters should dissect their impressions of everything that had been said on the dog walk with Lord Thorpe.

Valor remained entirely against him, as he posed a threat to her plan to keep her remaining sisters in the house forever.

Verity claimed she'd read that marquesses always preferred mastiffs as their dog of choice, so she found Lord Thorpe a very usual sort of person.

Winsome thought he was handsome enough and wondered

how he stacked up to his brother, though she satisfied herself that she would soon find out as they were both to come to dinner.

Felicity said the daily dog walking was very promising and applauded the lord for thinking of it.

Grace said he'd proved his interest by flying out of the house upon seeing Serenity.

Miles had nothing to say about Lord Thorpe, but he liked the lord's dog and spent a half hour trying to convince his mother that they ought to get one of their own.

But for Valor, everybody was satisfied with him. Was he as reserved as everybody said? She did not really know, he had not seemed so. On the other hand, nobody would describe him as particularly freewheeling either. There was a seriousness to him, she supposed.

It had struck her when they'd spoken of a temperament being fixed. Lord Thorpe had claimed that temperament was *mostly* fixed, but could be modified a little. That was just what she was trying to do! She was working hard to be less carried away by her feelings, as being carried away often led to a weep. She was certain Lord Thorpe would not be drawn to a weeping lady.

She had done well today; she'd controlled herself when she'd noted the snow that still covered the lower leaves of the trees sparkled in the sunshine. The majesty and beauty of nature was exactly the kind of thing that made her eyes water. She'd not even had to wipe her eyes over the developing friendship between Nelson and Havoc, though it had been so touching.

She must just go on this way, acting as a rational lady and not one who could be carried away by the glories of nature or the friendship between animals. Or rather, she could be a little carried away, but not too much.

It did occur to her to wonder about the rightness of attempting to change who she was for the sake of a gentleman. If one of her sisters had asked her the same, she'd advise against it. But then, none of her sisters were contemplating Lord Thorpe, and he was glorious in every respect. As well, she'd been attempting to rein in her feelings even before she'd met the gentleman.

THE DINNER HOSTING Lord Thorpe and Lord Charles was nearing and it had been the usual chaos in getting things ready. Mr. Cremble had finally descended from his room, though his coat bulged to one side. Charlie said he'd strapped a bible over his heart.

Serenity did not know what Mr. Cremble thought was to happen. Did he imagine Mrs. Right was planning on shooting him and he guarded his most important organ? That was Verity's speculation. She said it was a usual thing for a man fearing he would be shot to place something over his heart that would slow the bullet. Serenity did not know if that could be true or not. If that's what he'd done, it was very foolish. She'd never in her life seen Mrs. Right with a fowling piece in her hands.

She turned her attention to her looking glass as Mrs. Right fussed with her hair. Her cheeks were in high color from anticipation. She wore an aqua blue sarsenet dress with an embroidered bodice of tiny flowers that had lovely little cream silk bows at the cuffs of the sleeves.

"I see," Mrs. Right said, having just been informed of the daily walks at eleven in the morning with Lord Thorpe and his dog. "That seems like an awful lot of walking for one old housekeeper."

"You need not go every day, though," Serenity said. "Charlie could accompany me—he's a senior footman and practically the butler."

"We'll see how the duke feels about it," Mrs. Right said.

"Or, I could bring along Charlie, and my sisters."

"Aye, he might feel a bit better about that arrangement. Now what's to happen when it rains?"

"Goodness, we did not talk about rain."

Mrs. Right snorted. "Here you are, both living in London, and did not talk about rain, now I ask you…"

"It is only water after all, and I do have an umbrella."

"Aye, but I reckon he won't use one. Some gents do, some don't, and I'll guess the marquess is too manly to be seen shielding himself from rain. So there you are, him soaking wet and you struggling along with a leash and an umbrella. Of course, he'll offer to hold the umbrella for you, but somehow that never works entirely right—the far side of you will be firmly in the weather. You'll end with two wet people, two wet dogs, and wet whoever you dragged with you."

Serenity burst out in peals of laughter from the vision. "I suppose I'd better tell him the dog walking is off if it rains."

Mrs. Right nodded, satisfied she'd scored her point.

"I understand Mr. Cremble has strapped a bible under his coat," Serenity said. "Verity thinks he is convinced you will shoot him."

"That child," Mrs. Right said with a chuckle. "Her imagination never takes a nap. The very idea I'd visit the hangman over one of Lady Marchfield's butlers. No, I think the bible is there to ward off the evil he supposes just now surrounds him."

"I presume that means he still fears you are somehow connected to the devil?"

"Aye, last evening, when we had our tea before retiring, I suddenly clutched my head as if a great pain had struck it. Charlie and Thomas, having been briefed on the gambit, both looked at the ceiling and shook their heads in a disapproving way. Mr. Cremble was all aflutter and asked what was wrong. Charlie told him somebody above stairs was praying before bed and it made my head ache."

"And he believed it?"

"'Course he did," Mrs. Right said with a sigh of satisfaction. "Butlers are all alike, a regular bunch of lunatics. If we all claimed that fish can fly in the Dales, he'd probably believe that too."

"I do hope he moves on without inconveniencing you much longer. He'll be ever so much happier when he takes on a family that wishes for a butler."

"We'll all be happy, but for Lady Marchfield." Mrs. Right

paused. "She's not set to come this evening, is she? I'd not like for Mr. Cremble to describe what's going on. She might just set him straight."

"No, she knows nothing about the dinner. We all love our aunt, of course. She is our aunt, after all. It's just that she's so…stern."

"That she is. There now, your hair and your person look charming enough to tempt a marquess, I think."

Serenity certainly hoped so. She could already hear chatter from the drawing room. It was time to descend.

Mrs. Right fiddled with the hairpins on Serenity's dressing table. Softly, she said, "It is the same old puzzle—I am glad to see all my girls well settled and sad to see them leave the house."

Serenity kissed her cheek. "So far, I am only to leave the house for dog walks. Do not pack my trunks just yet."

"By the by, as fast I would pack them, Valor would unpack them. I caught the naughty little thing rearranging the seating but an hour ago. She had things set so you would be surrounded by your sisters at one end of the table, with Lord Thorpe and Lord Charles on the other end. I rectified it and you'll have the gentlemen on either side of you."

Poor Valor. But then, it had been fixed and Lord Thorpe would sit right beside her.

CHAPTER SEVEN

CHARLES ARRIVED TO Grosvenor Square a little bit on the early side. Not too early, as that would inconvenience the host and he intended to stay in the duke's good books. But hopefully early enough to beat Thorpe inside the doors.

He wore his best set of clothes which, thanks to his own duke's generosity, had been tailored by Weston himself for an exorbitant price. He could not recall when he'd attended a dinner that Thorpe also attended. In general, they traveled in different circles. Thorpe preferred the stodgy end of the *ton* and Charles preferred the more interesting end. Thorpe preferred the coffee room at Whites, while Charles preferred to take his opportunities on the dark walk at Vauxhall. Thorpe preferred to enter a horse at Doncaster, Charles preferred to while away the night and early dawn in a low gaming hell.

But here they both would be. This particular dinner would prove to be interesting. Charles was convinced that Thorpe had a strong interest in Lady Serenity, and therefore, so did he.

Charles supposed Thorpe would be frustrated when he realized his brother had sent a sketch of the mysterious dog, Nero. It was a personal gift and very suited to Lady Serenity—his brother would never have been so clever. If Thorpe dared to claim Nero had never existed, he would sadly shake his head and wonder at his brother's disregard for animals. How anyone could forget such a dog as Nero was beyond comprehension. Let Thorpe argue further if he dared.

Charles hoped Lady Serenity's dog would make an appearance so he could praise it to the skies. One would not usually expect the household's dog to turn up at a dinner, but this was the Nicolet household, so he had every hope of it. He must just mask his revulsion over the idea that it was missing a leg.

He used the door knocker and the door swung open to reveal an odd-looking butler. He could not tell if the fellow was deformed or had something stuffed underneath the left side of his coat. It was most peculiar. "Lord Charles Garner," he said.

"This way, my lord."

Charles followed the odd butler, whose eyes seemed to dart all over the great hall as if he were expecting somebody to jump out at him.

The fellow opened the drawing room doors to a crowd of people. "Lord Charles Garner," the butler said flatly.

It was an entire room full of women, right down to one who could not be older than nine or ten. Two he recognized, Lady Felicity and Lady Grace. Lady Grace came forward. "Lord Charles, I believe we met last season at Lady Peachbottom's musical evening."

"Indeed, Lady Grace, charmed," he said with a bow. Though there was an unusual number of women in the room and no sign of Lady Serenity, there was also no sign yet of Thorpe.

Lady Grace made the introductions, though Charles did not think he had a hope of remembering all their names. Except perhaps for the youngest—Lady Valor glared at him as if he were a housebreaker come to steal their belongings.

"Goodness, I am coming in late," Lady Serenity said, hurrying into the room.

"But you have still beat Papa," Lady One-of-the-sisters said.

Lady Another-of-the-sisters said, "It is a usual thing for a duke to run late."

Was it?

The duke strode in. "I see we've gathered one and wait for

the other one."

"And we wait for Stratton and Dashlend too, Papa," Lady Felicity said. "They come together from their club. There was some critical meeting in the offing."

"However," Lady Grace said, "they have both sworn they will not be late."

Charles was vaguely acquainted with both of those individuals. Dashlend was known as a Corinthian of the first stare. Stratton was one of those fellows who was a 'hail fellow, well met' sort that everybody liked.

They were not to wait long for at least one of the missing guests. The butler with a bulge under his coat reappeared and said, "The Marquess of Thorpe."

Irritating. Why could not the man just say Lord Thorpe? Why did he insist on bringing his full title into it?

Thorpe bowed. "Your Grace," he said. Then he greeted Lady Serenity, and proceeded to greet each and every sister. How did he remember their names?

Stratton and Dashlend came into the room in a rush, not having waited for the strange butler to announce them. "We are not late, I think?" Stratton said.

"No, no, here we all are," the duke said. "Well, let's get going to the dining room. Fingers crossed that the current resident butler has got it all sorted. But who knows?"

With that interesting idea, they proceeded to follow the duke across the great hall. Charles had intended to escort Lady Serenity in, but somehow Lady Grace got in his way and Thorpe was able to beat him to it.

They found the butler anxiously staring at the sideboard. There were place cards at the seats and Charles was at least gratified that he should be to the right of Lady Serenity. Less gratified that Thorpe was to her left.

The footmen brought the wine around while the butler stared at his staff as if he did not know what they were doing.

The duke looked down his table and said, "You see how it is,

I'm surrounded by daughters. Even when I get them out of the house, they somehow get back in it again."

The duke's daughters seemed to find this very amusing, though Charles wondered at it.

The doors, which had not been entirely shut closed, slowly pushed open. Charles looked behind him. There he was—the three-legged dog. A missing leg was not his only deficiency either. He was clearly of low parentage, his coat was neither straight nor curled, one eye was clouded over, and its tongue, which just now lolled out of its mouth, was really far too long. The thing was hideous.

"Ah," he said to Lady Serenity, "there is your dear Nelson."

Lady Serenity nodded. "Lord Thorpe was so good as to have a collar made for him that explains where to return him on the underside of it."

Did he, now. That was rather more clever than he'd imagined Thorpe would be. He kicked himself that he had not thought of it.

"Very thoughtful," Charles said.

Lady Serenity nodded. "Dear Nelson has made a friend in Lord Thorpe's Havoc. It is just a shame that he will never have the opportunity to meet your dear Nero."

What was this now? When had Lady Serenity's dog met Thorpe's mastiff? Charles presumed the dogs had not met on their own. Certainly their owners had been present. How had that happened?

Thorpe, looking very pleased with himself, leaned forward and said to him, "Nelson and Havoc took a turn around the square."

The duke laughed and said, "It's to be a regular thing is my understanding."

A regular thing? How was Thorpe getting a leg up on him? It was intolerable.

He supposed his brother had the advantage of location. Charles was at The Albany while Thorpe was two doors down.

Charles briefly thought of relocating himself into the Grosvenor Square house. He had the right to it. But he could not tolerate the irritation that would come along with that idea. He would not inherit that house, could not lord it over that house, and could not stand to watch Thorpe in the position of lord of the manor.

"We decided that since Havoc and Nelson got on so well," Lady Serenity said, "they should have future opportunities to meet."

Future opportunities to meet. How many opportunities?

Lady Serenity turned to Thorpe. "Goodness, I forgot to say. Our housekeeper, Mrs. Right, did advise that we not walk out if it is raining."

"Ah yes, very good thought," Thorpe said. "Though I suppose we ought to qualify what we mean by rain. I suppose a misting would not put us off?"

"Oh, a misting," Lady Serenity said. "I hadn't thought. Goodness, there really is not anything too inconvenient about a misting."

Charles willed his eyes to not roll back in his head over the current debate. A misting, indeed.

Just then, the horrendous-looking cur sat on his foot underneath the table. Charles shook it off. It staggered and then came back and bit at the leather of his boot. Then it moved off before he was forced to kick it halfway across the room.

This situation must be turned round somehow. Thorpe was beating him at a game and it must not be allowed to continue. His brother looked very smug at the moment.

He was not certain what he ought to do about it, but these walks with their two stupid dogs must not be allowed to go on. Thorpe could not be allowed to win.

Roland had not known who else would be invited to the dinner, but it turned out to be a family affair. He found that rather promising. Stratton and Dashlend were both fine fellows. He supposed the duke was too, though rather an eccentric version of a fine fellow. The only gentleman attending who was not a particularly fine fellow was his brother Charles.

He was not certain whether it was for good or ill that Charles had been apprised of his walks with Lady Serenity. It would be hoped that Charles would take the hint and turn his attention elsewhere. On the other hand, his brother was not very skilled at being a gracious loser and as far as Charles was concerned, everything in the world was a win or lose proposition.

The duke's table had been rather good. Roasts of beef and fowl, fricasseed chicken, thin-sliced potatoes in a creamed sauce, mashed parsnips, mushroom tartlets, Brussel sprouts with sauteed onions, rolls, and a chopped salad. It was the sort of thing one might have in the country—good food, not too fussy. He'd not paid much attention to the various cakes and trifles that came out, but the cheeseboard had been first rate. As well, the duke must have one of the finest wine cellars in Town.

All that, though, was of no matter. He would have been happy with a couple of rolls if it meant he was to dine with Lady Serenity. He'd discovered she and her sisters rode Dales ponies and he found himself interested in seeing the duke's stable. He understood they were surefooted, but then Lady Serenity was able to tell him of how courageous they were, and how their dark eyes were bright with intelligence.

Charles attempted to butt into the conversation, but he did so by describing a horse race. Roland did not believe Lady Serenity had any interest in such things. Her only question about it was if any of the horses had been hurt.

She was such a kind person; of course she would not care for which horse won the race or which gentleman won the purse, but just wished to assure herself that the horseflesh had come through it unscathed.

When that story seemed to go nowhere, Charles said, "I pray it was not presumptuous of me to send that sketch of Nero."

"Goodness, no," Lady Serenity said. "He seemed as if he were a charming little dog."

Charles had sent a sketch of the nonexistent dog. He really was beyond the pale.

"Dare I hope that it has become one of your personal possessions?" Charles asked.

What a smarmy idiot.

Lady Serenity wrinkled her forehead. "Now that you speak of it, I believe it is in the drawing room somewhere. Well, it's bound to turn up."

Roland suppressed a smile. A very good sign that she had no idea what she'd done with it. "I cannot express enough," Roland said, "how enthusiastic Havoc was to make the acquaintance of Nelson. He was really cheered by it."

Roland was satisfied to note the look of annoyance on Charles' face.

"I feel almost remiss in failing to see that Nelson might wish to have a friend. He seemed so pleased with it, I probably should have seen it all along." Lady Serenity dabbed at her eyes, deeply affected by the idea that she may have let Nelson down in some way.

This rather affected Roland too, and he worked to keep his features neutral lest he betray himself. He would not like Lady Serenity to note it, and if Charles saw it, he would be sure to make hay with it.

"I imagine Nero and Nelson would have been fast friends," Charles said. "They are more similar in size."

Roland wished Charles would shut up about that nonexistent dog. Further, Charles would not have the ability to see that size had nothing to do with it. It was a superficial idea, as were most of Charles' ideas.

"I believe it was their hearts that made friends, Lord Charles," Lady Serenity said. "I am not sure Nelson and Havoc even noticed the difference in their sizes."

"I only say, that mastiff could do some damage if he liked it."

As Lady Serenity recoiled from the idea, Roland leaned forward. "Havoc has never attacked or been cruel to any being on this earth, unlike some people I know."

Charles reddened. He generally did not have a retort when something hit too close to home.

"Stratton, Dashlend," the duke said from the head of the table, "are you to tell these two gentlemen what they can expect in not too long a time?"

Roland looked between the two sons-in-laws, presuming it was to be some sort of special port, or special cigars. Though, the longer he looked at those two gentlemen, the less confident he was about that idea. Why did they both look so downcast?

"Thorpe, Lord Charles," Dashlend said, shaking his head sadly as if he was apologizing for something.

"It cannot be helped," Stratton said with a shrug.

What could not be helped? Whatever it was, it sounded dreadful.

"It's Fact or Fib!" Lady Valor said, leaning forward to call down the table. "You will have to play it. Papa will bring the port and brandy into the drawing room and we'll all play together. I get to go first because I might suddenly get overtired and have an outburst."

"Trust her on that warning," Dashlend said, nodding.

"I'm sorry, I do not believe I am familiar with that game," Roland said.

His brother snorted. "Thorpe does not get out much," he said. "I am certain I played it at a house party last summer."

This caused the duke to roar with laughter. "He thinks he played it!"

"You can't have," Winsome said, "we invented it."

Charles reddened even further, which served him right. He was forever attempting to be a know-all. Somehow he'd failed to learn that it generally did not pay off.

"I imagine you played something similar, Lord Charles," Lady Serenity said kindly.

"Yes, I suppose I must have," Charles said.

"Do not be too sure of that," Stratton said. "I am not confident there is anything like it. Or that there ever should be."

His wife, Lady Felicity, laughed. "You know you adore it," she said. "Except when it is your turn."

Lady Verity nodded knowingly. "It was how we discovered that Mr. Stratton stares at Felicity when she sleeps."

"Because he stays in the same room all night," Lady Valor said in a tone that could only be described as disgust.

"I stared one time!" Stratton said. "Or twice at the most."

"Fib!" Lady Valor shouted.

"Ah, look!" the duke cried, "you have all given them both a look of foreboding. Never mind it, gentlemen—you cannot win. All you can do is drink to get through it."

"I plan to ask some pointed questions," Lady Valor said threateningly.

What was this game? He was to be asked pointed questions and then what? Was he to understand that Stratton and his bride's sleeping habits had been inquired into?

He did not know what he was in for, but as the duke had risen and directed the footmen to relocate the port and brandy bottles to the drawing room, he was about to find out.

CHAPTER EIGHT

SERENITY WAS MUCH buoyed by the evening so far. She and Lord Thorpe had settled the question of the weather between them. Were it only a misting, the dog walking would go forward. She'd sent up a silent prayer that nature would hold off on raining for the next days. Nature loved her rain so well, and it did such a lot of good, but if it could hold off just a little while, she would be most grateful.

She was beginning to not know what she thought of Lord Charles. He seemed somehow younger than Lord Thorpe. Of course, he was younger by a few years, but more than that. He seemed more boyish, perhaps. Really, it had been foolish to claim he had played Fact or Fib at a house party. It was the sort of thing Verity might do—claim to have knowledge she did not in fact have.

She supposed she must be lenient in forming her opinion, as certainly he'd said it to impress her and she could not condemn an effort at a compliment.

They had gone into the drawing room and arranged all the furniture in a wide circle with an ottoman in the middle. Verity and Winsome had made the separate piles of yellow and blue tickets. She was gratified to note that Lord Thorpe paid close attention to where she would sit and took the chair next to her with alacrity. Winsome was on her other side, and that left Lord Charles between Lord Dashlend and Verity.

"Well, now," the duke said, "Gentlemen, you'll be asked questions and my daughters will decide if it is a fact or a fib."

"That's the main thing," Dashlend said. "It does not matter if you tell the truth or not—*they* decide."

"That's why you cannot win," the duke said. "Do not bother trying. We'll all be drowning in blue tickets in no time at all."

"Blue is for fibs and yellow is for facts, and a blue cancels out a yellow," Winsome said.

"Valor has asked to go first," the duke said. "She rightly reminded me that last season she got overtired and threw a fistful of blue tickets in Stanford's face."

"I do get tired," Valor admitted. "If I get *too* tired, anything might happen. Now, Lord Charles, what is the first thing you noticed about our Serenity?"

Serenity looked down at her hands. It was no surprise that Lord Charles and Lord Thorpe would be interrogated ruthlessly. Though she knew it was coming, it was uncomfortable and thrilling at the same time.

"Oh, well I would say it must be her bright eyes," Lord Charles said.

"Fibber!" Valor cried, hurling a blue ticket at him. "You noticed her hair—everybody knows it."

"See?" the duke said laughing. "All right, who is next?"

"I am not done," Valor said darkly.

Serenity was getting the idea that her youngest sister was fast on her way to being overtired. It was not surprising, she supposed, as her usual time for retiring had passed hours ago. Hopefully, there would not be a repeat of last season's dramatics.

"Lord Thorpe," Valor said, "what did *you* first notice about our Serenity?"

"How joyous she was to be out in the snow," Lord Thorpe said. "Not everybody can appreciate the changing moods of nature. And then her hair was very charmingly escaping her bonnet."

Serenity's sisters all looked at one another in surprise. "Fact!"

Valor cried, throwing him a yellow ticket.

What an answer! It was positively perfect. It was as if Lord Thorpe really understood her.

"Very good," the duke said, laughing. "Now who will be next to interrogate our guests?"

"I am not done," Valor said, tears brimming in her eyes. "Nobody else can get married. No more weddings! Fact!" Then she took a pile of yellow tickets.

The duke motioned to Charlie, who understood it was time to retrieve Mrs. Right. "There now, my girl, you really are getting tired."

"Yes, I know," Valor said, sobbing into her father's sleeve.

Rather than continue on with the game while Valor was in such distress, they waited on Mrs. Right to collect her before they proceeded.

Lord Thorpe very kindly said, "Lady Valor, I am much impressed that you have remained in the drawing room to play the game with us. It is exceedingly late for a youth of your years."

As Valor wiped her tears with her father's sleeve, she said, "It really *is* late and I *am* just a youth."

Mrs. Right hurried in. "There you are, love. You'll never guess who's turned up—Mrs. Wendover has been returned and looks forward to a reunion."

"Oh Nelson," Valor said, climbing off the sofa, "you are very good to bring her home."

Nelson could not be entirely sure of what he was being thanked for and would likely make off with Mrs. Wendover at the first opportunity, but he wagged his tail. For now, the stuffed rabbit was back with its rightful owner.

Before taking Mrs. Right's hand, Valor gave a little curtsy. "Lord Thorpe, Lord Charles, a pleasure to know you. Lord Dashlend, you're wrong about what's happening on the moors—it's murder. Mr. Stratton, we'll all thank you to stop staring at Felicity while she's sleeping. You might sleep in another room if you cannot help yourself."

"I think that's quite enough of an adieu, Poppet," Mrs. Right said with a snort. She led Valor out of the room.

Serenity thought she'd at least better explain the comment about murder. "Valor is certain that when a fox screams, it is a woman being murdered on the moors. We cannot convince her otherwise."

"Deuced inconvenient those foxes keep her up at night," the duke said. "There is a bright spot, though—she accused my vicar of being involved in the murders. He's still not over it!"

Once Valor had gone, they played the game for a while longer. Winsome asked Lord Thorpe if he would be prone to Mr. Stratton's habit of staring at his wife while she was sleeping. He said not if she would not like it. This was deemed a fact, though Serenity had nearly gone through the floor with the embarrassment of prying so far into Lord Thorpe's personal attitudes.

Verity was not the slightest embarrassed by it and said, "So you do plan to be in the same room all night, then?"

Lord Thorpe did indeed plan on it. It gave Serenity shivers just to think of it.

Grace asked Lord Charles if it was true that he'd bet Lord Waltondell last season regarding how many spots Lady Alvinia's prize coach dog had. Lord Charles admitted to it, which was deemed a fact. He was further questioned on the nature of the bet by the duke and it seemed he'd lost one of his horses.

Serenity found herself horrified over the idea. She could not imagine putting her Dales pony at such risk for any reason. To play with her horse's fate for a bet would be unconscionable. She could not imagine how her dear Jupiter would feel to be taken away from her stablemates—they were her friends. It would be a betrayal of the worst kind.

Mr. Stratton, who had probably heard enough of his habit of watching Felicity sleep, finally rose to signal an end to the party. Serenity supposed that, had it been another house, the ladies of the household would stay in the drawing room. The Nicolets did not care for such constraints, though.

They followed the guests out the doors and to the pavement. Felicity and Mr. Stratton climbed into their carriage and Grace and Lord Dashlend got into their own. With much waving, they were off in their different directions.

Lord Charles' horse had been brought from the stables. Lord Thorpe had, naturally, walked over, as he was only two doors down. Serenity was pleased to note that he lingered.

Lord Charles noted it too. "Well, Thorpe, you have not forgotten which direction you travel?"

Serenity supposed that was a hint that Lord Thorpe should get going.

Winsome said, "It is such a fine night, I suppose it would do us good to walk with Lord Thorpe to his doorstep."

Very clever, Winsome!

"Indeed," Serenity said, "the night air is always good for one's health."

"Is it?" Lord Charles asked.

"Of course it is," Lord Thorpe said, looking eager to jump on the idea.

"It is very commonly known," Verity said.

"News to me," the duke said, "but I'll pretend to believe it."

"Thank you for attending us, Lord Charles," Serenity said. She did not wish to brush him off, but she did wish to walk with Lord Thorpe to his doorstep.

Seeing as he had no other recourse, Lord Charles tipped his hat. "Ladies, Your Grace." He turned his horse and trotted down the street.

Lord Thorpe put out his arm and Serenity gently laid her hand upon it. They proceeded, rather slowly, toward Lord Thorpe's house. The candlelight falling from behind window curtains along the square gently lit it with a soft romantic aura. Perhaps less romantic was being followed by her father, Winsome, and Verity. Her family were suspiciously quiet, and she felt put on the spot somehow.

They had reached Lord Thorpe's doorstep. "I believe the

weather will be fine on the morrow," he said.

"Indeed, yes, it is sure to be fine. In the morning at least."

"At eleven."

"Yes, at eleven."

"Well now, Thorpe," the duke said, "I suppose you'd best get inside. Despite claims of night air being beneficial, I should not like my daughters to catch cold."

Lord Thorpe nodded. "Thank you for the invitation to dine, Your Grace. Lady Verity and Lady Winsome, a pleasure. Lady Serenity, until tomorrow."

Yes, Serenity thought. Until tomorrow.

CHARLES HAD PRETENDED to set off for The Albany but had surreptitiously gone round the square until he was out of view and watched the proceedings from there. Why should they all walk Thorpe home as if he was too senile to find the place himself?

They'd walked with him and then lingered at his doorstep. They were probably talking about what they ought to do about the dog walking if it were misting again.

He felt at a disadvantage on several fronts. Thorpe had the advantage of location on him, though if he could stand it, he could rectify that by moving in. His brother might also have the advantage of being of similar temperament to Lady Serenity. Charles was finding it difficult to guess how she would view a thing.

His description of a horse race had fallen rather flat, though it was one that was widely spoken of and generally perceived to be of interest. He'd thought to bring the imaginary dog Nero into it, but that had not been satisfactory either. She did not even know where she left the sketch of it and she was not at all sold on the idea of Nero being of closer size to her wretched cur being superior to Thorpe's slobbering beast. He'd even thought to frighten her a little with the idea that Thorpe's dog was capable of injuring her own dog. Thorpe had got in the way of that idea. His remark about some people being more dangerous than his dog was beyond irritating.

And then that stupid game, Fact or Fib, they called it. His answer that the first thing he'd noticed about Lady Serenity was her bright eyes had been denounced as a fib? It was very usual to compliment a woman's eyes, whether or not they were particularly special. That would have been annoying enough, but then for Thorpe to get a yellow ticket for his nonsensical description of the lady walking in the snow and appreciating nature?

It was just the sort of thing Thorpe would think—sloppily sentimental. Why did they not seem to see that? They were all so approving of it.

He soothed himself with the idea that it was early days. There was still plenty of time to turn things to his advantage. He only needed the right ideas. This evening might not have gone all his way, but that could change. He could make it change.

He'd never lost anything to Thorpe, and he was not about to start now.

QUINN CAME INTO Roland's bedchamber with the usual glasses of brandy. Roland, as was becoming a habit, sat at his window overlooking the square.

"I presume things went well at the duke's dinner," Quinn said, taking his seat by the fire.

"Very well, I think," Roland said, watching as Havoc seemed to weigh the benefits of getting up and going to Quinn for a scratch. He finally did so, yawning and stretching his front legs out before ambling over to his butler.

"So things proceed, very good news. Did Charles behave

himself?"

"Charles behaved as Charles always does. He tried to score points in a game nobody else was playing. I do not think he got too far with it. I do not think he understands Lady Serenity. She is too different from him."

"But you do?"

"I think so," Roland said. "I am beginning to think she might be more sentimental than she lets on. She did seem teary-eyed when she considered that Nelson ought to have had a friend before now and perhaps she had been in some way remiss."

Quinn laughed. "Now that would be convenient, as *you* are more sentimental than *you* let on."

"Yes, but nobody knows it, including her. You will not be surprised that I was equally struck over the idea of Nelson needing a friend."

"But you did not show it."

"I worked very hard not to."

"Of course, to say nobody knows your real temperament is not quite correct. Charles knows it. Careful he does not somehow attempt to use it to his advantage."

"I do not see how he could," Roland said. "Should he outright say it in some derogatory fashion to Lady Serenity he would only look like a gossip telling tales out of school. I do not think she would approve of it."

"Or believe it, at this juncture."

"Likely not."

"You'll have to make some decisions there. Are you to be the emotionless marquess forevermore? I do not see how you keep it up day after day and year after year. Just think what it will be when you have children? There will be a thousand situations that will deeply affect you. Are you to always jump on your horse to shout in a wood?"

"I do not know. All I do know is that Lady Serenity seems to like me as I am now. I should not like to jeopardize it by introducing the teary-eyed marquess."

"Nobody says you have to weep," Quinn said. "You did far more of that when you were younger than you do now. Just be more yourself than you have been."

Roland thought that was good advice. He'd already determined that he would attempt to modify his temperament as much as he could. Perhaps he ought to loosen the reins a bit and see what happened. Perhaps Lady Serenity would welcome it. Perhaps.

It felt risky, but it also felt practical. And truthful.

In any case, he would see her again on the morrow at eleven. Even if it were misting.

PATIENCE HAD ARRIVED to the house for breakfast. She and Lord Stanford had come into London last evening and she'd been eager to see her sisters. As well, she particularly adored Cook's fried eggs. He had a way of burning them just a little around the edges that her own cook had not yet got the hang of.

They'd had a lively time at table, with their father, Winsome, and Verity weighing in regarding their opinions of Lord Thorpe and Lord Charles. Valor, very predictably, was against both of those gentlemen. Though, she did have to admit that it was gracious of Lord Thorpe to recognize what a heroic effort it took her to stay awake so late. He'd said most youths couldn't do it, which made her special. She supposed she already knew that, but it was gratifying to understand that other people were so struck by it.

Serenity did not recall him saying exactly that, but she supposed the sentiment was close enough. In any case, Valor was pleased with it. Before her youngest sister had even come into the room Serenity had heard her describing the compliment to Thomas and asking for his opinion on the matter. As they were great friends, Thomas had assured Valor that no other youth would be capable of her feats in staying awake.

Not surprisingly, she heartily agreed with the sentiment.

After breakfast, the duke had gone off to his library and Mrs. Right had commandeered Valor, Verity, and Winsome. They were to have their wardrobes inventoried and lists would be made for the shops.

Serenity supposed Mrs. Right was very astute in arranging it. She and Patience could have a quiet cup of tea without interruption. They went to the very back of the drawing room to a cozy corner settee.

"We did not expect you back so soon," Serenity said. "Are the renovations to the Brighton house done already? Papa asked you about it, but you were very vague."

"The renovations are not even close to being done," Patience said. "But I will tell you the cause of our precipitous return if you can keep it to yourself."

"Of course I can. It's Valor who repeats everything she hears."

"It will not stay a secret forever, but for now it is very early days."

"Early days? Oh, you mean—"

Patience nodded. "I am with child. But as I said, it is very early and it may not go forward. I will not be more certain of it for another month and a half or so. Then it will be safer to say."

Serenity nodded. It was such a frightening thing. A pregnancy might easily terminate itself in the very early months and nobody really knew why. She wondered what God was thinking to arrange such a situation. She'd asked the vicar about it once, but he got very cross and told her to stop questioning the lord's thinking.

"In any case, I did tell Stanford, which in retrospect may have been a mistake."

"How could it be a mistake? Surely, he of all people should know."

"Yes, of course. But I had not anticipated how he would receive it."

"He is unhappy? Why?"

"Because he has convinced himself that my chances of surviving it are exceedingly slim. If I am to live, every precaution must be taken. I slipped out of the house this morning and left a note with the butler, else Stanford would try to stop me. Somehow, the entire outdoors has been populated with dangers of every sort. My condition is why we are back to Town so early. He insists that we be nearby the best physicians at all times. So, we are here for the duration, whatever that may turn out to be."

Serenity dabbed at her eyes. "It's so touching, really, that he should be so worried."

"Of course it is and I love him to pieces for it, but gracious, I cannot even get out of a chair without him leaping to my side to hold me up as if I might...fall on the carpet, I suppose. The journey from Brighton took five days! He insisted on going very slow and had me sitting on pillows. He banished Carwyn and Cecil to the luggage coach with his valet as they are prone to jumping."

"Ah yes, the two little terriers you adopted when you were in Wales on your wedding trip."

"Yes, they are darlings, really. But let it be said that one terrier is ambitious, yet two terriers together create a sort of synergy that makes them greater than the sum of their parts. I sometimes feel as if we've got ten of them in the house, they are so full of mischief. Now, enough about my happy but rather ridiculous situation. I do not know if everything regarding Lord Thorpe was said at the breakfast table, or whether you held something back. My twin instincts tell me that you might have."

Serenity leaned back on the settee. She and Patience were really so different, but because they were twins, there was some sort of thread that connected them. She should have known Patience would press for details that had not been spoken. "Lord Thorpe really is glorious and I think he likes me. He very cleverly arranged that we should meet at eleven on the mornings it does not rain to walk our dogs together in the square. Even if it's misting we are to go."

Patience giggled. "You've examined the right course for a misting? Very promising, indeed."

"Yes, I do think so. Mrs. Right said we ought not go when it rains and then he challenged the idea and said we need not be afraid of a misting. It's just that, well, he seems rather reserved. At least, sometimes he does and then at other times less so. I do not mind it really, but I wonder if he would like… In any case, I have been very careful to not…you know."

"Weep," Patience said, instantly understanding her fear.

Serenity nodded. "I've had some close calls, you know how things can sneak up on me. So far, I've kept it under control well enough, I think."

"How long is that to go on, though?" Patience asked.

"Forever?" Serenity said.

"Do not be daft, sister," Patience said. "How long could you keep it up if you were living in close quarters? One remarkable sunrise, and you *do* think they are all remarkable, and there would be the weep over the glories of nature. Never mind come summer when you are forever finding dead bees in the garden. Goodness, it is almost as if you go looking for them."

Of course, she did go looking for dead bees. She'd been doing it for so many years that it seemed a duty or a habit by now. Patience's dubiousness over her ability to keep her wild emotions under wraps at all times was Serenity's primary concern. "Well, what I am working toward is to move my temperament a bit toward…less sentimentality. Not to be a different person, but to…modulate a bit better."

Patience was silent for a moment. "You might be able to do it. I have worked very hard to rein in my toe-tapping. Only last week, Stanford was weighing the benefits versus the costs of replacing the roof on the Brighton house. It did seem the debate he had with himself was going on for a terrible amount of time. I had the urge to get a ladder, climb up it, and start ripping the shingles off myself."

"But you did not do it?"

Patience shook her head. "No, I did not do it, or toe-tap, or say a word of complaint. I took a deep breath, stared at the tea tray, pinched my hand, pulled a loose thread from my dress, looked up at the ceiling for a while, pinched myself again, poured myself a cup of tea, and ate a biscuit. He eventually decided to replace the roof.

Serenity giggled over the strategy.

"As well, I find it helpful to remind myself of what care Stanford takes of me," Patience went on. "I could easily have wed a careless man who would not concern himself that his family might get rained on."

Just then, the drawing room doors crashed open. "There you are! Thank God, are you all right?" Lord Stanford said.

Patience snorted and whispered, "I am about to be rescued from nothing again."

CHAPTER NINE

M RS. RIGHT WAS not very often put on the back foot. She was very much on the back foot just this moment though. How on earth could she have guessed that Mr. Cremble would go to a local churchman for counsel regarding her burning eyes when nearby a cross?

"Mrs. Right," Mr. Cremble said, "I hope you are not offended, but if you have been in contact with…you know…and somehow been affected, as it seems you have, you need experienced help!"

The churchman, a certain Curate-in-Charge of The Grosvenor Chapel named Mr. Amesbey, stepped forward. "Madam," he said, "what I have heard was disturbing to the highest degree. I have come hither to investigate Mr. Cremble's claims and provide assistance if that is deemed necessary. I will go to the bishop if this situation reveals itself to be beyond my ken."

Mrs. Right steadied herself lest she stagger. Call on the bishop! The duke would not thank her for bringing in a bishop to inquire into his housekeeper's dealings with the devil. She took a breath. "What claims?" she said, attempting to sound all innocence.

Mr. Amesbey and Mr. Cremble looked at one another. Mr. Cremble said, "She knows what claims! She cannot be near a cross or nearby anybody praying! Her eyes burn and she clutches at her head. The whole house knows it! They all act like it's the most usual thing in the world."

Mrs. Right wrinkled her brow. "What on earth are you talking about, Mr. Cremble?" She moved her fichu and pulled out the small gold cross round her neck.

Mr. Cremble stumbled backward. "How can that be? I have seen her repulsion to crosses with my own eyes. I even hid one under the table and it hurt her eyes. She could not have known it was there, but she staggered back. I saw it."

Just then, Charlie and Thomas came bounding down the stairs. They stopped short upon noting a strange gentleman in the servants' hall.

"Boys, as we feared," Mrs. Right said before they could say a word, "Mr. Cremble is not at all well. He has dragged this poor clergyman away from his duties with a wild story of how I cannot bear to be near crosses or prayers. Have you ever heard the like?"

The footmen, clever and ever-ready to jump into one of the housekeeper's gambits, both raised their brows. "What an idea," Charlie said.

"Mr. Cremble?" Mr. Amesbey asked. "You have not imagined all of this?"

"I certainly have not!"

"Perhaps a cup of tea will help settle you, Mr. Cremble?" Thomas asked.

"I believe that might be a very good notion, young man," the clergyman said. "Mr. Cremble, do you have any relations we might contact who could attend you?"

"You think I've gone mad! I haven't, I tell you. I've seen it with my own eyes. I don't know how she's wearing a cross now when two times, two times I tell you, she has been repulsed by them."

Mr. Amesbey led Mr. Cremble to a chair. "Please do sit down and tell us who we may contact."

Mr. Cremble sat down, looking about him like a caged animal. Then he took in a breath and narrowed his eyes. "I know who you can call on, Mr. Amesbey. Are you perhaps acquainted with Lady Marchfield?"

"Oh yes, very well, we work on several charitable committees together."

"Tell her what's going on," Mr. Cremble said, in a low voice.

Mrs. Right bit her lip. That would not be a helpful development. "Now, Mr. Cremble, there is no need to bother Lady Marchfield."

Mr. Cremble took Mr. Amesbey's hand. "I beg of you, call on Lady Marchfield. Tell her what's happened. She placed me into this house and she ought to be informed. I'd write her myself but *she*," he said, pointing at Mrs. Right, "would likely steal it out of the post. The devil's work is being done here—anything might happen!"

"Certainly there can be no cause—" Mrs. Right said, trailing off as she was not particularly sure where to go next with the situation.

Mr. Amesbey considered Mr. Cremble's request. And probably the desperation in his eyes. "Very well, Mr. Cremble. I do not know how it could help, but I will carry out your wishes. Until then, I beg you to calm yourself."

Mrs. Right sighed. This was a fine kettle of fish.

PATIENCE HAD LEFT, laughing as she was practically carried out of the house by Lord Stanford. Apparently, he had interviewed several physicians who were skilled at attending births, and he and Patience had much to discuss between them. His idea of the physician moving into the house a month ahead of time had so far not been well received, but he was convinced it was the right approach. He had not even had a chance to begin interviewing midwives yet. He had asked around for a recommendation at his club, but that also had not been well received, so he placed an advertisement.

The next two hours had ticked by slowly while Serenity anxiously watched the weather. It was clouding over but, finally, it was near eleven and there was no rain. It was time to proceed out with Nelson for the proposed walking of the dogs with Lord Thorpe.

Serenity had hoped that it might be only Mrs. Right to accompany her, but Winsome, Verity, and Valor had been so downcast over the suggestion that she could not hold firm on it. They had all three promised to walk well behind and not interrupt. Valor's promise was not particularly convincing, though, and the effects of Lord Thorpe's compliment to her ability to stay up beyond her time had seemed to fade rather quickly. At least, she was still pleased that it was well known that her staying up past her time was remarkable. It was just that she'd somehow discharged Lord Thorpe from getting any credit for pointing it out.

They all stood in the great hall, staring at the hall clock, as Serenity did not wish to look overeager. As it struck eleven, pelisses were donned and they set off.

The terrible idea of Lord Thorpe failing to turn up gripped Serenity as she walked out the doors. It would be devastating! She would be shamed in some way. She'd have to carry on with the walk as if she thought nothing of it. Tears leapt to her eyes and she quickly wiped them away. It was well she did, as he was already at the gate that led into the square, Havoc by his side and wildly wagging his tail at the sight of Nelson.

Though she would like to proceed in some dignified manner, Nelson was equally enthused to get sight of Havoc and pulled her forward.

As the two dogs greeted one another in the rather off-putting way that dogs sometimes do, involving a lot of sniffing in unmentionable areas, Serenity averted her eyes.

"Lady Serenity, Mrs. Right, Lady Verity, Lady Winsome, Lady Valor," Lord Thorpe said.

There were curtsies all round, though Valor's was rather perfunctory. "Lord Thorpe," Serenity said.

"Shall we proceed?" Lord Thorpe said.

Serenity nodded and they passed through the gate. Now that the dogs had greeted one another in their own particular fashion, they seemed happy to walk ahead, relatively side by side. There were the occasional stops to sniff at something along the path, and then Havoc took the opportunity to relieve himself, which Nelson felt compelled to investigate.

Both Serenity and Lord Thorpe pretended they did not notice these inelegant activities.

"I wonder if you will attend Lady Jellerbey's candlelight picnic this evening," Lord Thorpe asked.

"Yes, indeed I will."

Valor sighed heavily behind her.

"My father claims it is rather ridiculous to go stumbling around in the dark," Serenity continued, "however, Lady Jellerbey's sideboards are said to be very good."

Lord Thorpe nodded. "Lady Jellerbey herself is very genial and unlike a usual rout, she does not fill up her rooms to the point that it's uncomfortable."

"I was a little surprised that we were issued an invitation this year. Last year, my papa singed the lady's curtains as he was demonstrating setting Lady Vanderwake's curtains afire."

"Ah yes, people do still mention Lady Vanderwake's experience from time to time. Lady Jellerbey is good-humored though."

"Yes, I suppose she must be, else she would have left us off the list this year."

"Maybe she did!" Valor said.

"She did not, Poppet," Mrs. Right said, "else they would not be going."

"Singed curtains are not all that unusual," Verity said, "at least, I have heard it often said."

"From who?" Winsome asked.

Lord Thorpe's eyebrows raised just a little over Verity's comment and Serenity could see he was attempting to suppress a smile over her sister's latest bit of nonsense.

"I had a thought this morning of hosting a dinner," Lord Thorpe said.

"Oh, a dinner?"

"I thought I might repay the duke's hospitality."

"Not necessary!" Valor said.

"Valor," Winsome scolded.

"I thought I might arrange things in a rather unusual manner," Lord Thorpe went on. "I thought we might dine early, at six, as that might be more convenient for Lady Valor."

There was not a peep behind them and Serenity supposed Valor was taking in this latest compliment. It was really very good of Lord Thorpe to take her youngest sister into consideration. And very clever too.

"It is a very kind thought, Lord Thorpe," Serenity said. "I am sure my father would be gratified by such an invitation."

"Excellent."

They had left the turn behind them and proceeded back toward their own side of the square.

Both Nelson and Havoc began to pull on their leashes to speed up. It felt very like what a horse does when he comprehends that he is headed back to the stables to be rubbed down and given oats. Far too soon, they were through the gate and back on the pavement.

Lord Thorpe said, "That was a very pleasant walk, I believe Havoc really enjoyed it."

"I feel confident I can say the same for Nelson."

"I will send over the invitations to my dinner this afternoon. I hope you do not have a prior engagement on Friday."

"We might," Valor said sulkily.

"I am certain we do not," Serenity said.

"There is nothing on the calendar," Mrs. Right said.

Lord Thorpe bowed. "I take my leave then. Mrs. Right, Lady Serenity, Lady Verity, Lady Winsome, Lady Valor."

He turned and walked Havoc back to his own house.

Serenity turned herself, as she did not wish to be noted staring at his departure. It had gone exceedingly well!

"Lady Serenity," Lord Thorpe called from his doorstep, "we will walk again on the morrow?"

Serenity turned her head. "At eleven," she called.

She and her sisters hurried into the house. Throwing off their pelisses into the waiting arms of the footmen, Serenity said, "What a glorious walk."

Valor took that moment to stalk up the stairs. She turned on the staircase and said, "Now I am torn! I want him to go away forever and, also, I'm being honored with an early dinner!"

Serenity hid a smile. "It really is an honor, Valor."

"I know it," she said, giving the stair rise a good stomp.

ROLAND FELT THE dog walking had come off without a hitch. Coming back into the house had not been so pleasant. A letter waited for him from his brother. Charles wrote that The Albany was not proving as comfortable as he'd imagined and he was weighing whether he ought not move into the Grosvenor Square house. He asked that his rooms be made ready in case he decided in favor of the idea.

At first, Roland was confounded. He did not wish his brother in the house, especially when he was poised to hold a dinner for the duke and Lady Serenity. However, he could not keep him out. It was not his house yet, it was the duke's, and his father would insist that Charles have access to his rooms.

On further reflection and a conversation with Quinn regarding Charles' habits, he became more sanguine about it. As far as Quinn was concerned, this was a typical Charles-like salvo. He would have no intention of moving in and finding himself second fiddle, which was why he went to The Albany to begin. It was only that Charles could not help needling Roland that he might relocate into the house because he *could* relocate into the house if he wished.

Now, Roland haunted Lady Jellerbey's dim rooms for her annual candlelight picnic, waiting for Lady Serenity to arrive. As was Lady Jellerbey's habit, candelabras of all sorts stood lit on tables throughout, but the chandeliers overhead remained dark. It gave the house a gloomy and haunted feel, but for the very good sideboard offerings which cheered the whole thing up.

He'd seen Charles was already in attendance, though he'd wished that he would not see his brother at all. When Roland had caught sight of him, he'd slipped off to another room, hoping the dimness of the place had masked his departure.

Unfortunately, it did not. "Brother," Charles said, hurrying after him, "one would almost think you were avoiding me."

"One would be right," Roland said drily.

"I presume you received my letter and have directed the servants to ready my rooms."

"I have received your letter and have not directed the servants to do anything," Roland said. "I will not put my staff through a pointless exercise. If you wish to relocate into the house, you can arrive and bloody well wait in the drawing room until they've had a chance to get to it, which I will inform them is not a priority and should not interrupt their regular duties."

Charles, as he always did when Roland spoke in a forceful manner to him, bristled. "I do not suppose Father would approve of this less than welcoming attitude."

"Then you'd better write him and tell him all about it," Roland said. "Though, I will not lose any sleep over it. The proud Lord Charles never places himself in a situation where he is not the most important man in the room, so I am not expecting you to arrive."

"Just because you will inherit the house does not make you the most important," Charles said petulantly.

"It does in that house. I think you would find that Quinn would take no orders from you and the footmen follow Quinn's lead in everything. You'd be lucky to get a tea tray when you asked for it."

"Quinn," Charles said derisively. "You must be the only marquess in England who holds on to his nanny."

"Quinn has more value, in both common sense and a moral compass, than you have as yet demonstrated."

At the mention of a moral compass, which Roland was certain Charles understood to be a failing, his brother looked as if he would explode.

"What ho!"

The conversation was interrupted by the arrival of the duke and Lady Serenity. Roland's attention was immediately diverted from his steaming brother. Lady Serenity was looking entirely smashing in a crème colored satin with a midnight blue gauze overlay that was embroidered with bees charmingly circling daisies in a matching dark blue thread.

"Your Grace, Lady Serenity," Roland said.

"Lady Serenity, Duke," Charles said, pushing himself forward.

The duke looked at Charles, frowning. Roland understood his brother had just done a very ill-considered thing. In an effort to attempt to somehow place himself above Roland, he'd assumed a familiarity with the duke that had not been invited and was clearly not welcome.

"Your Grace, I think you meant to say," the duke pointed out to Charles.

Charles reddened at the chastisement. As well he should. It was the stupidest thing in the world to assume equal footing with a duke unless and until that duke insisted upon it. Roland was not aware of anybody who'd been given the honor by the Duke of Pelham, and he speculated that it amused the duke to be monikered in any way graceful. He *knew* it amused the duke to put a person on the back foot, as it seemed to be his preferred sport.

"Of course, Your Grace," Charles mumbled.

"Well, now that we have that sorted out," the duke said, "Thorpe, I got your invitation to dine for Friday and as I was certain to see you here, I could not bother writing out an answer. We will attend."

Roland was both gratified that the duke indicated attendance, and aggravated that it had been mentioned in front of Charles.

"There is a dinner? At *our* house?" Charles asked.

It did not escape Roland that his brother put the emphasis on "our" house.

"A very early dinner," Lady Serenity said. "Lord Thorpe has been so good as to take into consideration my youngest sister's fortitude, or lack thereof, when staying awake past her usual time for retiring."

"I see," Charles said. "It is in consideration of Lady Violet."

"Lady Valor," Roland corrected.

The duke looked at Charles and said, "Hah! It doesn't look like you were invited to this early dinner."

Lady Serenity laid a hand on her father's arm and said softly, "Papa, do not tease."

"I do not mind an early dinner; I would be delighted to come," Charles said. "My father has been urging me to visit the house and this will provide a perfect opportunity."

Before Roland could inform him that he had not and would not be invited regardless of what their father thought of it, Charles bowed. "Your Grace, Lady Serenity, I excuse myself to greet Lady Sommersby."

The duke said, "I suppose I put my foot in it there."

"Certainly not, Your Grace," Roland said. It was very true that the duke had put his foot in it, but there could be no benefit to confirming the idea.

"I know what the problem is," the duke said.

Roland braced himself for some comment on the less than genial relations between him and his brother.

"I have not yet had a glass of Lady Jellerbey's fine claret. I'll take myself to a sideboard and try not to singe her curtains this time! Thorpe—show my daughter round the place."

The duke strolled off, laughing to himself. Lady Serenity turned to him. "You do not like your brother much."

CHAPTER TEN

LADY SERENITY HAD just questioned the relationship Roland had with his brother and he had no compunction to lie about it. "I do not, due to a long history between us. I do hold out hope that someday he will not be plagued over finding himself the second son. In essence, I hope that he matures and looks around and notices all the benefits he does have. He will have a life of ease and very little responsibility."

Lady Serenity sighed. "It is harder on gentlemen, I am sure. I cannot imagine being jealous of Felicity on account of her being the eldest. But then, she is not in a position to inherit. All of my father's holdings are entailed and his title will go to my cousin."

Roland had not been aware of what the situation had been regarding inheritance in the duke's family. "Ah, so the duke's nephew will someday take on the mantle. Do you like him?"

"We do not know him," Lady Serenity admitted. "It seems my father and his brother did not get on any better than you do with your brother. I believe that's why my grandfather put on the entail—to keep the land together, lest my father thought to break it up. When my uncle died, which was several years ago, my cousin went to live with more distant relations. In any case, he is still very young, near Valor's age, I believe."

"Perhaps the duke is lucky that he's only had daughters, despite the world thinking it some sort of disappointment."

Lady Serenity laughed. "I am quite sure that my father is well satisfied with his lot, though he is forever naming us setbacks that he is determined to get out of his house."

Roland smiled, as that did seem to be the duke's peculiar brand of affection.

From the corridor, a gentleman called out, "The Earl of Mumsby is setting off fireworks, you can see them from the garden!"

"Shall we go?" Roland asked.

LORD THORPE HAD held his arm out as he asked Serenity if she would care to go into the garden to view the fireworks being set off. "Indeed, yes," she said. "I have only seen them one time as my father will not take us to Vauxhall—he calls it the place people go to act like idiots and then hope it is not widely reported in the morning. He says if he is to do anything shocking, and sometimes he does like to, he will do it in somebody's drawing room."

Lord Thorpe held out his arm and they made their way toward Lady Jellerbey's back garden. "Yes, Vauxhall can certainly be that unfortunate place for some, as I believe Lady Highland discovered last season."

"What happened?" Serenity asked. She'd heard nothing about it. She supposed her older sisters probably had and thought it not the sort of information to bandy about.

Now she was almost sure of it, as Lord Thorpe looked uncomfortable to be asked.

"Well, let's just say she took an unfortunate stroll down the dark walk with an ill-advised companion. Where did you see fireworks the one time you did have the opportunity?"

Lord Thorpe seemed determined to change the subject back to fireworks and away from whatever Lady Highland had done on the dark walk with whoever she'd done it with. Serenity said,

"I saw them in the Dales. My father paid some fellow to set them off over Christmas one year. The first few went off without a hitch, but then there was some sort of explosion. In any case, the man ended with a very burned hand and a nearby barn burned to the ground."

"A barn?" Lord Thorpe asked. He looked positively stricken.

"I can see you fear for the horses, as did I at the time. They were all taken out once the roof caught, so it was only the structure that burned."

Lord Thorpe let out an audible sigh of relief.

"I remember we all stood out in the cold night air watching the flames and my father said, 'Well that was more of a show than I paid for.' He was such a dear to say it, as I think it must have cost him a deal of money to replace the barn and he must have been aggravated, but he wished to soothe Valor. She was terrified that everything in the neighborhood would burn."

"Lady Valor seems determined to stop her sisters from a wedding," Lord Thorpe said.

Serenity's breath caught. It felt like a daring statement. They had entered the garden along with a dozen others who'd come to see the fireworks. As a burst of orange and white could be seen in the distance, she said, "Valor has watched three sisters leave the house and she does not think she will wish to marry herself, so she would prefer the rest of us do not, either."

"Ah, because she does not like the idea of being stared at in the night."

"Or a gentleman being in the room all night either," Serenity said softly.

The fireworks burst on the eastern horizon and they were of such beauty that they did begin to affect Serenity's feelings. As a strategy, she pretended to look up but averted her eyes to the left so she did not weep over the majesty of it. Things were proceeding so well she would not allow herself to reveal any oversentimentality she might be afflicted with.

Their hands brushed and both of them pretended they had

not noticed. Nor did either of them move their hands away.

"There you are," the duke said, approaching from behind. "Stole my daughter out to a dark garden, did you?"

At that comment, they did move their hands away. "Certainly not, Your Grace," Lord Thorpe said. "We were alerted to the idea that Lord Mumsby's fireworks were visible."

"Yes, yes, I only jest," the duke said. "If I were serious, I'd demand a duel. Which, by the by, everybody knows I would not turn up for. Deuced early things. Don't know why anybody gets up for them."

Serenity could see very well that Lord Thorpe suppressed a snort. He seemed to understand her father, which she very much appreciated, as not everybody did. She also thought her father must very much approve of Lord Thorpe, or he would not jest about his daughter being located in a dark garden with the gentleman.

The three stood together watching the Earl of Mumsby's fireworks until the very last one faded to darkness in the night sky.

WHEN SERENITY HAD arrived home from Lady Jellerbey's candlelight picnic, she'd found that Valor was long abed and Winsome and Verity played lottery tickets with Mrs. Right. As was her sisters' usual habit, they grilled her with questions about the evening, and about Lord Thorpe in particular.

She told them as much as she wished to, but she did not tell them everything. She did not tell them one thing. That, she would keep to herself.

Their hands had brushed. And neither of them had pulled away. She wondered if it were shocking that she'd not pulled her hand away, though, much to her surprise, she found she did not care a whit if it *had* been shocking.

She'd almost wept there and then, so overcome was she. And of course, the majesty of the fireworks had almost set her off. She'd averted her eyes so she might more easily compose herself.

Serenity felt she'd done quite a creditable job of it too. The only problem, as Patience had pointed out, was how long could she keep it up? How long would it be before the marquess got a look at the real her? The dead bees and brushing hands and beauty of the dawn weeper, Serenity Nicolet?

What would he think? She could not bear to see the admiration fade from his eyes. He did admire her, there could be no other conclusion. She could not bear the idea that he was attracted to someone who was not quite herself, and that he might not admire her real self—the lady weeping over all and sundry.

Somehow, she was going to have to keep it up, though. She would have to toughen up. She had to remake herself into someone who would be a worthy marchioness, eventually to become a duchess. Nobody had ever heard of a weeping duchess and she thought nobody would prefer it. Certainly nobody had ever heard of a duchess who secretly kept a crypt of dead bees!

She lay in her bed, watching clouds gathering to shield the moon from view and wept over it.

THE COLD AND raining morning had brought a headache of massive proportions. Charles had perhaps drunk a bit more than was his usual habit at Lady Jellerbey's candlelight whatever that was supposed to be. It was Thorpe's fault. His brother just could not resist poking him where he should not be poked.

Ever since his father had once counseled him on the idea of acquiring a moral compass while Thorpe had been on the other side of the door gleefully listening, he'd had the idea constantly thrown in his face. That particular situation of so many years ago had been ridiculous to start with. All he'd done was throw a few stones at a village boy and he'd been hauled into the library like it was a hanging offense.

His father had gone on a long diatribe about how a ducal

family must lead by an example of dignity, kindness, and liberality. To fail to do so was to invite certain ideas the French had not so long ago explored. No lord lived behind high walls and moats guarded by a private army any longer. They held power not because they commanded it through force, but because it was afforded them through respect. If respect was gone, the guillotines were not so very far away. Nobody should ever be foolish enough to suppose it could not happen here, as that is just what every French nobleman who lost his head had mistakenly believed.

Charles had presumed it all nonsense. Since when was an uneducated village cur going to have the nerve to propose chopping off his head?

He winced as he was forced to remember what the uneducated village cur *had* found the nerve to do. Days later, Charles had been walking through the wood to a stream to fish for trout when he'd been set upon by the uneducated village cur and two of his uneducated friends. He'd been badly beaten and then informed that if he complained to the duke, it would be put about that he was responsible for a certain dairy maid's rather expanded condition. That would probably not have married well with the duke's ideas of a moral compass so he'd kept quiet about it and claimed he'd been thrown from his horse. He suspected Thorpe knew the truth, as his brother was always so friendly with the uneducated village curs.

Thorpe's barbs last evening had caused him to indulge too heavily. The factor that really sent him over the edge was when he'd looked all over Lady Jellerbey's rooms for Lady Serenity, hoping she'd since separated herself from his brother. He'd finally found her out in the back garden. She, her father, and Thorpe were watching Lord Mumsby's rather tepid fireworks display. He could not avoid noticing that Thorpe and Lady Serenity were standing closer than would be socially acceptable.

Thorpe was getting ahead of him. How was he doing it? Was it the ridiculous dog walks?

Perhaps he ought to borrow a dog from someone and turn up

for one of these dog walks. He would weigh that idea, but one idea did not need to be weighed. Thorpe was holding a dinner, an early dinner for Lady Violet or Valor or Vera. He did not need to debate if he would attend *that*, as of course he would. Let Thorpe attempt to bar the door against him if he would try it. It was his door too, and Thorpe was not yet the duke. Thorpe was just the son of a duke, as he was himself.

In the meantime, he'd spend the day holding a cold compress to his forehead, wondering who he might have offended last evening.

MRS. RIGHT HAD spent the morning in the drawing room, attempting to cheer up everybody in it. The rain was pouring down in buckets out of doors and not even the most cheerful sort of person could name it only a misting. The dog walking was off for that morning, at least.

Of all of them, Valor was the least affected and seemed to take the dousing rain as a definitive comment on Lord Thorpe and his dog-walking ideas.

Thomas had brought in a tea tray and Mrs. Right could see very well that Cook had gone to an extra effort. The miniature apple cakes were in abundance, along with the usual almond biscuits with the duke's stamp on them.

"Now girls, remember what we have always done in bad weather when we are in the Dales," she said.

Valor whispered the idea to Mrs. Wendover. She had so far managed to keep hold of her stuffed rabbit for the past few days, though Nelson rolled on his back and looked at it longingly.

"We can sometimes be very cozy when it rains in the Dales," Winsome said. "We should all find books in the library as we do there."

"Winsome can read from one of them," Verity said.

"Why must I always read, though?" Winsome asked. "Why do not you take a turn at it?"

Verity looked out the window and said, "You have the better voice for it, as everybody knows."

"If I have to read, then I will choose what it is," Winsome said.

"Of course, you should choose," Verity said, "but I hope you choose something that is educational, as I do like to know facts. Something about the Greeks would be efficacious."

"Perhaps efficacious, but not as interesting as something gothic," Winsome said, setting off for the library. "With any luck, I'll find some poor maiden trapped in a lonely and damp castle with no hope of escape."

Mrs. Right nodded, as she highly approved of the idea. There was nothing she liked better than tragic maidens in damp castles worrying over who kept murdering people. In any case, she could not fathom what Verity did with all the facts she gathered. She seemed to put them in her mind and mix them up like a cake.

As Winsome went out the doors, Charlie came through them holding a silver salver with a letter on it. "Addressed to Lady Serenity," he said. "Just delivered by one of Lord Thorpe's footmen."

Serenity sat up straight, as she had been rather slumped on the sofa in what looked like a state of ennui. She tore open the letter. She smiled and said, "He writes that he is shocked that nature has thought to punish them with heavy rain and made an urgent request to provide sunshine on the morrow. Or if not sunshine, then nothing more than a misting."

"Now that's a very cheering idea," Mrs. Right said.

"It is, rather," Serenity said.

"He's not read my letter yet then, or he would not be so cheerful," Valor muttered.

Mrs. Right took in a breath. Verity dropped her sewing. Serenity stared at Valor.

Winsome came back into the room and looked about.

"What? Why do you all stare at Valor like that?"

"She's written another letter," Verity said in a dark tone.

"Valor!" Serenity cried. "You were told you must not send any more letters."

"I wasn't going to," Valor said, burying her face into Mrs. Wendover's miniature India shawl.

"Then why did you do it?" Winsome asked.

"It got away from me, and also, Lady Margaret gave me some very good advice."

Mrs. Right sighed. Valor's letter writing was meant to come to an end last season after the rather unfortunate missive sent to Lord Stanford mentioning that Valor hoped he would die and the devil would burn him up. Now she'd gone to Lady Margaret for advice. That lady was very old and exceedingly eccentric and thought everything Valor did was very clever. Heaven knew what she'd told her young friend in their ongoing and very eccentric correspondence.

"What did that letter say, Valor?" Serenity said, her hands shaking as she laid down Lord Thorpe's letter.

Valor looked up at the ceiling as if the answer were to be found there. "Only that I had certain demands about him taking you away."

Good Lord.

"Tell me you did not sign it," Serenity said, brushing tears from her cheeks.

"I had to," Valor whispered. "Or else he wouldn't know who was making the demands."

"What demands?" Verity asked.

"Well, mostly just that you would sleep at our house and he could sleep wherever he wanted…somewhere else."

"He has not even asked for my hand, Valor," Serenity cried, sobbing. "You have humiliated me! He will never ask now."

This, not very surprisingly, caused Valor to sob. Then, once two sisters were sobbing, the last two must follow suit. Mrs. Right was not sure how it could have happened so quickly, but she was now in receipt of four sobbing girls.

"There now, Serenity," she said soothingly, "nobody who has ever been the target of one of Valor's outrageous letters has ever been much affected by it."

"They haven't?" Valor asked through her sobs.

"Of course they haven't, Poppet, and a very good thing too. You are sticking your nose in where it does not belong, whatever good intentions you had doing it."

"My nose knows it!" Valor cried.

"What am I to do?" Serenity asked.

"Nothing at all," Mrs. Right said. "Lord Thorpe will take the letter for what is is—a panicked younger sister lashing out."

"I really am panicked and I did lash out," Valor whispered.

"Now, enough of this crying and predicting disaster," Mrs. Right said, knowing that sometimes a firm hand was the best way to herd her girls back into sense. "I will go find the sherry decanter and pour a drop for Serenity, the rest of you drink your tea, and all will be well."

As she went off to do so, she passed Charlie in the great hall. "From now on, no letter written by Lady Valor leaves this house without me looking it over first."

Charlie nodded. "I did hesitate this time, Mrs. Right, but she told me that Lady Serenity had approved it."

Mrs. Right chuckled. "She's a daring little thing, but no longer believe a word she says. She'll grow out of this nonsense at some point, and that point cannot come too soon."

She had expected to find Mr. Cremble in the dining room, fussing over things as he liked to do in an attempt to avoid her. He was nowhere to be seen, though. She retrieved the sherry decanter and made her way back to the drawing room. Just outside the great hall, she heard a very ominous sound indeed. The front doors had opened and Lady Marchfield said, "I'll show myself in."

Mrs. Right was all but sure the curate from The Grosvenor Church had been as good as his word and gone to see the lady regarding the question of the housekeeper's aversion to crosses. Fortunately, the duke had left the house to meet with his solicitor at White's, so Lady Misery would not be getting in his ear about it. She backed away and set off for her quarters to make herself scarce.

There were times when she enjoyed crossing swords with Lady Misery, but this time was not one of those times. Like any good general, she would make a strategic retreat and live to fight another day.

ROLAND HAD THOUGHT it rather daring to write Lady Serenity on account of the weather. He'd done it anyway. After all, they'd practically held hands last evening. They had not, but things had come very close to it. Of course, had they actually held hands he would have needed to declare himself on the spot. He *would* declare himself, but he needed a little more time.

When the duke's footman had arrived at his doorstep with a letter, he had briefly imagined that Lady Serenity had responded to his wish for better weather on the morrow. The letter was not from Lady Serenity, though. It was a rather alarming missive from Lady Valor. He handed it to Quinn to have a look at it.

Lord Thorpe—I have found myself disturbed that you are alive. (I wouldn't mind if you were alive somewhere else, like America, I am a reasonable person.) I finally decided to consult with my very good friend Lady Margaret. We have had a correspondence for two whole years and she considers me her very dearest friend. (She admires my youth, as she is very old.) Lady Margaret sent several suggestions that might make it not so terrible that you exist. I thought you should know about them before we come to dinner.

First, I am hoping that you cannot convince Serenity to marry you (and I really don't know how Mr. Stratton, Lord

Dashlend, and Lord Stanford have been able to convince my three eldest sisters because as far as I can see it only leads to having a man stare at you while you sleep). BUT, if you can convince her, here are my demands: One, you must always be in London when we are here and you can't mind it when Serenity sleeps at our house, which would be on every night we are here. (You will stay at your house, obviously) Two, you must spend the summer months with us in the Dales. There is an empty gardener's cottage you can use and Serenity has her own room in the house. (Or else she could just come by herself, whichever is most convenient, I am a reasonable person.)

I do not expect any argument from you, Sir, as my mind is quite made up. Lady Margaret assures me that I am being very liberal with my terms because you do me the honor of planning dinner at an early time to accommodate my youth. Consider me reasonable! Valor Nicolet.

CHAPTER ELEVEN

Q UINN HAD JUST laid down the letter from Lady Valor with a laugh. "She's a bit of a corker."

"Or something like that," Roland said.

"Who is Lady Margaret?"

Roland shrugged. "I have no idea—an elderly relative, perhaps?"

"I suppose Lady Serenity remains unaware that her youngest sister has taken it upon herself to issue terms to the gentlemen in her sphere."

"That is just it, though. Lady Valor certainly has the idea that I will ask and will be accepted. Might she not have got that idea from Lady Serenity?"

"Perhaps so."

"That is a very good sign, then," Roland said.

"So you will ask?"

"Well…I intend to, naturally."

"What holds you back? And do not tell me it is some nonsense about her only having been introduced to the reserved marquess as of yet."

"Is it not a concern, though? Last evening, she told me a story about a barn burning down. You can guess where my mind went."

"To the horses in that barn," Quinn said, "which would have caused you to recall Balthazar, your poor pony that had to be put down."

"That is exactly it. I had a time of it keeping my expression neutral."

"You know, that's when it all started, this emotional flying up and down mountaintops. I've always wondered if that horrific scene did not permanently affect your mind in some way. It was not long after that you discovered that Clara, that housemaid, had been dismissed. You took that harder than you might have."

Roland smiled. "I took it hard enough to steal fifty pounds from my father."

"That you did. Never mind the father of her child was the local tavernkeeper who eventually married her. I reckon that fifty pounds set them up very well."

Of course, that was true. Clara's situation had not been as dire as he'd imagined. He'd thought if he did not do something, she would be left begging on the streets with a newborn baby in her arms. It had seemed imperative to act.

But the idea of a burning barn was not the only thing that had nearly set him off last night. "I had to avert my eyes while we watched the fireworks lest…well, what I say is that they were only fireworks. The way I sometimes react to things feels unnatural."

Quinn shrugged. "Nothing unnatural about it. In any case, it seems to me that married couples encounter all sorts of surprises after the wedding. I distinctly remember your mother being a bit taken aback by what she termed your father's snores that could wake the dead. They kept separate bedchambers, but she insisted she could hear it from her own. She'd spoken to her lady's maid about it, wondering why the duke had not mentioned it beforehand."

"I am not sure that is the same."

"A lady could do worse than to discover her lord is rather a soft touch. I do not suppose you would deny her any amount of pin money or anything else she wished for."

Roland considered it, as that was probably true. Too many ladies discovered just the opposite. Once the wooing was done, she might discover she'd wed a rather hard character. He was very afraid that anybody who agreed to wed Charles would discover precisely that.

"What do you plan to do about this letter, though? I do not suppose you intend on meeting this little lady's demands."

Roland laughed despite himself. "No, I certainly will not. I thought I might answer the letter, but then I decided that, for now at least, I'll leave it."

Quinn nodded. "Just what I would advise. If Lady Serenity has been made aware of this effrontery, she will be highly embarrassed. No need to pile on the embarrassment with an acknowledgement."

Roland nodded. "I will just ignore it, as if it never arrived here at all."

"Very encouraging that the young miss considers a wedding as a thing practically done, though."

"Yes, it is very encouraging indeed."

SERENITY WAS RATHER distressed that Lady Marchfield had arrived right when the drawing room was overflowing with weeping sisters. The look on her aunt's face indicated she was rather distressed too.

"What on earth is going on in here?" she asked, throwing her cloak to Thomas.

"I couldn't help it!" Valor cried. "I sent another letter."

"To Lord Thorpe," Verity said, wiping her eyes. "As is becoming a usual thing."

"She listed her demands," Winsome said, wiping her nose on her sleeve, "mostly about Serenity sleeping here and him sleeping…somewhere else."

Lady Marchfield sat down on the settee. "Am I to understand that Lord Thorpe has asked?"

Serenity went to sobbing again, as that was the real crux of it. He had not asked and Valor had written him a letter presuming he would.

"He hasn't," Winsome said.

"He will, though," Valor said. "They always do, no matter what I write."

"Let me understand this," Lady Marchfield said gravely. "Lord Thorpe, a marquess who will someday inherit a dukedom, has paid some attention to Serenity. And you, Valor, saw fit to write him about who knows what, though it is the height of effrontery to write him at all?"

Valor shrugged. "That's the size of it."

"May I ask how you ever thought that was appropriate?"

Valor, looking very cornered, glanced down at Mrs. Wendover, the stuffed rabbit hanging limp in her arms. Seeming to see that blaming Mrs. Wendover for her misdeeds was an idea that had run its course, she said, "Lady Margaret told me to do it."

"Then Lady Margaret is an idiot. I really do not understand you girls at all. Whenever anything promising seems to be developing you go out of your way to ruin it."

"Ruin it?" Serenity asked softly. "Do you say that Lord Thorpe will be so offended that he will lose interest on account of it?"

"I would presume so. What is a highly placed gentleman to think of such a thing? He will be looking for a bride who will do him credit and a family connection he can be proud of and all I see here is eccentricity and uncultured boldness run amok."

Serenity's heart sank even lower than it had sunk. She'd been afraid the letter would put Lord Thorpe off, but to hear it spoken so decidedly by her aunt made it seem more certain.

"I have tried and tried to help you girls, but you will have none of it. I suppose the piper will finally have his due. It seems you will only learn through experience, as painful as that is bound to be. I wash my hands of it. Now, where is Cremble?" Lady Marchfield turned to the rather stunned footmen standing at the doors. "You. Thomas, is it? Retrieve Mr. Cremble for me this instant."

Serenity sat on the sofa feeling as if she had almost left her body. Her aunt could not be right. Just because Lord Thorpe would one day be His Grace, that did not mean he would not be stalwart in the face of a younger sister's ridiculous letter. Mrs. Right had all but said so.

But then, Mrs. Right was always attempting to make them feel better. On the other hand, Lady Marchfield just stated things she thought were a fact. She could not be right. Perhaps her family did not do every single thing just as the *ton* would have it done. It did not make them bad people. She did not think.

What if her aunt was right, though? What if Valor's letter had been a step too far? If Serenity were to take out Nelson on the morrow at eleven, would she be humiliated to find herself abandoned? If that happened, how could she bear to go to his house to dine, knowing she was not wanted?

How could she bear it, when they'd brushed hands last night?

Thomas had set off to locate Mr. Cremble and came back with him after not too long a time. As Serenity brooded and swiped at her tears, Mr. Cremble said, "Lady Marchfield, thank heavens you have arrived."

The lady nodded. "I heard all about what's gone on from the curate. I assured him that I would not be at all surprised to discover that Mrs. Right *was* in league with the devil as it would explain quite a lot."

Mr. Cremble nodded sadly.

"Furthermore, I told him there is not the least chance you are losing your faculties. I can assure you he intends to investigate this matter. I suggested he bring the bishop into it."

"Thank you, Lady Marchfield," Mr. Cremble said with relief in his voice.

Serenity, of course, knew of Mrs. Right's gambit to frighten Mr. Cremble with ideas about the devil. She'd not imagined the bishop might be lured into it, though.

"Once I was alerted to what has gone on in this house, I gave it some deep thought and consulted with Lord Marchfield. As it happens, our vicar is intending to retire in two years' time. If you are agreeable to be a curate for Mr. Hartshorn for that amount of time, Marchfield will give you the living."

The joy that overtook Mr. Cremble's features could not be overestimated. "Lady Marchfield, I accept! Heartily! It is my calling to make the church my life's work."

Serenity stared at him and thought she ought to be happy that at least one person in the house was happy.

Lady Marchfield nodded graciously. "Go and pack your bags, Mr. Cremble. I will put you up tonight and send you to the estate on the first coach out on the morrow, with a letter of introduction to Mr. Hartshorn. I am certain you will find the vicarage very comfortable—it is exceedingly roomy and affords a pretty little view. Mr. Hartshorn will be grateful for your arrival, as he has been inquiring into when we might send someone. He is arthritic, you see."

"Mr. Hartshorn will find a willing servant in me, my lady! The lord has sent me through the fires to prove my worthiness, and I have come out of it unsinged," Mr. Cremble said, hurrying out the door.

Lady Marchfield turned her attention to the tea tray and poured a cup while she waited for Mr. Cremble to pack up his things.

All four sisters surreptitiously glanced at their aunt, waiting for a further scolding. As she did not scold, they did not know what to make of it.

Winsome said, "So I suppose that's it for the butlers. There won't be another one coming next year, I would guess."

Lady Marchfield set her cup down and said, "If you knew what I was thinking on that score, Winsome, it would send a chill down your spine."

Serenity stared at Lady Marchfield, wide-eyed. Valor cried, "It's going to be scary!"

"What will be scary, young miss," Lady Marchfield said gravely, "is if you have the audacity to write one more letter to a gentleman of the *ton*. I advise you do not try it or you will never wed—society has a very long memory."

"I'm never getting married anyway! It's terrible!" Valor wept into Mrs. Wendover's limp body.

Nelson, seeming to come to his own conclusions regarding the tone of the room, staggered up on his three legs, nipped a biscuit off the tea tray, and loped out to have it elsewhere.

"I hope you are all satisfied to have come to such a pass," Lady Marchfield said.

The last thing Serenity could claim to feel was satisfied. It felt as if all her hopes were crumbling like sand through her fingers. She felt like she could weep for a hundred years, though little good it would do her. Little good it had ever done her.

MRS. RIGHT HAD very sensibly taken herself to her quarters upon the arrival of Lady Marchfield. As she was the senior-most servant in the house, aside from the odd butler coming and going, she enjoyed a large bedchamber and a generous sitting room attached. Both rooms had a view of the back garden, and both had cheery little fireplaces. There was even a very small and narrow dressing room. Though it was not as large as her accommodations in the Dales, she'd always been well satisfied with her quarters in Town.

Just now, though, she paced those quarters. At least Lady Marchfield had not arrived with the bishop in tow, though that might be next.

But what was a poor housekeeper to do when faced with an unwanted butler? It was not as if she'd had any choice. After all, the duke had made clear that he did not wish for a butler. If she was not to rid the place of him, then who would?

There was always the idea that the duke could order Mr. Cremble out of the house, just as he could have with the others who had come and gone. But Mrs. Right knew the duke better than anybody. He would never be satisfied with that idea, as he liked the game of seeing how they would be driven out. He'd been all his life in a cat and mouse game with his sister. He liked to be amused and there was not much amusement to be had in simply ordering them out.

So there it was. She'd had no choice but to convince the pious butler that she was in league with the devil. Anybody would have done the same.

Mrs. Right heard a firm rap on her door and went to answer it, presuming it was one of the maids come to tell her that Lady Marchfield had departed. She opened the door and was accosted by a heavy cross waving in her face.

"Hah!" Mr. Cremble cried. "Are your eyes burning?"

"Mr. Cremble!" she said, fighting him off, "what on earth are you doing in the women's quarters?"

Mr. Cremble stepped back, still waving the cross as if it afforded him protection. "I came to give you my final adieu, you diabolical woman. Lord Marchfield is to give me a living and I am leaving this godforsaken house forever! And guess what? Guess what, Mrs. Wrong? That's right, I called you Mrs. Wrong instead of Mrs. Right, which I thought up days ago! Guess what? Lady Marchfield is going to the bishop about you. What do you suppose that great and pious man will make of a wicked housekeeper causing havoc in the town he is sworn to protect from evil forces? Maybe he'll bring back burning at the stake! Au revoir!"

With that, Mr. Cremble picked up his travel case and fairly skipped down the corridor.

Lady Marchfield was going to the bishop. The very stern and conservative Bishop Porteus.

Well that was a fine kettle of fish.

THE FOLLOWING DAY did not dawn bright, but it was not raining either. It was a rather foggy sort of day and Serenity was wracked with all sorts of thoughts. She and Lord Thorpe had not discussed the efficacy of dog walking in the fog. And then, what if the weather was no matter anyway after Valor's ill-conceived letter outlining her outrageous demands?

She must go and find out, whatever it was to be. Lord Thorpe would either turn up or not turn up. But if he did not turn up, how was she to be certain of the cause? Perhaps he would not turn up because he thought *she* would not turn up in foggy weather.

Serenity had been teary-eyed all morning, her thoughts wildly swinging between imagining the best and fearing the worst. Her dear father had, of course, noticed her distress at breakfast.

"What's setting you off," he'd asked. "It cannot be the sunrise, as its as foggy as an old man's mind out there. Fog doesn't set you off, now?"

"No, Papa."

"You cannot be still brooding over Valor's letter," the duke said, "no sensible man in receipt of such nonsense will take it seriously."

"I wish somebody told me that to begin," Valor said.

"We all wish that, Valor," Winsome said.

"Regret is a very usual thing, as I understand it, Valor," Verity said.

"Papa, our aunt was very decided about it yesterday," Serenity said. "She said he is a marquess and will be a duke someday, and will expect his future duchess to be a credit to him."

"Oh, let me guess," the duke said, "Lady Misery imagines a duke must be all dignity and restraint, and wish the same from his duchess."

"Well, yes, I think that is what she meant."

"*I'm* a duke," her father pointed out. "When was the last time you caught me worrying over dignity or restraining myself in any fashion?"

None of them answered that, as they could not say.

"Never mind what Lady Misery thinks about it. She's taken that latest butler out of the house which is the most useful thing she's done in years. I count on Mrs. Right to tell me how it all came about and am prepared to be amused! Now, at eleven you'll take Nelson for a walk. I'll venture you'll find Thorpe at the gate into the square. Valor will make a heartfelt apology, and then Winsome will escort her back into the house as she's done enough for one season. All squared away."

"What am I to say, though?" Valor asked. "Should I pretend to be very sorry?"

"You should *in fact* be very sorry, Valor," Winsome said in a scolding tone.

"Well, I am when you talk like that to me," Valor said, crumbling her toast.

"Say you are sorry, it was a fit of pique due to your youth, and you have been punished by foregoing dessert for a week," the duke said. "That ought to do it."

"I'm not to have dessert? For a week?" Valor asked, in the panicked tone that can only come from a young person watching cakes and trifles slip out of their reach.

"No, no," the duke said. "Just say it—it will make Lord Thorpe feel better."

"You should tell the vicar about the making people feel better part," Valor said. "He says you can never lie, but I said you could do it to make people feel better. Like how I tell Winsome her hair looks great, even when it doesn't. He said I am too defiant and should repent of it. I said no."

"What about my hair?" Winsome asked.

"It usually looks all right," Valor muttered, "but then sometimes it doesn't, and what's the use in saying?"

The breakfast had gone on in such a manner, as the Nicolet

household's breakfasts usually did—wide-ranging debates from one subject to the next.

And now the hour approached eleven and they stood in the hall ready to don their pelisses and bonnets while Nelson pulled on his leash. They would proceed out and Valor would apologize and they would walk. If he was there.

If he was not there, Serenity was counting on the fog to hide her stupid weeping.

The clock chimed. "Come now, love," Mrs. Right said. "As your father would say, let's get this circus going."

They proceeded out with Valor trudging behind them. It really was a heavy fog, the warmer air that had descended on London taking advantage of what was left of the snow on the ground to cast up a blanket of grey.

Serenity squinted in the direction of the gate, but though squinting might work in sunshine it did nothing in the fog. She walked closer and saw the outline of a man. Her heart beat faster and she hurried forward.

Then she stopped short. She could not see the man's face yet, but the build was not right and the dog certainly was not right. It was not the great beast Havoc, but a much smaller dog.

CHAPTER TWELVE

SERENITY HAD HOPED to see Lord Thorpe at the gate of the square, but even through the fog she could perceive it was not him. Then she came close enough to discover it was Lord Charles.

He bowed and said, "Lady Serenity, I hope you do not mind me pushing into the dog walking. I was pressed by Lord Furtherington to walk his dog while he is out of Town. Apparently, the dog will not allow a servant to do it. It occurred to me that my home neighborhood would be a more pleasant location than the environs of The Albany."

"Oh. Goodness," Serenity said, really for lack of anything better to say.

"Lady Serenity," a deep voice said, emerging from the fog. It was him. Lord Thorpe. He had come.

"Charles. What do you here?" Lord Thorpe said, the scowl in his voice rather apparent.

"I'm walking Lord Furtherington's dog as a favor to him. I decided on this neighborhood as being the most amiable, which happens to be my own family's neighborhood, I would remind you."

"Silence!" Valor shouted.

Serenity sighed. Valor was meant to apologize. That was not a very promising start.

Valor stepped forward. "Lord Thorpe, I am very sorry about

anything I may have written and then may have had delivered to your house. It was a fit of pique due to my youth and I am forbidden to have dessert for a week. Though, I have not checked about having dessert in other people's houses, so that might still be all right."

She curtsied.

Lord Thorpe bowed. "Thank you, Lady Valor, but I have not seen such a letter. I imagine my butler removed it from my mail tray, suspecting it to be a pique of youth."

"That was lucky!" Valor said, entirely believing that bit of nonsense. Though, Lord Thorpe was very gracious to pretend he'd not read it.

"As that is the case, I am certain that dessert at my house must be all right."

"I would think so!" Valor said.

Just then, Nelson edged toward Lord Charles' dog, which was a liver and white colored spaniel. The two dogs growled at each other. Then Havoc growled and the spaniel backed away and hid behind Lord Charles' legs. Nelson wagged his tail as if he'd won the point.

"Perhaps separate those two dogs," Mrs. Right said. "It seems they do not care for one another's company."

"Very good idea, Mrs. Right," Lord Thorpe said. "Lady Serenity and I can walk ahead."

"I have to go back in the house," Valor said. "Winsome is to take me in, as my papa says I've already done enough this season, whatever that means."

"She knows perfectly well what that means," Winsome said, grasping Valor by the hand and pulling her away.

"I'm to stay, as I am the oldest but for Serenity, Patience, Grace, and Felicity," Verity said. "Lord Charles, I will walk with you, as I understand quite a lot about spaniels and would wish to compare notes. What is his name?"

"Oh, uh, well, Lord Furtherington never said."

"Ah, a usual thing for a lord to forget his dog's name," Verity said. "In particular with spaniels, I have heard said."

Serenity smiled. Lord Charles was about to have a time of it. Whenever Verity claimed to know quite a lot about a subject it was bound to be peppered with nonsense and hopeful imaginings.

They proceeded through the gate and Nelson playfully jumped around Havoc who put up with it in all good humor. The fog that Serenity had at first found so inconvenient was now thought lovely. It blanketed the square in a soft hush. But really, it could be raining rocks and she would have found her circumstances lovely at this moment.

He had come. He had played off Valor's ridiculous letter as if he'd not even read it. Lady Marchfield had been wrong.

They walked ahead in silence as Verity chattered on about all sorts of spaniel nonsense. Was Lord Charles really expected to believe that the word spaniel came from the original Latin for sprightly?

Apparently not, as Lord Charles had just pointed out that the word *alacer* was Latin for sprightly.

"You misunderstand, Lord Charles," Verity said, "I am referring to the older Latin."

Was there an older Latin? Serenity peeked up under her lashes and saw Lord Thorpe tightly pressing his lips together lest he laugh. It was a very good sign. Lady Marchfield thought her father's household was drowning in eccentricity, but if it was, Lord Thorpe did not seem to mind it.

She was to the lord's right and she noticed him switch his leash to his left hand. Her left hand was already currently free. His hand brushed her own. He was doing it again.

Serenity went happily round the square, brushing Lord Thorpe's hand by accident while Verity waxed on about spaniels. It was the best day of her life. A single tear rolled down her cheek but as she did not have a free hand to brush it away she let it fall and counted on the fog to disguise it.

They returned to their original starting place far too soon.

"Lady Serenity," Lord Thorpe said, "an excellent walk, I think."

"Indeed, yes."

"Charles," Lord Thorpe said, "one hopes Lord Furtherington is not long out of Town. Of course, if that be the case, I am certain Lady Verity would be indulgent enough to speak to you further about spaniels."

Serenity could hardly control her laughter as Verity said, "Oh yes, there is a lot more to say."

Lord Charles bowed and said, "Until this evening, Lady Serenity. At the early dinner taking place at my family's house in Town."

He turned and stalked off, dragging his unnamed spaniel with him.

"Come loves, we will take our leave," Mrs. Right said. "Good day to you, Lord Thorpe."

"Mrs. Right," he said.

Her dear housekeeper pulled Serenity in the direction of the house, followed by Verity positing all sorts of spaniel information that might be communicated to Lord Charles at his earliest convenience.

In not too many hours she would set off again, but this time to Lord Thorpe's house to dine. She wondered what it looked like inside. She wondered if she would one day find herself the mistress of it. Life could not be more wonderful.

ROLAND HAD NOT been at all enthused to see Charles pushing into his walk with Lady Serenity. Nor was he enthused to understand he was determined to come to the dinner. He'd hoped it had just been an idle threat, but apparently it was not.

However, aside from those minor irritations, all went forward swimmingly. He'd wondered what Lady Serenity would do when he'd switched his leash to his opposite hand and allowed his right hand to brush her own. She did not pull away. No, not at all. They'd brushed hands all the way round the square. It felt as if it were an unspoken engagement, almost. After all, a lady like that did not go round brushing a gentleman's hand for nothing.

"When do you think you might ask the question?" Quinn asked. "Tonight might be as good a night as any."

"I must approach the duke first, I think," Roland said. "I believe he would approve the match, but when it comes to a duke I imagine it's best to afford them every courtesy. At least, my father always expects it. I will arrange an appointment with the Duke of Pelham. Soon."

Quinn suppressed the smallest of sighs, and Roland was very much aware that he wished him to get on with it. He did not bother explaining that *he* wished for a little more time to introduce Lady Serenity to something closer to his real nature, as he already knew what Quinn thought of the idea. His butler thought the reveal of the real Marquess of Thorpe could be a surprise after the wedding.

But, he could not be comfortable with that idea.

"Typical of Charles to crash in on your walk. I wonder where he got the dog?"

"Probably from some lazy fellow at The Albany who was delighted to have him take out his dog," Roland said. "He claimed it was a certain Lord Furtherington, who I have never heard of."

"He is determined to come to dinner too?"

Roland nodded. "Have the place cards been arranged as I wish?"

"They have. Charles will be in the middle of the table with Lady Valor on one side, Lady Verity on the other, and Lady Winsome across. Lady Serenity will be to your right. As you do not have a hostess, the duke will take the far end of the table."

"Excellent. With any luck, Lady Verity will tie up Charles about spaniels on one side and Lady Valor, well, who knows what she'll want to talk about."

"It is such a small party, consisting only of the duke's family. Certainly that is a heavy hint regarding the direction this is going."

"I would think so, though I also think Lady Valor will remain convinced it's all being done in her honor. Which I suppose she has a right to, since I did say it was to be early on her account."

"Lady Valor should be very flattered by the attention paid to the arrangements—the menu is exquisite. The champagne is iced, the aged hock gently cooled, and the claret uncorked to breathe. Orgeat has been prepared for the younger of the sisters. White soup to begin. The venison and partridges from the estate arrived this morning. Cook has made up a plate of quince paste cut in the shape of the duke's house. The rest of it, boeuf en croute, broiled game hens, baked turbot in a dill sauce, vegetables of all sorts roasted, mashed, and sauteed, two salads, an excellent cheese-board, trifles, cakes, and ice creams, all being prepared."

Of all the things Roland might worry over, the components of the dinner were not on that list. Quinn and his housekeeper led the staff forward and each one of them, down to the scullery maids, were an expert at their jobs.

"The water is being heated for your bath and I," Quinn said, rising, "will poke around the dining room to ensure the footmen have got the places set correctly with the right porcelain and crystal. I sent Jeffrey in there with a ruler an hour ago, so it should be in order."

Roland rose too. The time was fast approaching that Lady Serenity would step through his doors. It felt a rather momentous occasion, as it was not just a dinner. It would be an opportunity for the lady to have a look at his house. The house that, with any luck, she would become the mistress of.

CHARLES HAD RETURNED the stupid dog he'd borrowed from Mr.

Robbins. What a morning. He'd had some idea that the dog and Lady Serenity's dog might take to each other, but they had not. At the very least, he'd hoped to interrupt whatever progress Thorpe was making with the lady. He had not got anywhere with that either.

Rather, he'd been relegated to walking beside Lady Verity with the housekeeper bringing up the rear. Had he ever had to listen to such drivel in his life? What was the girl thinking to invent a litany of facts that were not facts at all? Ancient peoples had once kept spaniels to warn of floods? Noah, himself, relied on his spaniel to know when to get on his boat? The girl was deranged.

It was possible they were all deranged. The youngest had practically shouted something he supposed was meant to be an apology about some letter she sent that Thorpe claimed he'd not bothered to read. The other one, Lady Winny or some such, seemed always to be scowling. And then Lady Serenity herself. If she preferred Thorpe, it did not say much for *her* mind.

He'd seen the hand brushing that had gone on.

It began to occur to him that merely presenting himself was not proving sufficient to divert Lady Serenity's attention from his brother. Perhaps she was set on becoming a duchess. But then, she hardly seemed to have enough sense for such practical ambitions.

Now there was to be the dinner at the ungodly hour of six o'clock on account of Lady Vera or Velma or whatever her name was not being able to stay awake. The girl should be in the nursery under the strict control of a starched governess, not shouting out apologies and attending dinners. He would go mad if he were seated next to her.

He must do something to move things in his direction. Thorpe was positively smug at the moment. The high and mighty marquess believed he was winning. It could not be allowed to stand. If Thorpe were to prevail it would be a competition lost. Thorpe would wed the lady, and Charles' defeat would be thrown in his face in perpetuity.

He just must think of something that would once and for all turn the lady's attentions away from his brother.

SERENITY HAD CHOSEN her very best dress to wear to Lord Thorpe's house. She'd been saving it for the most special of occasions and what could top this?

It was the darkest green silk dress with a matching velvet overlaid skirt that fell down from either side of her hips and showed the silk underneath to good effect. A gold thread band, patterned as lace, wound round the waist of the silk as the only embellishment. She wore one of her mother's necklaces, a square cut emerald in a gold setting. She was determined to wear the most delicate green satin slippers, despite the damp of the pavement.

As Mrs. Right had fussed with her hair, she could hardly breathe. She'd forced some deep breaths in and counseled herself to stop being such a ninny. It was only that she was soon to walk into his house. *His* house.

She'd gone downstairs and found the rest of the family waiting in the great hall, including Valor. Serenity was pulled up short regarding her youngest sister's alarming appearance.

Rather than the usual silk ribbon tying back Valor's hair, it had been swept up in a style suited to a lady twice her age. She'd also raided somebody's jewelry box, Winsome's, she thought. They all had such pieces, inherited from their mother. Except for Valor, as she'd been so young when they'd made their choices of the various jewels that she'd chosen the most worthless but most colorful. Including the enameled parrot pin she wore on a regular basis. This night, she'd donned a heavy pearl necklace and a pearl-encrusted tiara that was too big for her head and in danger of slipping down over her eyes.

"Goodness," Serenity said, staring at her youngest sister.

"I know," Valor said, looking pleased as Punch. "It's my first dinner out in society, so I convinced Mrs. Right to put up my hair so I could look elegant."

"Well now," the duke said, "a hundred points for originality, I'd call it. Shall we proceed? We do not have far to travel, but it gets on six."

They set off and as Lord Thorpe lived just two doors down, they arrived in moments. A very starched butler took them into the drawing room, where Lord Thorpe and Lord Charles were waiting.

As the greetings went round, Serenity could not help but to notice the rather wide eyes upon encountering Valor's current mode of dress. She could also not help but notice that Valor took it as a compliment.

"It goes together, you see," Valor said. "The necklace and tiara are both pearls, so they match."

"Indeed, yes, they certainly do," Lord Thorpe said.

Two footmen entered carrying silver trays and handed out crystal coupes of chilled champagne.

"Good idea, I may take up the habit myself—champagne before dinner to grease the convivial wheels," the duke said.

It was indeed a charming idea and the coupes given to Winsome, Valor and Verity were just a quarter filled to supply a few sips. Though, there was something faintly ridiculous in the sight of Valor weighed down by pearls, her hair swept high, sipping from a coupe and then wrinkling her nose over it and putting it on a table.

The drawing room was of similar dimensions as their own, but far different in appearance. It had a man's stamp on it with dark leather abounding. Bookshelves of leatherbound books lined the far wall and ran over top of the fireplace. Where there were not books, there were various portraits of the family. One in particular struck her as being most probably Lord Thorpe's mother, based on the style of the lady's dress. She was exceedingly pretty.

It was a manly room, but a very fine room.

The starched butler once more appeared. "My lord, you may go through at any time."

"Thank you, Quinn," Lord Thorpe said.

His butler's name was Quinn and he had just smiled at her. Did he know something about her? Had Lord Thorpe told him anything? She did not really understand what the relationship would be between a butler of longstanding service and the lord of the house. She'd never seen it in her own household, having only distant memories of their first butler, Mr. Herring, having a mental collapse and fleeing the estate.

Lord Thorpe held his arm out, though Serenity saw Lord Charles attempt to push forward. Lord Thorpe seemed to have been ready for the gambit. Rather hilariously, Valor held out her arm toward Lord Charles and he was all but forced to take her in, though he had to bend down to put out his arm. The duke laughed aloud over the picture, though Valor proceeded with all dignity.

The dining table was magnificent, a snowy linen cloth set with superb porcelain dishes painted with roses and edged in gold, crystal goblets, highly polished silver, a dozen fine wax candles—the table practically sparkled.

Serenity was most gratified to find herself sitting to Lord Thorpe's right in the place of honor. She noted Valor on one side of Lord Charles and Verity on the other, which he did not look very enthusiastic about. He likely feared he was to hear more about spaniels, and he was likely correct.

Valor picked up a fork and examined it as the footmen came round filling glasses. She said, "I thought the person being honored would be where Serenity is sitting."

"It is," Winsome said, shaking her head in a warning from across the table.

Valor raised her brows as if she did not understand why she was not sitting in her sister's place. Serenity was beginning to fear that this idea of an early dinner to accommodate her had quite gone to Valor's head.

"Lady Valor," Lord Thorpe said, "I placed you thus as my brother made it known that he was very eager to further his acquaintance with you."

"Oh, I see," Valor said. "Well, just so you know, Lord Charles, I will never marry, so you spin wheels if that's what you're thinking."

The duke guffawed into his napkin and motioned for the footman to fill up his glass more than it had been.

"And then of course," Lord Thorpe said, "my brother is quite keen to take in further information about spaniels, Lady Verity."

Lord Thorpe was clearly teasing his brother and Lord Charles did not seem to take it very well. He wore a very tight smile.

"Consider it my pleasure," Verity said, "I am always happy to share what I know."

Goodness, Lord Charles was in for it. And, he seemed to know it. She might feel sorry for him, but on the other hand, Verity and Valor occupying Lord Charles and her father being entertained by it gave her more chance of conversation between herself and Lord Thorpe. Except for Winsome, who was very determinedly leaning in their direction to hear what was said.

"I hope you approve of my house, Lady Serenity. What you've seen of it anyway."

"I very thoroughly approve," Serenity said, certain she was blushing up to the tops of her ears. To mention what she'd seen of it hinted at what she'd *not* seen of it, which was above stairs in the more private areas of the house. Like the lord's bedchamber.

She gave a nervous little laugh apropos of nothing. Winsome wrinkled her brow, and Serenity silently scolded that she was not to make a cake of herself just because any rooms not viewed had been hinted at.

The first course had come round and Serenity felt the honor of it. A white soup was quite an onerous thing to make and must be got just right. At least, that was what Mrs. Right said about it.

It was generally made for occasions more elaborate than a small dinner, so it must be a compliment of sorts.

Though Verity was just now positing that the spaniel was well known for its ability to warn people of fire while her father snorted into his napkin, Lord Charles turned from her and said, "By the by, Thorpe, I suppose you've told Lady Serenity all about Clara."

Serenity dropped her spoon into her soup. Who was Clara? Why had she not heard the name Clara mentioned before? She was not a sister, Serenity already knew that it was only Lord Thorpe and Lord Charles in the duke's family. If she was not a sister…

CHAPTER THIRTEEN

THE DINING ROOM had gone quiet as Serenity held her breath and waited to hear who Clara was.

Lord Thorpe was glaring at his brother. Serenity also noticed the butler, Quinn, frown. Was Clara some lost love that was never to be mentioned? Perhaps Lord Thorpe had been deeply in love and this Clara individual had broken off an engagement? No, nobody would break an engagement with Lord Thorpe, how could they? That could only mean she'd died! Was it of consumption or being thrown from a curricle or a winter fever?

"Oh, I see," Lord Charles said, "you did not mention her yet."

"Did she die?" Serenity nearly cried out, dabbing at her eyes.

"Die?" Lord Thorpe asked, sounding very surprised. "Certainly not, she wed the local innkeeper and goes on quite happy."

Now Serenity was thoroughly confused. The duke said, "Thorpe, you'd better spell out the story your brother has so gleefully hinted at lest we all imagine strange ideas."

Lord Charles reddened at the idea that he'd gleefully hinted. Then he said, "She was a housemaid."

What did Lord Charles say? Why should there be some story of a housemaid having to do with Lord Thorpe? She would not believe he had meddled with a servant. No, that was not at all his nature.

Lord Thorpe sighed. "I do not have the first idea why this would be a topic of conversation at dinner, but as it has been raised, I will relay the circumstances. Clara was a housemaid who was dismissed on account of being with child. It was very early days and she would not have been found out, had not she told the housemaid she shared a room with. I was sixteen and had just arrived home on a school break at the time. I became certain Clara was to end up begging on the roads with an infant in her arms. I took fifty pounds out of my father's library and gave it to her."

"You see?" Lord Charles asked. "He stole fifty pounds from our father."

All eyes turned to Lord Charles. "What else was he to do?" Winsome asked. "Allow poor Clara to starve on the road?"

Lord Charles appeared to be embarrassed to be asked that question. Serenity did not give a toss about Lord Charles' embarrassment. Lord Thorpe had acted nobly. Of course he had, she would expect nothing less.

"It's not on, you know," her father said, "allowing one of your household to starve on the road."

"She was never going to starve," Lord Charles blurted out. "She married the local innkeeper."

"Well, thank heavens for that," Serenity said. She did not think she understood Lord Charles. He had seemed to hint at that story being something that would put Lord Thorpe in a bad light when it had been quite the opposite. Certainly, his father the duke would have seen that he ought to have given Clara the fifty pounds himself, and been sorry at being so remiss.

"Well now," the duke said, "that's settled. It seems everything worked out satisfactorily for all involved."

"Lord Charles," Verity said, "are you aware that the spaniel has a long history of being able to detect gold? They have very sensitive noses, I'm given to understand."

Serenity pressed her lips together to stop from laughing as Lord Charles gripped his fork. Verity was about to lead the lord down a long garden path of nonsense.

Lord Thorpe turned to her. "I am sorry my brother thought

to bring up that particular interlude."

"Why did he, though?" Serenity asked. "He made it sound as if you had some terrible confession to make when you acted quite rightly for poor Clara."

Lord Thorpe laughed. "I felt it right and in fact urgent at the time," he said. "But I *did* steal fifty pounds from my father."

"I do not suppose my own father would mind it," Serenity said. "But then, I suppose he would not have thrown Clara out to begin."

Lord Thorpe nodded. "My father thought it brought disgrace on the house."

"But that is so unfair. It should only bring disgrace on the gentleman responsible for poor Clara's condition."

"He thought that too," Lord Thorpe said.

Valor, who apparently was not entertained by Verity's long explanation of how and why spaniels could detect gold, said loudly, "When I am grown and out, I will go to all the parties but marry nobody." She stared pointedly at Serenity as if she hoped her sister would take on that novel idea.

"Oh, I see," the duke said jovially, "you're to cost me all the money with no end in sight. What about my plan to empty my household of every last one of you? What's to come of that?"

Valor had seemed to have given that idea some thought. She said, "Papa, by the time I should go to Almack's for my debut, you will be very old and decrepit. You'll barely be able to walk and might not be able to use your legs at all. You'll be happy I'm there to wheel you from room to room. You'll see."

"I rather hope I will not see, if that's to be my fate," the duke said. "She paints a cheery picture, eh?"

As her three younger sisters debated the idea of whether the duke would or would not be able to walk when Valor turned eighteen, Lord Thorpe said, "You are lucky to have such a genial family."

"As I think so, too!" Serenity said. "So many people do not understand my father."

"I believe it takes multiple encounters to perceive it."

"Yes, I can see how it would. Felicity says our father is like a windstorm that likes to blow off hats and bonnets."

Lord Thorpe laughed. "Very apt."

And so they went pleasantly on through the rest of dinner. Her dear sisters had seemed to make a game of keeping Lord Charles' attention on one ridiculous matter after the next. When they lagged at any moment, the duke picked up the slack.

As for her and Lord Thorpe, their conversation was wide-ranging and easy. He spoke of his estate and Serenity got the idea that he particularly wished her to know of it.

As far as she understood it, Mariton Hall was a rather large estate in northern Suffolk nearby the Norfolk border. She listened intently as Lord Thorpe described the extent of the rooms and grounds. She was delighted to understand there was a good-sized lake on the property and a host of sailboats, as well as a yew hedge maze of some magnitude. The gardens were filled with roses and wisteria, and there were several greenhouses. Perhaps what affected her most, and she did have to control her feelings over it, was the description of the stables. Every possible comfort had been thought of for the horses belonging to the estate. She supposed Jupiter might be quite comfortable there.

She supposed she might be very comfortable there herself!

CHARLES HAD NEVER endured a more tedious dinner in his life. More than tedious, actually. It was positively enraging. He spent most of it wishing to stab the spaniel girl with his fork over her stupid spaniel stories. Apparently, spaniels could do everything in the wide world—warn against fire and flood, find gold, and finally, tell the time. Maybe they carried round pocket watches! Maybe he should inquire into that with the all-knowing Lady Veracity or Veritable or whatever her godforsaken name was!

He pleasantly imagined killing Lady Very-Tedious with his fork, removing the utensil, and using it to stab Lady Vera on his other side. If he could manage it, he'd retrieve the fork once more and aim it across the table at Lady Winny. Then, and finally, they would all stop talking.

What did the duke mean by countenancing these girls? If he were their father, he'd lock them up until they could conduct themselves with some modicum of sense. As it was, the duke seemed to find them all amusing.

They were not in the slightest amusing.

More aggravating than that, though, was the girls' constant chatter had boxed him in while Thorpe went on in conversation with Lady Serenity. He'd heard snippets of that—Thorpe described the gardens at Mariton Hall while the lady professed a particular admiration for roses and wisteria.

He wanted to overturn the table over it. Mariton Hall, had the fates had any sense at all, should have been his. He should have been born first. Every time he went home he could barely stand looking around at its architecture and contents, knowing it had been all but stolen from him.

His story about Clara and the fifty pounds had not gone over as well as he thought it must. He had presumed that the duke, at least, would be condemning over the theft of fifty pounds. Why had they all been so sympathetic to Clara? She'd been only a housemaid stupid enough to get herself in trouble.

He really did not understand these people. However, understand them or not, something must be done. Thorpe seemed to be doing far too well with Lady Serenity.

He'd tried to darken Thorpe's character with the story about the theft, but it had not worked. Something drastic must be done.

Even now, as they had retreated to the drawing room, things were looking bad. Thorpe had decided to take on the duke's habit of bringing the port and brandy into the drawing room with the ladies.

Charles suspected his brother had thought ahead of what he

would do when they got there. He'd suggested a game of piquet with Lady Serenity, which she'd happily accepted.

How convenient to suggest a card game that only admitted two people. He was left playing Commerce with the duke's deranged daughters while the duke himself had commandeered the brandy bottle and made good use of it.

They were all very lucky that there were no sharp objects within his reach. Perhaps he could not kill those girls, but he could kill whatever was currently brewing between Thorpe and Lady Serenity. He just needed the right idea. A big and bold idea.

Thorpe never won against him and Charles was determined that they would not begin a new precedent now.

As he sat and stewed over it, not giving a toss if he won at Commerce or not, an idea began to form. Perhaps more could be made of the story of Clara and the fifty pounds. After all, was it not rather hard to believe that Thorpe would have stolen the money out of the goodness of his heart? Who ever heard of such a thing? It might be the truth, but it did not sound like the truth. Surely, another truth might be communicated.

Anonymously, this time.

ROLAND HAD THOUGHT well ahead how he would manage the drawing room after dinner. He intended to flatter the duke by following his example of bringing the port and brandy into the drawing room. It also held several other benefits. He would not be long parted from Lady Serenity, which was the whole point of the dinner. As well, he would not have to spend a tedious amount of time with Charles over port.

Charles, it was becoming apparent, did not understand the duke's family at all. His bringing up the story about Clara had flown as well as a butterfly with lead wings, crashing down just as fast. To Charles, staff were barely people and not to be sympathized with as one might with another more elevated person. In truth, Roland was fairly sure that the only person walking the earth who'd ever garnered Charles' sympathy was Charles himself. If one was forever mulling over one's perceived slights, there was not room for any other consideration.

Roland had wasted no time inquiring if Lady Serenity were willing to engage in a game of piquet. Now, they had sat at a small and round card table he'd had brought in ahead of time for the very purpose.

The only impediment to this plan was that he was rather wretched at piquet. He found the game unnecessarily complicated and tiresome.

Lady Serenity was staring at the cards with a look of something. Was it alarm? Perhaps she imagined she was to be trounced by a card sharp?

"I have an admission," he said, "I am only glancingly acquainted with the rules of this game."

Lady Serenity let out a long sigh and then she laughed. "I have a bigger admission. I am not at all acquainted with the game. I tried to learn it once, as my sister Patience likes it. However, it seemed the rules were endless and confusing and she was rushing me, so I gave up."

Roland shuffled the packs and said, "Perhaps we change our minds to vingt-et-un?"

"Oh yes, that game I know."

They both rather lackadaisically made attempts to get to twenty-one without going over, though they mostly did go over. Their conversation was easy-flowing and interesting and resulted in little attention being paid to whether or not a card was picked up. Roland had just counted up eighteen and foolishly picked up another card. No surprise it put him over to twenty-eight.

He laid it down and Lady Serenity laughed. "That really is very bad," she said.

"Yes, I know," he said laughing himself.

"Will you attend Lady Darlington's masque on the morrow?"

Roland asked.

Lady Serenity nodded. "Indeed, yes."

"Dare I inquire what costume you wear?"

"I think it should be a surprise," Lady Serenity said. "I will only say you will probably find it exceedingly silly."

"You will find my own costume boring, which is a far worse crime."

"Ah, you wear a domino, then."

"Exactly."

As they began the card game again, Roland's thoughts began drifting far into the future. He could imagine this very scene taking place at Mariton Hall. His children would be long abed and he and Lady Serenity would sit nearby one of the massive fireplaces in one of the drawing rooms, playing cards. Perhaps the snow would whip the windows, roaring out of doors. For, what need would they have to spend too much time in Town in the winter season? They must go for his attendance at the House of Lords, but they need not extend their time there unless Lady Serenity wished it.

Perhaps the following morning he would discover that one of his sons had stolen money from him to help somebody in need of it. He would not be at all cross about it, he hoped. That afternoon, the family would gather together and walk to the village, stopping by the tavern to see Clara and her children. Even now, he often stopped by the tavern when he was on the estate. He knew well enough that his arrival lent a stamp of approval to the couple, despite how late in the day they'd finally wed.

As his thoughts wandered, he saw the village decorated with boughs of greenery on every available surface in anticipation of Christmas. They would walk home, leaving the village as candles were lit in windows, under the dying light of a winter sun.

These ideas were so affecting that he had to whip his thoughts away and force them elsewhere lest he betray himself.

"Are you quite all right, Lord Thorpe?" Lady Serenity asked.

With all the might of the self-control he could muster, he

said, "Indeed, yes. I apologize for appearing too solemn for a moment. I was just considering what must be done to rectify an estate matter."

Had he been right to play it off in such a manner? It was really beginning to disturb him that he appeared to Lady Serenity as one way, when in fact he was another way. He really had to do something about it. And hope she was not disappointed with whatever she discovered.

MRS. RIGHT HAD felt, for the past several days, as if the Sword of Damocles hung over her head. Each knock at the door had threatened to bring an unwelcome visitor.

She had thought to tell the duke that there was the smallest possibility that he might receive an uncomfortable visit from Bishop Porteus. And yet, there had never been the right time to casually mention it. Since Mr. Cremble had left, the duke had seemed to have put the whole butler situation out of his mind.

The housekeeper had taken to looking over the mail as it came in, in case the disaster was to arrive by post. This morning, however, she'd missed it when it came in. Charlie had already moved the letters into the duke's library.

She supposed she might have told Charlie and Thomas to monitor the mail arriving for the duke, but she did not wish to embroil her boys in any contretemps with a bishop. The local vicar was one thing, and they often did toy with that gentleman's temper, but a bishop was quite another.

Fortunately, she was the housekeeper and had every right to go into the duke's library to inspect the maids' work. And have a look at the post while she happened to be in there.

Letting herself in after the duke had left for his club, she saw the stack on his desk. Some of the letters had already been opened and lay there too.

She casually strolled over and had a look.

And then another look. And then another. She could hardly believe her own eyes.

She picked up a particular letter and read it for the third time.

For the eyes of the Duke of Pelham:

Your Grace, I write this anonymously to alert you to a danger. Believe me, if I had the power and standing to reveal myself I would, but I am only a lowly servant who has had the bad luck to observe certain outrages. I do not have the power and riches to speak aloud, but I must speak nonetheless!

It is my understanding that the sad case of a certain Clara Woodrow, a housemaid in the Duke of Mariton's household, was communicated to you. Your Grace, you have not been told the truth of it! Lord Thorpe was in fact the man who compromised young Clara and then the fifty pounds was used to bribe the local innkeeper to wed her. As these things often are, it was all hushed up.

This was just one of the outrages that Lord Thorpe has visited on his father's house. Having been a long and close observer of the family, I can tell you that it has been a stain on the nobility that Lord Thorpe is the heir rather than Lord Charles. Beware, Your Grace, of the growing attachment between your daughter and that devil—he is not what he seems!

CHAPTER FOURTEEN

M RS. RIGHT DROPPED the letter she'd just read. The letter sent to the duke that outlined who Lord Thorpe really was. The rogue! The scoundrel! The unprincipled rake! She'd heard all about Lord Thorpe's supposedly noble actions regarding this Clara and all along he'd been the author of the poor girl's troubles!

Mrs. Right could see it all in lurid detail—the powerful marquess catching the defenseless girl in a dark corridor and overpowering her. Or perhaps he'd sweet-talked and promised things that could never be. And then, though she was the victim of the lord's depraved needs, she'd been accused, found guilty, and thrown from the house.

Poor foolish Serenity. She was quite besotted with Lord Thorpe. Or, at least who she thought Lord Thorpe to be. Mrs. Right reminded herself that the duke would not put up with such an outrage. She would not be at all surprised if he were to order the trunks packed and take his daughter home to remove her from the danger.

That would be the right course, she was sure. She could not be against it. It would remove her dear Serenity from what could be her undoing. It would also solve a little problem involving a bishop. After all, a bishop could not come storming into the house when nobody was at home. The churchman was likely to have forgotten all about it by next season.

Yes, certainly, she would just wait for the duke's orders that they were to go back to the Dales. In the meantime, she did not countenance the idea of Lord Thorpe getting away with this outrage to one of her girls.

He must be made to pay for it.

Mrs. Right had the smallest moment of hesitation when she reflected on what had occurred over the past three seasons. She had been mistaken when she'd meddled with Mr. Stratton's laundry, grocery order, and wine merchant. And then, it had turned out to be unnecessary to convince Lord Dashlend's hysterical valet that he was being let go. And then, perhaps she ought not to have infested Lord Stanford's house with case moths. She was perfectly sanguine about recognizing her mistakes, as anybody with a maturity of spirit would be. In any case, all of those missteps were water under the bridge and no harm done. Or at least, not an insurmountable amount of harm done.

She could not be wrong every time though, could she? Here it was written out on paper what had happened to poor Clara. Lord Thorpe was a villain who imagined he would lure innocent Serenity Nicolet into his web of immorality. A man like that would not stop at one housemaid. Oh no, there would be other housemaids to come. Lord Thorpe's wife would be shamed again and again.

She would not stand for it. Lord Thorpe must pay. He would pay.

Mrs. Right drummed her fingers on the desk as she considered how Lord Thorpe could pay. She might set his house alight, but it was too close to their own. He seemed to be fond of his dog but she could do nothing there either, as she was fond of dogs herself and would not hurt a single hair on their heads.

Then she recalled an idea she'd had when she'd considered her revenge on Lord Stanford. She'd only tossed aside the idea because of the logistics. But Lord Thorpe was just two doors down, making the whole thing much more feasible.

She imagined she would find the right tools in the shed in the back garden. It would only be a matter of slipping over there under cover of darkness. She could wear her dark cloak and go on a moonless night. Certainly, it could be done.

It all hinged on what her father had done all those years ago. A gentleman had stopped at the local inn and had strolled round the village with his head held high. That would have been nothing. But then, the fellow had the audacity to make a lewd comment to Mrs. Right's mother. Her father could not do anything outright. It was one of the injustices of England—a powerful lord could not have his ears boxed on a public road without dire consequences. However, something could be done under cover of darkness.

Her father paid for the grooms in the stable to buy themselves some ale, which they took to the far back of the inn's garden. Meanwhile, her father loosened the bolts on the springs of the lord's carriage. He loosened them just enough that they would hold for a bit, but not forever. Mrs. Right knew the tale as she'd grown up hearing it. Her father had a hundred times described it step by step as he liked to spin it out in a long story when he was in his cups. Everyone in the village had been delighted when the gentleman's carriage left the inn, made it thirty feet, and then tipped to one side. That the lord ended with a black eye from the tipping was the icing on that cake.

Perhaps Mrs. Right had a few more details to be worked out, like how to get rid of Lord Thorpe's stablemaster and grooms while she worked on the springs, but certainly it could be done.

SERENITY THOUGHT THE weather was somehow against her. It had poured buckets all morning, meaning her walk with Lord Thorpe was off. Then, it had the gall to clear up at the end of the day. The sun had even peeked out from the clouds. Still, there was always tomorrow and she would see Lord Thorpe at the masque soon enough.

Just as Patience had done before her, Serenity had been visited by Madame LaFray in the Dales for the months leading up to the season. The modiste had designed an exquisite wardrobe, though she found her customer far more interested in the design of a masque costume than anything else.

Upon consideration of what she wished for, Serenity had instantly seen that she ought to honor the bees. Once the idea had arrived in her head, it had seemed almost traitorous to think of any other idea.

Madame LaFray had at first been perplexed by how to go about it. Or why she was to go about it. But, as Serenity was so insistent, a notion finally arrived.

The final result was just what Serenity had imagined. She would wear a half mask painted in a gold honeycomb pattern with a matching honeycomb patterned fan. The dress itself was made from heavy flannel that had been brushed and roughed to replicate the fuzziness of a honeybee. The top of the costume was a brownish yellow and below the waist it alternated with black horizontal bands. Madame LaFray had even constructed light organza wings held up with wire for the back of the dress.

It was not that the dress was beautiful, as it was not, it was that it honored the bees. Serenity Nicolet, bee killer, must honor the bees. Though there was the rational part of her that knew perfectly well it was absurd, her feelings would not be swayed on the matter. As far as her family was concerned, it seemed to make sense to them. She'd always been fixated on bees and they did not give much thought as to why.

Mrs. Right had dressed her and, while it was not the most attractive costume, their dear housekeeper had seemed very out of sorts over it. She had several times mentioned that Serenity ought to be wary of false flattery. Serenity had pointed out that any high-flown compliments over the attractiveness of the dress certainly would be false.

It had not seemed to soothe the lady.

Since then, she'd gone downstairs and met her father in the costume he'd worn last year. A white domino with flames painted round the hem of it. It was meant to represent the two times her papa had set a lady's curtains on fire, though most people who viewed it, including her aunt, took it to be a churchman's white surplice going up in flames. Serenity supposed her father decided to wear it again this year as it had taken so many people aback last year.

Serenity found herself leaning forward in her carriage seat so as not to crush her organza wings. She had been startled when her father said, "I believe Lord Charles is a troublemaker and ought to be avoided."

"Goodness," Serenity said. "Because he brought up that story about poor Clara, the housemaid?"

"That was just brotherly one-upmanship in which Lord Charles misjudged his audience. No, I have other reasons to think he might make more trouble for his brother if he can manage it. I'll have a word with Thorpe about it."

Serenity could not imagine what her father had discovered. Though, she did trust her father's judgment. People might think him eccentric, but he was never wrong about people. At least, usually. Or at least, eventually. There had, of course, been those moments when he'd been mistaken. He'd been the author of the pile of chains left on Mr. Stratton's doorstep, and he'd filled Lord Dashlend's front hall with flowers that all carried a terrible meaning, and then he'd sent Lord Stanford a jar of molasses to comment on his lack of speed regarding his courtship of Patience. However, he always came to the right conclusion at the end.

What conclusion had he come to about Lord Charles?

"Papa, I am a grown lady. Do not you think I should know what has caused you to think badly of Lord Charles?"

"I do not," the duke said. "I know how to stop trouble in its tracks and that's what I am doing."

It was all very mysterious. However, she ought not fret over it. After all, she did not have an interest in Lord Charles. Her interest was all in for Lord Thorpe. Really, she had at times found Lord Charles a bit off-putting. If her father thought Lord Charles should be avoided…

"But Papa," Serenity said, "what am I to do if he wishes to dance with me? He is Lord Thorpe's brother. Will I not offend Lord Thorpe if I outright refuse his brother?"

"There will be no dancing this evening. Lady Darlington has her own ideas about a masque. We will all mill around and vote on costumes and eat from the sideboards and the occasional little trays that are brought round."

"Oh yes, I had forgotten. But if I refuse to dance with Lord Charles at some other place, will I not have to sit out?"

"If Lord Charles finds the opportunity to attempt to dance with you, feel free to refuse on my account. Do not sit out, we do not give a toss for the *ton's* more stupid rules. Lord Thorpe will not give a toss for his brother's feelings. In fact, I suspect he'll be flattered."

"I cannot imagine having such a hateful relationship with my sisters."

The duke snorted. "That's because there is no property to inherit. If there were, you'd all be clawing each other's eyes out."

"We certainly would not!"

"Or something like it," the duke said, laughing. "Anyway, I know from my own experience that a second son feels badly used. Your uncle spent most of our childhood looking very injured. Hard to be around, really—he was always staring at me as if I ought to apologize for landing on the sheets first."

The carriage had rolled to a stop. They were here. Now that they *were* here, Serenity did feel the littlest bit foolish to be dressed as a bee. She supposed other ladies would come as queens or otherwise looking lovely. Even a milkmaid would be far more charming.

"Papa," she said, "I suddenly feel that I look ridiculous."

"Nonsense," the duke said. "One of the benefits of being a

duke's daughter is one never has to consider anybody else's opinion."

Her father often said so. It was just hard to believe it was true. She very much cared what Lord Thorpe would think. Perhaps she ought to have dressed in a costume that made her look pretty.

But then, she could not forsake the bees. Because she was a first-rate idiot!

ROLAND HAD BEEN let down by the weather in the morning. It had been raining hard and not even the most hopeful imagination could claim it a misting. As the hour of eleven had approached, he'd looked out the window and willed the rain to stop but it ignored his wishes entirely.

He spent the rest of the day attempting to read and thinking ahead to the masque that was to be this night.

Though he only wore a simple domino and black half mask, he always did feel a bit ridiculous at these masques. He'd not even attended last year and only heard later that Lady Patience, Lady Serenity's sister, had collapsed on the floor and had been taken home.

He never did hear what had ailed the lady.

This year, though, he had come. He'd asked Lady Serenity if she would attend last night and she'd said she would. So of course, he would come. He'd even arrived on the early side.

He milled round Lady Darlington's ballroom, greeting people he knew and ever keeping an eye out for Lady Serenity. Rather than the lady he sought, he saw his brother enter the ballroom. Charles wore what he could only guess was a costume of Richard the Lionheart—gold crown, burgundy velvet, ermine-lined cloak, and a dark blue tunic with a large white holy cross leaving not much doubt. Roland supposed Charles meant to say something by it, as he always did.

Perhaps it was the idea that Richard the Lionheart was not a firstborn son and yet had succeeded to the throne, just as Charles ought to have succeeded to the dukedom. Or maybe it was a comment on Charles' perceived bravery and daring being very like that king.

He looked away, as he did not much care what Charles was trying to say.

As always at Lady Darlington's masque, the evening would consist of food and drink being brought round on trays and sideboards lining the room to fill in any gaps. The orchestra would play music, but softly and there would be no organized dancing. Though, he'd heard that Lady Underwood and Lord Welscott had daringly waltzed a few years ago. Perhaps not unsurprisingly, neither *Lord* Underwood nor *Lady* Welscott had been enthusiastic to hear of it.

The food served at the masque would be in very small portions that did not require a knife and fork, mostly consisting of thin sliced ham with cream cheese rolled into a small packet, or the same small packet made with beef and horseradish cream, tiny puff pastries, squares of hard cheeses, boiled and chilled prawns stuffed with herbed butter, toast points topped with dill and Scottish salmon, rolls, and miniature cakes. It was an exceedingly odd menu, but he supposed a hostess must be hard-pressed to come up with items that could be passed round on trays. In any case, the wines and champagnes that came round were always first rate.

Tables were scattered throughout the ballroom and the end of the room was lined with the voting booths, each manned by a footman. At some point in the evening, everyone was to cast their votes on the costumes present—most elaborate, most original, most beautiful, most historically accurate, most like the person who wore it, and et cetera.

He cast his eyes back to the doors, and then he saw her. Lady Serenity. Her costume was not at all what he'd expected. He had supposed she'd do what most ladies did. They took the opportunity to stand in a particular alluring attitude. They might be queenly, or a coquettish maid, or an alluring sultana. The costumes were all meant to complement the lady's looks in ways that ordinary dress could not.

Lady Serenity had come as a bee. It really was both a dreadful and somehow endearing costume. There was nothing at all flattering about it and the colors were awful, but she came off very charming.

He could not make heads or tails of the duke's costume. Was he in a vicar's surplice going up in flames?

He hurried forward. "Your Grace, Lady Serenity."

"Ho there, Thorpe," the duke said.

Lady Serenity gave a pretty little curtsy. Or as pretty a curtsy as one could do in piles of drab flannel.

"You are a bee," Roland said. "It is charmingly original."

Lady Serenity laughed and said, "Our housekeeper warned me to be on the lookout for false flattery and here it is. I feel a little bit ridiculous, especially now that I am in view of so many fine ladies arrayed in splendor."

"Serenity has an obsession with bees," the duke said, "best to know about those sorts of oddities up front."

"Papa," Lady Serenity scolded.

"Gracious, Serenity," a lady said to Roland's right. He turned to find Lady Marchfield frowning.

"Aunt," Lady Serenity said, not looking particularly delighted to see her.

Lady Marchfield sighed. "Lord Thorpe, please pretend you've never set eyes on this concoction of a costume. I will guarantee that it was the duke's uncouth housekeeper's influence that led to it."

"It was not Mrs. Right's idea, though," Lady Serenity said. "I thought of it on my own."

"She's very fond of bees," the duke said, "which you would know, Lady Misery, if you spent ten minutes attempting to understand your nieces rather than scolding them all about one ridiculous thing after the next."

Lady Marchfield seemed taken aback by this idea, as Roland imagined she must be. The lady sniffed and said, "I had intended to introduce Serenity to the Countess of Pembroke. She is Lady of the Bedchamber to our dear queen and a very influential woman. I think I will put it off, considering."

"Take my daughter to meet the countess or I will tell everyone I am dressed as *your* vicar, going up in flames to meet the devil, as that poor fellow thought it preferable to spending another minute in your company," the duke said.

Lady Marchfield stiffened.

Roland supposed the duke really would tell people that, and he supposed Lady Marchfield knew it.

"It is *your* housekeeper that has gone to the devil, I will remind you," she said. "I have rescued Mr. Cremble from her clutches but do not imagine you have heard the end of it."

Roland assumed that meant the butler had departed the Nicolet household under unusual circumstances.

"Ha! Why would I imagine I've heard the end of it? There never is an end to your nattering. Now, get going to find Lady Pembroke. I wish to have a private word with Thorpe."

"Shameful!" Lady Marchfield muttered. "Come, Serenity, I cannot say what's got into your father, but he is somehow more offensive than usual. I'd not have thought it possible!"

Roland might have been shocked by the duke's and his sister's exchanges if he'd not been witness to it before. What private word did the duke wish for, though?

He watched Lady Serenity being marched off by her aunt, her charming white organza wings bouncing behind her. He looked enquiringly at the duke.

"Your brother has sent a preposterous letter to my household," the duke said.

Roland felt his jaw clench. Charles never stopped making trouble, it had turned into his life's work.

"The idea of the letter was to convince me that it was you

who got that housemaid in trouble and it was all hushed up."

"Did he, now," Roland said.

"He did, but as it happens, your brother's star does not shine very bright in the sky. It was clumsily done and he very obviously gave himself away on quite a few fronts. One, the account of the circumstances you gave at your dinner, which he did not challenge, was that you had just returned from school and discovered the girl had been thrown from the house."

Roland nodded. "That is true."

"Seems rather impossible that the girl was in early pregnancy, then. Had you meddled with her over your last school break she'd have been well along and you did not have time to meddle with her when you arrived. You're an Oxford man, I presume?"

"I am."

"And your estate is in Suffolk. Quite the lengthy trip during term to meddle with a maid, unobserved no less. Had you been interested in such things, I suppose you might have located a lady more conveniently situated. You are not interested in such dalliances, I hope?

"No, Your Grace," Roland said. He thought he knew what the duke wished to hear, which was nothing but the truth anyway. "I would never disgrace my future duchess in such a manner."

"As I thought. Now, on to number two, the letter claimed to be from a lowly servant, but if so, that servant inexplicably attended Oxford or Cambridge, such was the sophistication of the language and composition. Three, that lowly servant either stole paper from his employer or spent all his wages on it, as it was very fine quality and sealed with good wax. Four, the top of the sheet was cut off, indicating a monogram had been removed. Five, I was just arriving to the house when the letter was delivered by a porter wearing livery from The Albany. And finally, six, and I did find this the most hilarious, this supposed lowly servant ended the letter noting that everyone wished that Charles, the second son, had been the heir."

"That devil."

The duke nodded. "I have not told Serenity, nor will I. Though, I have told her to avoid him when she can and that he's not to be trusted. In any case, Lord Charles did not get anywhere with it." The duke took that moment to punch his arm. "What about you? When are you going to get somewhere with it? Something to think about, Thorpe!"

With that, the duke grabbed a glass of wine off a passing tray and strolled off.

CHAPTER FIFTEEN

ROLAND WATCHED THE duke stroll off after having informed him of the absurd letter Charles had sent to him, claiming that he was the author of poor Clara's troubles. His brother was outrageous. Did he actually think he would have got away with such a thing? He supposed he had thought that, as he'd done it. He might have, had the duke been a different sort of gentleman.

All along, he'd been so distracted by the duke's eccentricity that he'd not noticed how astute the gentleman really was. Another father might have fallen for the ruse, or at least not been certain of the truth. That father would err on the side of caution and cut off all contact. He was very lucky that the duke had seen through it.

Of course, there was also the duke's hint that he ought to get on with it. At least, he'd taken it so. That would indicate the duke's firm approval of a match between himself and Lady Serenity. He had thought that would be the case, but it was well to hear it.

Roland's eyes searched the ballroom to locate Lady Serenity. Lady Marchfield had indeed introduced her to the Countess of Pembroke. She was an older and very stately lady and she seemed to be looking kindly at Lady Serenity. He supposed the countess would—she was known to be kind and full of good sense.

Just then, Charles approached Lady Pembroke's party. Though Roland could not hear what was said and was left trying to read expressions, he did not think his brother was particularly admired by the party for doing it.

Charles never understood when it would not be welcome to push in. Lady Marchfield wished her niece to be introduced to one of the grand dames of London, she did not need Charles to crash into the conversation.

At first, Charles was all smiles. There seemed to be an exchange between him and Lady Serenity. Then she flushed and turned away from Charles. Of course, his brother did not know that Lady Serenity had been warned off him. He'd just put her in a very uncomfortable position, and he'd probably been insistent about it.

Charles curtly bowed and strode away. In Roland's direction, unfortunately. He took a glass of claret from a passing tray and turned round. With any luck, Charles would pass him by.

"What did you say to her?" Charles practically growled into his ear.

"To who?" Roland said, turning round to face his brother.

"You know who," Charles said. "Lady Serenity."

"Ah, Lady Serenity. I said nothing, that would have been the duke's doing."

"What do you mean the duke's doing?" Charles asked.

Roland knew his brother well enough to see that he was making rapid calculations and speculations in his mind.

"Well, let's see," Roland said, taking a sip of his claret, "the duke received a letter. After reading it, he concluded that it would be best to keep his daughter well away from you."

"Did you dare to send some kind of letter denouncing me?" Charles said, his outrage simmering.

"No," Roland said, laughing, "*you* sent a letter attempting to denounce *me*."

It was fast dawning on Charles that not only had the duke not believed the letter from the "lowly servant," but had easily deduced who had sent it.

"I have no idea what you are talking about," Charles said,

clearly in a play for time.

"Ah, I see. Well, perhaps ask your porter from The Albany, as he was the one who delivered that letter. Really, you ought to consult with him in any case. If the fellow is to go round delivering anonymous letters, perhaps he should not wear his livery—it gives the game away, you see. That was just one of the tip-offs to the duke that all was not as it seemed, though he had quite a hilarious list of your missteps."

Charles had gone very red in the face. Roland had seen that look before, especially when they'd been younger. At those moments, Charles was likely to break something or throw fists. He could not do so here, though. He was careful of appearances and would not dare damage his reputation in such a manner.

Rather, he stormed off. Such was the violence of his departure that his tin crown flew off his head, clattered on the floor and rolled into a corner. He did not stop to pick it up.

Roland assumed that would be the end of Charles' meddling. His younger brother had flown a little too close to the sun with that gambit. It would unnerve him that the duke knew he'd sent that ridiculous letter and, knowing the duke, His Grace might decide at some later date to talk about it. Or rather, joke about it. Roland could easily envision such a circumstance, and he imagined Charles could too. The one thing Charles absolutely could not bear was to be laughed at.

Perhaps this was all for the best. Whenever Charles went too far, which was often, he always retreated to lick his wounds. He'd done so a hundred times when they'd been schoolboys. After a suitable time had passed he would reappear as if nothing at all had occurred, as he seemed to think that time washed all crimes clean.

Roland would not be at all surprised to discover that his brother had set off for the continent again, only to return at some later date looking blameless.

He would be glad to see the back of his brother for a while. He had more important things on his mind than Charles' bad behavior. As soon as Lady Serenity had concluded her conversation with the countess, he would approach and suggest a turn around the room.

SERENITY HAD BEEN whisked off to meet the countess, as her father wished a word with Lord Thorpe. And, he had threatened her aunt with telling all and sundry that he was dressed as her vicar going to the devil.

She supposed the word her father wished for with Lord Thorpe was the mysterious problem with his brother, Lord Charles. She tried to avoid being over-curious about it, as it would not do her good. However, she really was curious about it.

Her aunt had led her to Lady Pembroke and she'd curtsied deep as Lady Marchfield made the introduction.

"Charming," Lady Pembroke said upon her rising.

Serenity could not think the lady really thought so, though. She was, after all, costumed as a bee.

"Lady Pembroke," Lady Marchfield said, "The plight of a motherless girl. I assure you that if I'd been on hand for the costuming we…well, we would have done differently."

"Gracious, I do hope not, Lady Marchfield. Lady Serenity is dressed as everything emblematic of our bucolic great estates. Without our bees there is not the sweetness of honey that graciously arrives at our tables each day."

"I believe they are very sensitive creatures, Lady Pembroke," Serenity said. She probably ought not to be so bold, but Lady Pembroke did seem so sympathetic to the bees.

"I presume you subscribe to slatted skeps, Lady Serenity," Lady Pembroke said.

Serenity nodded. "Yes, certainly. We would not kill our bees with sulfur every September on any account. I should just die to think of it."

Serenity willed the water that drifted to her eyes to go back where it came from. The very idea of killing bees en masse had almost overtaken her. She could see that her aunt was not exactly approving of her niece being so decided in her opinions. However, she did feel rather strongly about that point. She'd all but shamed the villagers attached to her father's estate to adopt the slatted skeps so the bees might live.

"Excellent. Well, Lady Marchfield, you may take pride in such a connection," Lady Pembroke said looking kindly at Serenity. "And I might also mention, it is pleasant to encounter such a costume. After all, need we see one more Queen Boudica running round the place?"

"Oh, as to that…" Lady Marchfield said. Serenity thought she hardly knew what to do with Lady Pembroke's approval, so unexpected had it been.

"Countess, Lady Marchfield, Lady Serenity," Lord Charles said, pushing into their party.

"Lord Charles," Lady Pembroke said. "I suppose you have a particular reason for interrupting our conversation?"

Serenity thought this was how a lady with real power spoke. Lady Pembroke sounded as she imagined Queen Charlotte would speak—she did not mince words. It was very like her father, though the tone was so different.

"I did, and I beg pardon," Lord Charles said smoothly.

Serenity did not know what he wanted, but as her father had told her to avoid him, she wished he would go away.

"I wondered if Lady Serenity would consent to a turn round the room?"

Now he'd put her on the spot, exactly as she'd feared he would. She'd just not thought it would be so soon after her father's directive. There was nothing for it, though. "I am sorry, Lord Charles, I must regretfully decline."

That certainly did take Lord Charles by surprise. "No matter," he said, in a more jovial tone than his expression would suggest. "Well then, perhaps at the next ball where we meet, I might escort you through a dance."

He was so persistent! She would not answer that. Her sister Patience had always advised simply going forward and jumping a fence when one got there. Whenever it was that she encountered Lord Charles at a ball, that would be time enough to decline him then.

"Lady Serenity?" he asked.

Serenity suppressed a sigh. He was so pushy he would force her to answer. "I have been directed to decline," she said, "I am sorry."

"Oh. I see," Lord Charles said. "Well, excuse me for interrupting."

With that, he sharply bowed, turned on his heel, and strode off. Her aunt looked as if she would disappear through the floor. Had Lady Pembroke not been within hearing, Serenity was certain she would just now be enduring the scolding of the century.

"Goodness, I do not know what that was all about," Lady Pembroke said.

"My father directed me to avoid Lord Charles, though I am not privy to his reasons," Serenity said.

Lady Marchfield sighed, and Serenity was certain that she thought the duke wrong, regardless of whatever reason he had. She always did think the duke wrong.

"If your father has directed it, quite right that you do it, to my mind," Lady Pembroke said. "It is pleasant to regard a young lady with respect for a parent's natural authority—I do not care for this new idea of certain young ladies putting themselves forward as independent of everyone and flaunting the rules in an effort to raise brows. In any case, Lord Charles has always struck me as a bit too smarmy, so I suppose nothing is lost there."

Lady Pembroke had taken herself off to speak to her friends, the other great ladies of London. Lady Marchfield said, "I will question your father about this idea of snubbing Lord Charles. It is not exactly sensible as it appears that his own brother has been paying you attention."

Serenity did not bother to respond, as that brother fast approached.

"Lady Marchfield, Lady Serenity," Lord Thorpe said. "Lady Marchfield, might I escort Lady Serenity for a turn around the room?" He addressed her aunt to request her permission, which her aunt was clearly flattered by.

"By all means, Lord Thorpe," she said, giving her permission with an air of gracious condescension.

He held out his arm and they strolled off. "I hope you are not offended that I asked your aunt for the honor of escorting you, as if you could not decide things for yourself," Lord Thorpe said. "I was certain if you did not wish it, you would say so. It was just that Lady Marchfield looked as if she might need some propping up just now and nothing soothes a matron more than deference."

Serenity smiled. "You seem to understand my aunt very well. She was all turned round because Lord Charles…"

"I noticed he pushed into the conversation with Lady Pembroke. It did not seem as if it went well."

"He asked me to take a turn round the room, and then when I declined he asked if he could request a dance at the next ball. I was forced to tell him I had been directed to say no. It was very uncomfortable."

Lord Thorpe nodded thoughtfully.

"I imagine you know the reason, though I do not," Serenity said. "I will not inquire into it, as my father did not like to say."

"I suspect he is right to leave you out of it. Not because you are his daughter or could not weigh the matter yourself, but because it is unsavory and the less said about it to anybody the better. However, it is nothing to fret over. My brother likes to attempt to stir trouble, he is forever unhappy and cannot seem to help himself. Your father, however, is a shark to my brother's goldfish and he was soundly routed."

Serenity could not imagine what Lord Charles had done. "I wonder, if Lord Charles has done something untoward and is not to be chastened over it, will he not attempt something else?"

"No," Lord Thorpe said, stopping a footman and offering Serenity a glass of champagne. "Charles always operates the same—he goes too far and then he lays low for a period of time. I expect we will not see him for the rest of the season."

Serenity gratefully took the glass. She was cheered to hear that whatever lord Charles had been up to, it was at an end. She was even more cheered to be strolling round the ballroom with Lord Thorpe.

"We must not forget to vote over the costumes or Lady Darlington will be put out," Lord Thorpe said. "I at least know who I will vote for as most original."

She laughed. "I am very afraid it is me. Surprisingly, Lady Pembroke seemed to admire my bee costume."

"As do I," Lord Thorpe said.

Serenity did not answer that, as what was there to say? He was so kind though the idea that she looked ridiculous had been growing in her ever since she'd arrived.

"Perhaps we might try the card room? We might attempt to sensibly get to twenty-one this time."

"Oh let's do," Serenity said, feeling that was indeed a very good idea. "I am certain we will pay far closer attention and will acquit ourselves admirably."

"You are certain of that?"

"No, not really," Serenity said, laughing.

CHARLES LEFT LADY Darlington's masque in a blind rage. When he arrived to his apartments in The Albany, he paced back and forth with the assistance of liberal glasses of brandy. That duke! That damn duke! If he had been like any other father in the wide world, he would have reacted decisively to even a whisper that one of his daughter's suitors had meddled with a servant. He would have cut off all contact with Thorpe and that would have been that. Victory would have been achieved.

What a victory it would have been, too. It was the kind of thing he could remind Thorpe of forevermore. "Ah, brother, you thought to secure Lady Serenity but her father did not find you up to the mark."

There were small moments in his frenzied pacing when the idea that he'd not executed the scheme perfectly presented itself to him, but he just as quickly brushed them away. Perhaps the execution had not been perfect, but it had been close enough for any reasonable father. In any case, the next time he needed to do anything similar, he'd send a man who was not wearing livery.

As the brandy began to numb his thoughts, it also began to turn them in a new direction. Both brandy and port had the unique ability to soften the edges of any disappointment and then swirl ideas all round until a far happier conclusion was reached. Why was he moping like all was lost? He was a victor, he always had been. Perhaps the duke *had* seen that the porter delivering the letter was wearing The Albany's livery. Perhaps he *did* know Charles was the author of that letter. That did not mean he would not come to believe it. In fact, it might just dawn on that duke that a brother on the scene was the likeliest to know what had happened regarding that maid.

If only Thorpe did not come off as such an upstanding citizen. That was the real sticking point. His damn brother was always so careful not to put a foot out of place. Worse, the one weakness he'd had, his mopey sentimentality, seemed to have fled.

Charles paused. He'd not got anywhere attempting to affect the duke's estimation of his brother. It was not entirely clear if Lady Serenity was aware of the letter. She'd said she'd been told to decline. That might have been all she was told.

If he could not bring Thorpe lower, was there a way to raise himself higher? Certainly, that must be the ticket. Prove himself superior in her eyes.

What would Lady Serenity admire? His mind ran through all

the likely things a lady might admire. He might claim to have been in a duel or maybe he was beset by a gang of footpads and roundly defeated them. He might even darken one eye so that people were all but forced to inquire into what happened.

But then, that might not work with her. She might fan herself over the violence. He could perhaps pretend at being a poet—she seemed a rather dreamy and impractical specimen, she might admire that quite a lot. Was there somebody living in The Albany and finding themselves short on funds that might whip up some sloppy and overwrought phrasings for a price?

What did Lady Serenity admire, what would affect her feelings? What would put him head and shoulders over Thorpe?

Charles stumbled and dropped his glass, spilling brandy across the cream carpet. He stared at the amber liquid seeping into its fibers. He was such an idiot. It had been staring him in the face all along.

It was that dog. That ridiculous three-legged dog. He could rescue the dog.

All he'd need to do was devise a situation in which the dog needed rescuing. He would be the hero, while Thorpe would appear befuddled, having no idea where to even look for that cur. Charles would know, though.

"It is all right, Lady Serenity," he mumbled, "I have rescued…whatever its name is…from…very bad people. It is my honor to return it to you."

THE NIGHT BEFORE, Serenity felt as if she'd all but floated up the stairs to her bedchamber. She and Lord Thorpe had spent the rest of the evening playing vingt-et-un. Or at least, pretending to play at it. Their conversation was such that there was little attention paid to the number twenty-one or any other number. It felt as if they'd spoken of everything in the wide world.

Of course, there had been moments when her feelings threatened to run away with her. She had relayed her conversation with Lady Pembroke, which had led to a discussion about slatted skeps. Lord Thorpe admitted that he did not know what sort of hives were used on his estate and that idea had very naturally led Serenity to imagine the worst. He did promise to find it out and switch to the slatted skeps if it was discovered that they'd not yet been adopted. It was very kind of him to do so but she'd had a time of it blinking the water back in her eyes at the thought of a colony of bees being murdered. She supposed her honeycombed mask had hidden it well enough, though.

They might have gone on agreeably in that situation had not Lady Darlington rounded up everybody in the card room and herded them to the voting tables.

Soon enough, Lady Darlington had tallied all the votes, quieted the orchestra, and read aloud the results.

Serenity could not claim to be too surprised to win the most original costume. Other ladies won the prizes for costumes that were deemed beautiful in some way but nobody else had arrived as an insect.

She had really been very touched at the applause that accompanied the announcement and she was certain Lord Thorpe applauded the loudest. She'd received quite a few congratulations, though some of them mentioned her daring so she supposed she was right to feel ridiculous in her bee costume. Lady Darlington gifted her a very charming India shawl as a prize.

At the end of the evening, Lord Thorpe had proposed to ride his horse alongside her father's carriage. He claimed there were no end of footpads and would-be highwaymen lurking on the London Streets and he might be called on for protection.

Her father's coachman had looked down his nose at the proposal and patted his pocket as if to point out he was well-armed, and well able to protect the duke.

The duke had snorted and told Lord Thorpe that he did not care to cause talk until there was something decided to talk about.

Lord Thorpe had nodded as if he'd expected as much but thought to try it out anyway. They had said their goodbyes and Serenity had made a spectacle of herself, hanging her head out the window to watch him ride off.

CHAPTER SIXTEEN

AFTER THE MASQUE, Serenity had gazed out her window at the flickering of the lamps around the square as tears of happiness streamed down her cheeks. Certainly, there would be something definite to talk about soon.

She had hoped a walking of the dogs would commence on the following morning. The walk might be just the opportunity for Lord Thorpe to say something decided. Once more, though, nature ran against her. The icy rain did not even come down straight as the day dawned, but rather hurled itself at the windows as if determined to get inside.

After breakfast had come and gone with no let up of the rain, she resigned herself to it. Her family had gathered in the drawing room and even her father had not wished to go to his club in such weather. He said the carriage horses would be exceedingly cross about it, and rightly so.

Mrs. Right had come in and Serenity was becoming not quite sure of what their dear housekeeper thought of Lord Thorpe. She had liked him. She had liked him exceedingly, Serenity had thought. But now, it seemed that every time his name was mentioned, she frowned.

She supposed she ought not read too much into it. A housekeeper must have a thousand matters to consider and was probably hardly listening to the chatter as she straightened the mess Valor had made with a pile of books.

In any case, she would see Lord Thorpe soon enough. It could not rain all the time. There was every chance that the morrow would bring only a light misting.

The drawing room doors were thrown open and Thomas hurried in and closed them behind him. He looked a little panicked and just stared at the duke.

The duke pulled a curtain back to look outside to the square. "Don't tell me," he said. "Lady Misery has arrived. Well, tell her I am not at home. None of us are at home. We've all gone on an extended trip somewhere so she need not return on any other day. We'll see her in five years!"

"Your Grace," Thomas whispered. "It is not just Lady Misery…I mean, Lady Marchfield. She's brought the bishop!"

Mrs. Right dropped the pile of books that had been in her arms.

Serenity looked to her father. Gracious, why was the bishop coming to see them? Did he know they did not attend church while they were in Town?

MRS. RIGHT STARED at the books strewn on the floor, her mind racing back in time over the last twenty-four hours. It was not a very good time for the bishop to turn up! What if Lord Thorpe's carriage was to collapse right in view of him? There would probably be an inquiry. It was her experience that no good could come of the church looking into a thing.

Last night, she had been careful to clean the oil from her hands, though there was still some telltale evidence lodged under her nails. Her outing had been thrilling and terrifying—she had felt herself one of the twelve spies of Moses sent to survey Canaan.

She had finally hit on a strategy of emptying Lord Thorpe's stable of his staff so she might tiptoe into the carriage house and meddle with the springs on his coach. She had discovered the name of his stablemaster and then hired a boy to deliver a message to him while Lord Thorpe was at the masque.

Baxter—

I write on behalf of Lord Thorpe. We are at the scene of a terrible accident between two carriages who had engaged in a race. There were multiple injuries as there were hundreds of people come to watch. Bring every soul in the stables to the Wapping High Street to provide assistance. Do not bring Thorpe's carriage as it is not suited to the task. Rather, hire as many hackneys as you can find so we might provide transport for the injured.

Meckelton

Poor Baxter would not have the first idea who Meckelton was supposed to be, but he would not be expected to know every lord of the *ton*.

At precisely eleven o'clock, Mrs. Right had donned a dark cape and carried her bag of tools to the back garden. She threw a step stool over a short wall and climbed over, making her way across Lord Luddington's garden. On the far side she encountered a higher wall and used the step stool to get over it to Lord Thorpe's mews. She lurked in the shadows and it was not too long a time before she saw her messenger, and then the flurry of activity that accompanied it.

The stable hands were gone off to the Wapping High Street to assist in the tragic carriage accident that never was. It would take them ages to secure hackneys, get there, wander around looking for evidence of an accident, and finally return home. She had arranged more than enough time to do her work.

It was well she did so, too. It had taken her a while to determine where she ought to apply a hacksaw and which bolts to loosen. She'd done her best with it, not being an expert on disabling carriages. She'd had no choice, Lord Thorpe must be made to pay for tricking Serenity into thinking he was an upstanding gentleman when really he'd compromised a poor maid in his household.

Of course, the going back to the house was complicated by the step stool being on the other side of the higher wall. With all her might she'd somehow got over the top of it, though she'd left her bag of tools behind. She really ought to have thrown them over first, but they were very heavy.

Nevertheless, she had accomplished it. The carriage springs meddled with was her goodbye gift to Lord Thorpe before the Nicolet family disappeared from his view. Though, Mrs. Right was still wondering when the duke would announce they were all returning to the Dales. She'd thought it very peculiar that the duke should take Serenity to the masque. Lord Thorpe would be there—what plan did the duke have to keep his daughter away from the rogue? And then it seemed he hadn't.

Mrs. Right consoled herself with the idea that the duke could be a very deep character. She was certain he had something in mind and she would discover it in due course. In the meantime, she had done her bit to remedy the situation. That bit must always be behind the scenes, as it was one of the deficiencies of England that a housekeeper could not give a loud and violent what-for to whoever she pleased without consequences.

With any luck, Lord Thorpe would set off for an important appointment only to have the springs of his carriage collapse underneath him. She hoped she was nearby a window when it happened!

For now, though, all in the household remained unaware of her accomplishment. They had just now been gathered in the drawing room having a merry time of it. Or at least, it seemed they were trying to cheer Serenity over the weather. It was not just raining, but mother nature had kindly added in a whipping and icy wind. Serenity's walk with Lord Thorpe, which the duke had inexplicably not yet put a stop to, had been off for this day at least.

Mrs. Right had surveyed the dining room to assure herself that all was in order. Mr. Cremble was out of the picture and she was back in her rightful place as the general of the duke's household.

Once the dining room had been deemed in order she'd made her way to the drawing room to see what plans were being made for the afternoon. She was hopeful that the weather might clear and they would go for a drive in the park—the fresh air would do her good after her exertions of the night previous.

"Mrs. Right," Winsome had said when she gone in, "Serenity was just telling us that Lord Thorpe was very admiring of her bee costume."

"Oh, aye?" she'd said, noncommittally. She could not understand it. Had the duke allowed Lord Thorpe to continue his wooing? She could not understand what the duke's plan was. She knew him well enough to know that he would not give over one of his precious daughters to a scoundrel, so why was he allowing this to go on? He would not countenance a philanderer, he'd never been one himself and looked askance at that sort of thing.

As she turned that question over in her mind, Thomas had come in and it was understood that Bishop Porteus was at their doors.

Now she scrambled to pick up the books she'd dropped and acquire an expression of bored disinterest. Or mild surprise. Or gladness. Or righteousness. Or piousness. Anything but guilty, pretending to have dealings with the devil, and being a person who might meddle with a lord's carriage.

"THERE WAS ALSO found," Quinn said, as he and Roland sat in the library, "a bag of tools in the garden by the wall. Wrenches of every description and a saw."

"What could have been the purpose of it, though?" Roland

asked. "Was it housebreakers who thought they'd need the stable staff away, but then they'd somehow lost their nerve?"

Quinn shrugged. "Something frightened them off. I was thinking it might have been your brother up to something?"

"Up to what, though?" Roland asked. "If he wanted something he could have walked through the front doors."

"I cannot say and I imagine it will remain a mystery. I will have a guard hired for the back of the house in case they return."

"And nothing has been found meddled with? Nothing has been stolen?"

Baxter says not even a harness is missing," Quinn said. "He also had some choice words for whoever was at the bottom of this. He and the boys had quite the evening searching the Wapping high street in three hackneys for the terrible carriage accident."

"I will write to our neighbors and inform the nightwatchman on the square. Perhaps we are not the only house targeted. Though, it seems farfetched that this could have been some gang of housebreakers. Whoever it was went to the trouble of seeing that the stables were emptied of people but what were they proposing to do about the staff in the house?"

Quinn nodded. "Also, very odd that the step stool was left behind. Are they very short sorts of criminals? Lord Luddington's butler claims that stool does not belong to his household."

"And why did they come that way in the first place?" Roland asked. "They must have entered the square by road somewhere. Why go down the wrong mews and then climb over a wall?"

Quinn snorted. "Perhaps they are both short and stupid."

"I hope they are not stupid enough to return."

They fell silent for some minutes. Then Quinn said, "Very sorry about the weather not cooperating this morning, by the by. Hopefully, your dog walking venture will be back on for the morrow. Are you inching ever closer to a proposal?"

"I am. I had thought possibly this morning, if I could find the right moment."

"So I gather all your doubts are at an end?"

"No, they are not. I am determined that she must know the truth. I am not the reserved marquess she has come to know. She deserves to know the truth, and then she came make a decision based on the facts."

Quinn sighed. "The facts are you are an upstanding gentleman with a care for your fellow man. And fellow creatures. I do not see how she can be opposed to it."

Roland did not answer, as his friend and butler was always downplaying his affliction. The real facts were, he sometimes rode out to a lonely green at dawn to shout out his feelings and he could be taken down in an instant over the sight of a suffering animal. That really was the worst of it and there were so many opportunities for disaster on an estate. A litter of pups and the smallest did not survive. A horse to be put down. A stalwart and loyal hunting dog of the pack growing too old to keep up and retired, watching longingly as his brothers set off. All of those things very ridiculously stopped him in his tracks.

Children would likely be a thousand times worse. Those were the facts. He did not, at this point in his life, expect much improvement in those facts. The question was, would Lady Serenity find she did not care for those facts? Did she look for a stern and unfeeling marquess who was not buffeted by suffering? For if she was, he was the wrong marquess.

If nature would cooperate, he would find out on the morrow, sometime after eleven o'clock while they walked the square's gardens. If it were to go against him, he would retreat to the estate. If that were to be the outcome, he knew well enough that he could not bear to be in view of the street that had once seen Lady Serenity Nicolet glorying in a snowfall. If that were to be the case, he might never return to the Grosvenor Square house, as it would contain too many painful memories.

And there he went again. Such thoughts as those were far too dramatic for a marquess!

Serenity looked toward her father. They'd all risen, but for him, as the bishop was led in. She and her sisters curtsied, as did Mrs. Right, who was looking very suddenly pale. Their aunt, Lady Marchfield, had hurried in behind the bishop and wore a look of supreme satisfaction.

Charlie, looking wide-eyed, said, "The Right Reverend Porteus, Bishop of London, Member of the Privy Council, and…and…"

"Dean of the Chapel Royal," Lady Marchfield heatedly whispered.

"Dean of the Chapel Royal," Charlie said, before backing out the door.

"Your Grace," the bishop said in a sonorous voice, "I thank you for admittance to your house. I would request a word in private on a very serious matter."

"What? Come to scold us for not attending church, have you? Well, Lady Misery here knows well enough that I only attend my own church in my own neighborhood in the Dales. Having one vicar in my life is quite sufficient!"

The bishop looked positively horrified. "You do not attend church?"

Serenity got the idea that was not why the bishop had come but was rather new information.

"Did I not tell you the state of this household, Bishop," Lady Marchfield said.

The bishop nodded gravely.

"I am sure she told you quite a lot, Bishop," the duke said. "She tells everybody quite a lot. Perhaps what she did not mention was that she goes round acting all pious without a sympathetic bone in her body! Not very Christian in my view. What about that?"

The bishop did not seem to know anything about Lady

Marchfield's unsympathetic bones. "Your Grace, if we might have a word privately?"

"Nonsense," the duke said. "Anything you have to say can be said in hearing of my family and my housekeeper."

This seemed to pull the bishop up short. Serenity was feeling pulled up short herself. Why had he come? What were they supposed to do? Could they sit down? She did not know—she'd never been visited by a bishop before.

"Very well," the bishop said. "Lady Marchfield and the curate of the Grosvenor Church have given me a full accounting of what has transpired here with Mr. Cremble. Including the unfortunate, and may I say alarming, involvement of your housekeeper."

If the bishop had thought those ideas would strike the duke hard, he was to be disappointed. The duke laughed uproariously. "An amusing tale, is it not?"

The bishop pulled himself up straighter. "Amusing? Your Grace, there is every indication that something is spiritually amiss in this house!"

"Oh, is there?" the duke asked. "From my view, I would think a bishop would be a little concerned that a fellow churchman would fall for such ridiculous stories! A meeting with the devil on the moors and now my housekeeper cannot be anywhere near a cross? Preposterous."

Lady Marchfield stepped forward. "Then how do you explain that this housekeeper of yours fell back at a moment when a cross was nearby though she could not even see it? It was lodged under a table and she could not have even known it was there! Roland, this woman has had you under her thrall for years and I have never understood why. But now, I believe the truth is beginning to show itself!"

The bishop turned to Mrs. Right. "Madame, how *do* you explain that point, as that really is the crux of the matter. Why did you fall back from a cross you could not see?"

"Because Cook saw him put it there," Mrs. Right said, raising her eyes defiantly. "I was instantly informed of it, as my staff are loyal to me. Since your Mr. Cremble decided he was to act as a Spanish Inquisitor, I decided to play along." The housekeeper took that moment to pull the cross around her neck from under her fichu. "I am a god-fearing woman, Bishop Porteus. But I am not a butler-fearing woman."

"You see? Gullible is what that fellow Crumble or Bumble or whatever his name is. They all are, in my experience," the duke said. "My sister throws them into the house and my housekeeper throws them out. It's become a family tradition!"

Serenity did her best not to laugh. It really had become a tradition. They all knew well enough that their father could put a stop to it, but he was always too amused to discover how the situation would play out.

The bishop seemed to take in Mrs. Right's words and the cross around her neck. "Lady Marchfield, perhaps we have been precipitous in a leap to judgment. There is the possibility that Mr. Cremble misinterpreted events."

"Do not let them fool you," Lady Marchfield said. "That woman is evil in one way or another, even if we cannot see exactly how."

"Bishop," the duke said from his place lounging on the sofa, "my advice is to drop Lady Misery at home and be done with her. Her lord won't be happy to see her, he never is, but that's his problem, is it not?"

"Roland!" Lady Marchfield exclaimed.

Serenity was not certain why her aunt looked so shocked. Her father had said the same or something like it a hundred times.

The bishop seemed to think for a moment. Then he said, "I will take my leave. Though, before I do, I must point out, Your Grace, that attendance at church is not to be at your convenience. Not even a duke can put the Sunday service aside. I highly suggest you begin attending while you are in Town, to protect your immortal soul. As well, I suggest you carefully monitor your household for any suggestion that all is not as it should be in a

God-fearing house."

With that, the bishop bowed and took his leave. Lady March-field hurried after him, but not before casting a last glare at her brother.

After the doors shut and Lady Marchfield's carriage departed the square, Valor said, "What do you think, Papa? Should we go to church to protect our immortal souls?"

"Go if you like, somebody will take you," the duke said. "However, I think our quiet reading of the bible for an hour on a Sunday morning and attending service in the Dales is quite sufficient. The bishop and his ilk would like us all to think that God is at every church doorstep taking attendance. Very convenient of them to think it, too, but I do not see it that way."

Valor seemed well satisfied with that answer, as did they all, Serenity supposed. Perhaps Verity did not look wholly convinced but she was likely only searching her mind for facts on the subject.

Mrs. Right seemed the most pleased, the color had returned to her cheeks. "Well now," she said, "I reckon I ought to send a tea tray in."

"Very good notion, Mrs. Right," the duke said. "One requires sustenance after tangling with a bishop."

Valor laughed. "You did tangle with him, Papa. Just think, when we go home you can tell the vicar that you gave the bishop a what-for! He'll be so mad about it."

The duke laughed. "I suspect I will do that, Val. Nothing more brightens a day at home than confounding our vicar. Especially as that fellow was good enough to send Mr. Cremble our way."

"Wait until he hears Mrs. Right tricked him into thinking she was friends with the devil," Winsome said. "He'll have steam coming from his ears!"

"Speaking of the Dales, do we have any particular plans to return home soon, Your Grace?" Mrs. Right asked.

Serenity turned to stare at their housekeeper. Why would

they have plans to go home? They could not go home now! Lord Thorpe was on the verge, well he seemed as if he might be getting close to, it seemed as if something might be said. They could not go home!

"I know you miss the Dales, Mrs. Right, as do I," the duke said. "But I feel as if I am getting nearer to unloading another of my daughters and cannot do it from there. No peace for the wicked, I imagine the bishop would say. Of course, what *I* would say is my dream of an empty house is within reach!"

As Serenity's sisters roundly denounced their father's idea of unloading them, Serenity watched Mrs. Right. She seemed a bit let down to hear they would not go home. Serenity supposed she'd never taken into account how much their dear housekeeper must miss her home and her friends and neighbors each time they came to Town. The dear lady had been very stoic about it.

"Let us all hope," the duke said, "that the weather clears on the morrow and a certain gentleman might take aim and fire in my daughter's direction at the hour of eleven."

"Papa!" Serenity said. Though really, she was hoping just the same.

CHAPTER SEVENTEEN

C HARLES HAD DISCOVERED that it was not as easy as one might imagine to find a dognaper for hire. He did not understand why—dog-stealing was rampant across England. Every other advertisement in the newspapers was about a lost or stolen dog, generally offering a description, the location last seen and the offer of a reward or threat of the law.

Finally, though, one low contact led to the next and the word was put out in the low streets of the Rats' Castle and eventually one was found. Or, if the fellow did not specialize in such activities, he was willing to try it out.

Wilkes, as he claimed his name was, looked as if he'd be willing to try out anything at all. His face was rather gaunt and his clothes full of holes. Along with the fee to be paid, Charles had put him into some of his old clothes. It was entirely necessary, as anybody turning up in such shabby and threadbare attire in the vicinity of Grosvenor Square would instantly be marked suspicious.

Wilkes had been haunting the environs of Lady Serenity's garden in the early morning hours before the sun was entirely up for two days. He'd claimed that as soon as the kitchen fires were lit, somebody would let the dog out, as dogs always did demand to be let out first thing. He'd been right, though he'd no luck on the first day, as a footman had stood at the doorway.

On the second day, though, Wilkes had found success. The

footman had only opened the door and then gone off somewhere. Wilkes had lured the cur close with a bit of meat and then grabbed him and made off with him.

Charles had been the smallest bit alarmed when Wilkes had delivered the dog to The Albany an hour ago. He'd been loaded into a traveling case and the growls coming from the case were not promising. Further, Wilkes had a rather nasty bite on his hand.

As it happened, Charles had very good reason to be alarmed. Despite the thing only having three legs and one working eye, it had gone after his ankles with determination. It was just now locked in the sitting room with a bowl of water and another of chopped up beef. Wilkes was long gone and Charles was nearly jumping out of his skin listening to the scratching and clawing at that door.

What a time for his valet to be away. Richards had gone off to Cornwall to assist his dying mother, despite Charles pointing out that the only way he could *help* her die was to put a pillow over her face. He supposed he'd meant that as a joke, though Richards had not seemed to see it that way. He was not even entirely certain his valet was coming back, so affronted had he been.

Charles had thought he might keep the dog around for a few days. Then, just when Lady Serenity was convinced that all was lost, he would return it. He'd have to wait long enough for an advertisement to be placed in the newspaper, else how could he explain even knowing the dog was lost? The duke had ordered his daughter to steer clear of him, so he could not call at the house and discover it that way. He was certain he would not be admitted.

Perhaps he could hire somebody to move into his rooms at The Albany to mind the creature until such time as it could be returned? He had to do something—how could he sleep at night with it clawing at the door? Charles had every confidence that were the dog to get out in the night, it would happily get him by the throat.

He would ask around The Albany. There was always somebody with empty pockets, having gambled too high. There was always somebody wondering how they would explain it to the old soldier back at home. Some of them did not even have the means to gamble as high as they did. A night of drink and dice and all of the sudden a mortgage was needed to save the family honor. He might not offer enough to stave off a mortgage, but for a gentleman with empty pockets, any amount would be welcome.

That's what he would do. He would hire somebody to keep an eye on the dog and feed it. He'd thought to go off to a comfortable inn, but perhaps he need not do that. Michaels was in the apartments next to his own and was in rather terrible financial straits. He could pay the fellow fifty pounds to switch apartments with him.

Let Michaels sit here and listen to the growling while Charles lounged in his set. He could tell Michaels that he looked after the dog for an old and infirm aunt. After all, Michaels was shortly to leave Town—he'd already been recalled home by his father on account of his debts. Charles was confident that Sir William, Michaels' father, would never allow his ne'er-do-well son to set foot in London again. He'd never know who the dog actually belonged to.

From the comfort of Michaels' apartments, Charles would monitor the newspapers for the advertisement about the Duke of Pelham's lost dog—brownish in color, answers to the name Nelson, missing a leg, blind in one eye. It would be hard to miss. It would also be hard to imagine anybody stealing such a creature. He must be lost, and that is exactly the story Charles was intending. As far as Lady Serenity would know it, he'd discovered the dog in a lonely area of the park, wandering round forlorn.

Had Thorpe scoured the park for any sign of her beloved dog? Apparently not, if results were anything to go by. Could the duke keep up his disapproval of the gentleman bringing home the family dog? He did not think so. The duke had no end of women wandering round his house—the screeching over the missing dog would be window shattering.

More scratching and growling drifted into the room. He backed up at the sight of the dog's nails appearing in the gap between the bottom of the door and the floor. He would likely have to pay for repairs to that door the dog was just now mauling. He really had to find a nanny for that cursed dog before the sun set. He could not sleep with it so nearby him. He would not get a wink always wondering when he'd find canine jaws choking the life out of him.

Charles jumped up and put on his coat. It was time to see Michaels.

THE SUN WAS doing an excellent job peeking through the clouds and it was a fine morning. At half past ten, Serenity had been dressed and gone down the stairs. Her dog-walking with Lord Thorpe was set to commence at eleven. Her mind went round in circles over the same idea—something might be said, something might be said, something might be said.

If something *were* said, this would mark the greatest turning point in her life. She must face it with bravery.

Serenity sighed. She did not suppose any other lady had to face a proposal with bravery. Nerves, probably. But not bravery.

However, she was determined that Lord Thorpe be informed of her weepy nature before she would accept. She intended to tell him all of it, even about the crypt of bees. He must know her for who she really was, not this composed lady she'd pretended to be. Else, he would be so disappointed later, when he did find it out. It would be as if she'd tricked him, and he would resent her for it.

She must just pray that he found it of little matter that his marchioness looked round the garden for dead bees, or wept over a sunrise, or might weep for no particular reason other than to relieve her feelings. She supposed a usual marchioness was very regal and composed. If that was what he looked for, she was not that lady.

She must think positive, though. For all she knew, he'd be delighted with her weeping. But maybe not think *that* positive. Perhaps the best she could hope for is that he viewed it as a trifling inconvenience.

Winsome passed her by in the front hall. "Nelson is hiding somewhere, the rascal," she said. "I'd have thought he'd be below stairs with Cook, but he is not."

Oh do find him quickly. I do not wish to be late, I cannot be late."

A few minutes later, Winsome called down from above stairs. Nelson was nowhere to be seen up there either. This set all the sisters to looking for Nelson and rechecking places that had been checked. Then all the staff looked for him. Voices filled the house, calling for him. Nobody seemed to know where he was last seen. Mrs. Wendover was in her rightful place on Valor's bed, so he'd not made off to some corner with the stuffed rabbit. Thomas had said he'd let him out to the garden hours ago, just after sunrise, but he'd been sure somebody else had let him back in. Nelson was very good about scratching at the door when he was done patrolling the paths.

That was when Serenity really began to worry. Nobody below stairs had heard any scratching on the door that led to the garden. Every soul in the household had been interviewed. Nobody had let Nelson back into the house. Thomas had been sent to the stables to speak with the grooms but he was not there either.

Serenity and Winsome had run out to search the garden together. Serenity had the sudden thought that perhaps Nelson had injured himself and was even now lying under a bush. Perhaps he'd been bitten by an adder! Were there adders in

London? She did not know! Why could not her papa be here? Why had he set off to his club just when they could not find Nelson?

There had been no sign of Nelson, but there had been a sign of something else. She and Winsome stared down at some bits of meat sprinkled nearby the garden wall.

"Look, Serenity, there is a footprint too. Large, from a man's boot."

Serenity clutched her sister's hand. "It cannot be true!"

"It is true, though. Somebody was here and tempted him with meat. Somebody made off with Nelson. You always said it was a possibility, though I did not see much in the idea. You were right."

"I do not want to be right," Serenity said, sobbing. "What's happened to him? He must be so frightened! Who took him?"

Winsome patted her hand. "Calm yourself, your weeping will not help Nelson. He has a collar on and somebody might look at it. It says who he belongs to. We should advertise a large reward in the newspapers and somebody will bring him back."

"Do you think so?" Serenity said, grasping at any hope at all. "Do you think they would take him and then bring him back for money?"

"I hope so. We should put in the advertisement that he wears a red collar and has only three legs and one working eye. Then if someone has seen him, and really he is distinctive looking, they will remember and want the reward."

"We must send Thomas or Charlie for Papa. We must get an advertisement in for tomorrow. Oh, I can't bear the idea of how frightened he is and what might be happening to him. He will be so bereft and sad to be taken from his home!"

"I'll send for Papa," Winsome said. "You've got to tell Lord Thorpe that dog walking is off on account of our dog gone missing."

"Lord Thorpe!" Serenity cried. She picked up her skirts and ran toward the house. If she could not run to her father at this very minute, she would run to Lord Thorpe.

ROLAND HAD BEEN girding himself all morning. This was the momentous day. He would ask Lady Serenity for her hand and God willing she would accept.

Quinn had gone so far as to suggest a nip of brandy, but Roland had declined. If ever in his life he must be clear-eyed and clear-headed, it was this morning.

The hours had ticked by tortuously slow. Why did they go so slow when usually they were moving at a much faster pace? He crossed and recrossed his drawing room as Havoc looked on with interest. He occasionally stopped and pulled out a velvet box from his pocket—a token for his future bride.

He'd spent some time at Rundell & Bridge the previous day, examining what was on offer. There were some very grand pieces, and Lady Serenity deserved every one of them, but then something more modest had arrested his attention. A small gold pin, fashioned as a honeybee. It housed two pearls comprising its body, one smaller for the head and the other larger for the body. The fashioning of the gold had been exceedingly detailed and the whole was surrounded by diamond chips. It was not elaborate or prohibitively expensive, but it was charming and would suit Lady Serenity. After their talk of slatted skeps, it would show that he cared for her concerns. She really had been concerned, too. Then, of course, he had recalled the duke claiming she had a particular affinity for bees and the pin had seemed just right.

Finally, the minute hand on the clock inched toward eleven. Roland turned to his dog. "Come Havoc, it will not hurt us to be on the early side of things."

The mastiff got to his feet and lumbered over to him, ever agreeable to be going somewhere. Roland leashed him and set out to the square, determinedly ignoring any curtains on any of his windows that might just now be pulling aside to watch him.

He arrived at the gate to the gardens a full five minutes ahead of time. Therefore, he'd been surprised to see Lady Serenity running toward him. In a state too, and without Nelson.

She reached him out of breath. "Lady Serenity, what has happened? Has someone been taken ill?"

"Nelson," she said, brushing tears away from her cheeks. "Somebody has taken him! He's gone and my father is at his club and we need an advertisement in the newspapers right away so somebody can bring him back!"

This was all said in such a rush that it took Roland a moment to take it all in. "You are certain? You have looked everywhere in the house?"

Lady Serenity nodded.

Just then, Mrs. Right came running out of the house after her charge. "Lord Thorpe," she said coldly, "as you can see, we are in the midst of an emergency. Serenity, do come back inside."

Roland was not at all sure why the housekeeper was glaring at him just now. *He* did not take the dog. "Lady Serenity, I will put an advertisement in immediately. Please tell the duke that I did so and I offer a sum of a thousand pounds for Nelson's safe return, which I am happy to do."

"A thousand pounds!" Lady Serenity cried. "Gracious, I was thinking of pressing my father to offer a hundred pounds. Certainly, somebody will bring him back for such an amount. But is it too much to ask of you? It is an excessive sum."

"It is nothing at all, to guarantee Nelson's safe return."

"I am not sure the duke will approve it, Lord Thorpe," the housekeeper said. "He might have a mind to decline your help in this matter."

Lady Serenity stared at Mrs. Right, aghast.

"Do not fear such a thing, Lady Serenity," Roland said. "Nobody, not even the duke, can stop me if I wish to offer the sum. We will have Nelson returned."

The housekeeper sniffed at the idea. Lady Serenity, however, looked very much comforted. Mrs. Right took her by the hand and walked her back to the house.

Roland sprang into action. He hurried Havoc home and directed Quinn to see to the advertisements himself. It was to be a large ad, run in all the major newspapers regardless of the cost, and offer a thousand pounds. It would catch the attention of every person who picked up a newspaper.

While that was being done, he ordered his horse saddled. He would tour the neighborhood, attempting to discover if anyone had seen the dog. He would discover if anybody had seen anything at all.

As he waited for his horse to be brought round, Havoc stared dolefully at him, no doubt wondering why they'd not gone on a walk. Roland could not help thinking of poor Nelson. He could not help thinking of what his own feelings would be if it had been Havoc. It was precisely what he had feared when Havoc had been small enough to take.

He willed himself to stay in control, but it was just the sort of thing that set him off. A poor animal taken from his home. The little dog must be terrified.

Who would take him? For a brief moment he wondered if somehow whoever was responsible for sending his stablemaster and his grooms on a goose chase to the Wapping high street and Nelson gone missing were connected. He could not see how it made sense though.

The only idea that did make sense was that somebody had taken Nelson in order to ransom him back. The duke was known to have deep pockets, making him a target for that sort of thing. Roland was in no doubt that somebody would come forward to collect the reward. Likely with some ridiculous story of finding the dog on their doorstep and kindly taking him in from the cold out of Christian charity and a pure heart.

"Your horse is out front," Quinn said. "I'll take a hackney to Fleet Street, it will be faster than waiting for the horses to be hitched to the carriage."

Roland nodded. He could not say much, as his feelings were teetering on the edge regarding Nelson's current situation.

"You are sure? You will offer a thousand pounds?"

"Very," Roland said, striding out of the house.

Roland rode round the square, questioning passersby. When that did not lead to any information regarding the whereabouts of Nelson, he expanded his search to nearby streets. Then, finally, the park.

Nelson was nowhere to be found. Nobody knew anything about it. Whoever had taken him had been careful he was not observed. Nelson must have been hidden from view in some way. Anybody who'd even glanced at that dog would remember him. He had a very original appearance. Nobody had seen him, though. The reward was the only thing that would bring Nelson back.

He reluctantly turned his horse and headed for home. He must at least confirm with Quinn that they'd made the deadline for an advertisement. That was the only hope for Nelson now.

Mrs. Right was well used to dealing with an upset from one or another of her girls. Not since their mother died, though, had the roof been raised in such a manner. And even then, Valor had been an infant and Winsome and Verity still too young to really take it in.

Notes had been speedily sent to the three eldest sisters to relay the unfolding emergency and they had all three made their way to the house with alacrity. So now, on top of Serenity, Winsome, Verity, and Valor weeping, they had added in Felicity, Grace, and Patience.

The duke had been called back from his club, and he did do his very best to comfort his girls. But what was one man to do with seven crying daughters?

Mrs. Right had finally, in the late afternoon, put Serenity to bed with a bit of laudanum. The girl really did need to calm herself and sleep for a few hours, else she would make herself ill.

As the rest of the girls consoled one another in the drawing room, Mrs. Right softly knocked on the library door. The duke had taken a momentary refuge there to regroup.

Summoned in, the duke said, "Still hysterics in the drawing room, I imagine?"

Mrs. Right nodded. "Aye, they'll be drained of all tears by the end of it."

"I hope the end of it is we get that dog back," the duke said. "He's an odd little thing and awful to look at, but he's grown on me."

"I am certain things will come right," the housekeeper said, though she was not certain at all.

"I expect so, the reward is big enough. I'd like to know who would look at Nelson and then think about becoming a thousand pounds richer and have things come down on Nelson's side. Very gracious of Thorpe to offer such a sum. I expect a proposal is in the offing."

Mrs. Right did not quite know what to do with that statement. The duke would allow Lord Thorpe to propose? Was there some scheme here she could not see?

"A fourth daughter wed, and Lady Misery had no faith that I could do it. Hah! The jest is on her."

"You mean to allow it to go forward, then?" Mrs. Right asked. She could hardly believe it to be true, but what else could she think?

"Why shouldn't I? Thorpe is an upstanding sort of man and he's a marquess. Serenity likes him and she will be a duchess someday. Good all round, I'd say."

"But Your Grace! Do you not fear—" Mrs. Right did not finish that sentence, as she did not exactly know how to mention that she'd read the duke's correspondence.

The duke had leaned back and folded his arms. "Mrs. Right,

we have known each other a good long while. Whatever it is on your mind, out with it."

She had no choice. She'd have to admit what she'd done to have any chance at talking some sense into the duke and saving her dear Serenity from that rogue of a marquess. "Well, as it happens, I do not know if you are aware, but there are times when one is dusting and straightening things when one's eyes, terrible traitors that they are, will take in words suddenly thrust upon them. Words written down. On a paper. Those words might be anywhere at all and a person cannot always direct their eyes in a preferred direction—"

The duke held his hand up. With a snort, he said, "A person cannot always direct their eyes in a preferred direction? I'd find it rather uncomfortable if my eyes were going off doing things without me. Mrs. Right, if you were to put that idea in plain English, do you mean to say that you accidently read some of my correspondence?"

"Aye, that would be the plain English of it."

"I see. And I will make a giant leap and imagine that correspondence was from some lowly servant in Lord Thorpe's household."

"Yes, and so you can see why I did not think—"

"That I would allow one of my daughters to wed a scoundrel who had meddled with a housemaid."

Mrs. Right nodded sadly. She really could not understand it. It seemed so unlike the duke!

"That letter was not written by a servant in Lord Thorpe's household, but rather, an unhappy younger brother."

Mrs. Right staggered back and fell into a chair. The letter was written by Lord Charles?

CHAPTER EIGHTEEN

MRS. RIGHT SLUMPED in the chair she'd collapsed in as the duke went on to outline all the reasons he had instantly known that the damning letter was from Lord Charles. Not the least of which was it had been delivered by a porter wearing The Albany's livery. He concluded by saying, "You may put your mind at ease, Mrs. Right. I would hardly throw my daughter into the jaws of a lion."

Mrs. Right had fairly staggered out of the library. The revelation that Lord Charles was the author of the letter was both welcome and unwelcome news. It was gratifying to understand that Lord Thorpe was not the rogue she had imagined him to be. On the other hand, there was the unfortunate circumstance of his carriage springs having been meddled with.

How could she have known, though? The letter had spelled out that Lord Thorpe was a reprobate of the first order. That was the sort of thing that had to be avenged. She'd really had no choice. She could not be expected to imagine that Lord Charles had invented the story out of pique.

Nobody could have guessed at that. Of course, the duke had guessed it, but that was beside the point! She really had no cause to feel badly about the carriage springs, as it had been kindly done.

As the day wore on, Mrs. Right did begin to feel much more sanguine about it. After all, nobody would imagine that she had anything to do with damaged springs. Also, she did have very good reason for it. At least, at the time she had good reason. As well, any stablemaster or coachman worth his salt must regularly check the springs. She could not know that for certain, but it seemed like it would be a good idea. It was very likely that whatever damage she'd done had already been repaired. And then, it was not as if Lord Thorpe could not easily afford the repairs. He'd just gone and offered a thousand pounds for Nelson! What was repairing carriage springs to that? It really was a trifling matter.

By the end of the day, she'd really shaken off any worry or concern she'd had about it. If there had been any moments of reflection, any wanderings down the lanes of memory to consider any past mistakes she'd made with the gentlemen who'd gone on to become the duke's sons-in-law, well what was the advantage of it? One could not live in the past!

The past was just more water under the bridge.

She resolved to put the entire adventure out of her mind, and that is exactly what she did.

ROLAND COULD NOT settle or at all be at ease until he discovered what the morning's advertisements would bring. As it was still early evening, he had quite a few hours of not knowing. Where was Nelson? How was he being treated? How was Lady Serenity holding up under such stress and worry? All unsolvable questions until somebody stepped forward to claim the reward. All questions that threatened to set him off on one of his trips to the park to shout out his feelings.

He did comfort himself over the amount of the reward, though. It was such a figure that it seemed impossible that Nelson could be hidden for long. A prying neighbor, a lad with his eyes open, a butcher receiving a request for beef bones from a customer who'd never before asked for them. A thousand ways a villain might be found out. Every person of limited means in this town would be watching and searching for any clue as to Nelson's location and would be more than happy to turn in the culprit.

Quinn bustled into the drawing room. He held a folded paper forward and said, "I noticed that you left your father's letter sitting on the hall's table."

Roland nodded, as he'd done so purposefully. He had so much on his mind at the moment and he well knew his father was writing to ask him the same thing he always asked—did you find a bride yet?

He'd hoped to very soon answer in the affirmative.

"Yes, I know," Quinn said, reading his thoughts. "However, he is your duke. You owe him the respect of reading his letters, even though you know what they will say."

Roland took the letter and opened it as he settled into a chair.

Thorpe—

How goes it on the wedding front? I did advise in my last letter that you ought not allow your younger brother to beat you to it. For one, you are to be a duke and ought to have no trouble securing anybody you like. For another, you know Charles. If he beats you to it, you'll never hear the end of it and neither will I!

I just received a letter from your brother this very day and I am afraid that, unless you've got something up your sleeve, he is well on his way to an altar. At least, he tells me it is almost assured. A certain Lady Serenity Nicolet catches his eye.

She's the daughter of a duke, which runs in her favor. Of course, that particular duke is as mad as a spring hare, which is not as promising. (Last I heard of the Duke of Pelham, he was setting a lady's curtains afire and finding it a grand jest.) I imagine you've met her—the Nicolets are your near neighbors on the square. Well, one can hope she's nothing like her father, else we'll have to keep sand buckets near all the curtained windows.

Get on with it, Thorpe. I must have an heir before I depart to meet my maker. Would it help to say I feel the life draining from my body? I don't, but it's an idea you might keep in mind at the rate you are going.

Mariton

Roland handed the letter to Quinn. "I am reasonably sure this particular letter was written with the assistance of brandy."

"You must admit, he can be amusing in his admonishments. Though, very reckless of Charles to go so far as to write your father regarding Lady Serenity. Could he really have been that confident when all the facts ran against him?"

"I suspect Charles' letter was written shortly after he sent the Duke of Pelham that anonymous letter claiming I had meddled with Clara, and before he discovered the duke did not believe it for a minute. Charles always has a great faith in his schemes."

"As I said, reckless."

Roland agreed. It really had been reckless. But that was Charles all over. His brother found he could not wait to claim victory to their father, even though victory had not been at all assured. He supposed the next letter his father would receive would outline some impediment to pursuing Lady Serenity that was not at all his fault and, by the by, he'd set off for the continent again.

He glanced at the postmark. He was rather surprised his father had not already received such a letter. When had Charles sent news of his pursuit of Lady Serenity?

His father was a terrific correspondent. One could always rely on the idea that when a letter arrived, an answer would leave the house the very next day. The letter Charles had sent about Lady Serenity must have been more recent than he'd initially thought.

Roland sat up a little straighter. They'd just assumed that Charles would be back on his way to the continent to lick his wounds and haunt whatever gaming establishment he frequented there. They did not positively know that, though. And if Charles had decided to stick around, even knowing the Duke of Pelham was on to his ruse…what would he do?

What he would do was come up with another scheme. That's what Charles would do. He'd attempt to prove the duke wrong about him somehow. And just this minute, Lady Serenity's dog had unaccountably gone missing.

Roland leapt from his chair. "I think it might have been Charles," he said.

"What might have been?" Quinn asked.

"Nelson. I think it might have been Charles who took him."

Roland could see Quinn's mind working through the idea.

"You see it, don't you?" Roland said. "He could be a hero if he returned Nelson. But in order to do that, he'd have to take Nelson."

Quinn tented his fingers. "It is a possibility, though you cannot be certain. Charles is reckless, but this would be beyond the pale."

"I can be certain if I go and find it out, which is exactly what I'm going to do. Don't bother calling for my horse, I'll go to the stables myself."

"Be careful," Quinn said. "You never know with your brother's temper."

Roland nodded, as Quinn lived in fear that one day the two brothers would end firing on one another on a green. He did not imagine it would ever come to that, though. For one, Roland would never challenge Charles and cause such disrespect and upset to his duke. For another, Charles would not challenge *him*, as he would have the choice of weapons and would demand swords. Charles could not out-fence him and he knew it. Roland would not kill him, but he would rip his younger brother's shirt to shreds to make his point. Charles, for whatever else he got up to, would not put himself in the position to be humiliated in front of the seconds looking upon such a scene.

Roland strode out of the room, out the doors, and down the mews. If Charles had Nelson, that dog would shortly be returned home.

SERENITY HAD BEEN put to bed in the afternoon and as Mrs. Right had put some laudanum in her tea, she had slept for a few hours. It had not lasted, though, and as soon as she'd woken, she'd hurried down the stairs to be with her sisters.

The drawing room had been a rather grim scene, as all in the house were fretting over Nelson. Her eldest sisters had come to hold vigil and were determined to stay over and be on hand for the morrow. That was when they would discover if Lord Thorpe's reward had enticed someone to return Nelson.

The duke had made a terrific effort to cheer them, claiming every person in Town would be searching their little corner of London for a sight of Nelson in order to collect the reward.

Lord Stanford had eventually turned up, even though Patience had written him that she was perfectly well and must stay with her sisters. Serenity imagined he'd thought he might take his newly pregnant bride home, but he was speedily apprised that would not be the case. Therefore, he'd settled into the drawing room with the rest of them, looking exceedingly uncomfortable over all the weeping but keeping a sharp eye on his wife's comfort. Nobody but Serenity yet knew what possessed the fellow, though Valor mentioned that she found his love-staring sickening.

Now they'd gone into the dining room to half-heartedly consume whatever the cook had managed to put together. They did not expect much, as the down stairs of the house was just as fretful as the above stairs over the disappearance of Nelson.

"Seems to be a broth of some kind," the duke said, staring into the soup urn.

Thomas, who was at the sideboard and looking greatly affected by the events of the day, said, "Made from bones from the butcher that were to go to Nelson. Cook makes him a special broth to put on his dinner. But he's not here to have it!"

"I see," the duke said quietly, "we're to have the dog's bone broth."

Charlie came into the dining room, having checked outside the doors again. He'd been doing the same every few minutes all day. He shook his head sadly to indicate there was no sign of Nelson.

This set half the table weeping again. Once the sobs began to quiet, Valor said, "Papa, does a person get hanged for stealing a dog?"

"I doubt it," the duke said. "Very hard to prove, in any case."

Valor shook her head in disgust. "If I were a judge, I would hang anybody who stole a dog. I would hang anybody who even one time *thought* about stealing a dog. I would hang all the people who knew about the person who thought about stealing a dog. Or even heard about it in the shops!"

"And the bodies pile up," the duke said with a smile.

"Why would anybody talk about stealing dogs in the shops?" Winsome asked.

"People talk about everything in the shops," Valor said. "Mrs. Right took us to get gloves and ribbons and two ladies talked the whole time we were there. They said Lady Gentian, whoever she is, wore a terrible puce colored dress to Mrs. Maybee's musical evening and her daughter was clunky on the pianoforte and really should those people be invited anywhere? We had to leave before I found out."

"It's a very common thing," Verity said, "to denounce people while shopping."

Serenity did not know if that were true or not. But she thought it might be true.

"I have an idea," Felicity said. "It will do us no good at all to carry on as we have."

"Amen to that," Lord Stanford muttered, draining his glass of wine.

"We must think positive. A thousand pounds has been offered for our dear Nelson and I am confident that we will see him back in the house before the sun sets tomorrow. Now, I think we ought to spend our time on happier ideas—what are our fond memories of Nelson? What can he expect for his first dinner back at home? What new comforts might we provide? How might we spoil him more than he has ever been spoiled before?"

This really did cheer the table as it gave everybody something to think about rather than horrid imaginings of Nelson shivering in the cold, alone and hungry.

"I will allow Nelson to borrow Mrs. Wendover for a while," Valor said generously. "I will not even complain about it."

"I will set out to knit Nelson a blanket of his own," Verity said. "It is a well-known fact that dogs prefer a blanket made specially for them. Mrs. Right can show me how to knit and I am sure I will take to it in a trice."

Winsome looked out the corner of her eye over the idea that Verity would suddenly know how to knit. She refrained from challenging her on it, though, considering the gravity of the situation they all found themselves in. "I'll give him a bath," she said. "He does not like it, but he likes it when he's dried off and clean."

All eyes turned to Serenity. "I will never allow him out of my sight forevermore. If anybody tries to take him, I will club them over the head. Papa, could you buy me a proper club so I am prepared? I am very much opposed to violence, but it will be necessary."

"A club? Why not?" the duke said.

"And Serenity, after you club them," Valor said, "we could drag them to a judge and demand they be hanged immediately. No mercy!"

The duke reached across the table and patted Valor's shoulder. "Perhaps enough with hanging everybody in the wide world. It will give you nightmares."

"Oh yes, it might," Valor said softly. Then she perked up. "I know what, Papa, they could all be hanged together on the same day, but I won't go to the hanging to watch it. You see? Then it could not sneak up on me in my dreams."

And so they went on, doing their best to struggle through a rather original dinner. After the broth made from beef bones that had been meant for Nelson, there were platters of chicken and beef, both clearly left in the ovens for far too long, burned rolls, and a salad that had not been dressed. Vegetables had not made an appearance at all, and dessert was slices of stale cake from yesterday.

Lord Stanford summed the whole thing up by saying, "The wine is good, though."

ROLAND HAD GOT his horse saddled and set off for The Albany. Spartacus was delighted with the cold air, it was brisk and had that feeling to it that hinted of snow. The streets were fairly empty; it was that time of night when most people going somewhere had got there, and yet still early enough that nobody was yet on their way home. There was an ebb and flow to the traffic on London streets and this was an ebb. Oil lamps lit the wet roads in intervals, the pools of light guiding his horse forward through the mud and revealing any dips and divots to be avoided.

As the place was not far, he arrived in under ten minutes. Roland did not know which apartments his brother occupied at The Albany and at first the night porter had been reluctant to say. Roland did not believe this to be any delicate care for the inhabitants' privacy, but rather a typical opportunity for a night porter to find some money deposited in his pocket.

The porter was adamant that he could not reveal the information. As Roland had not brought any money with him, he was forced to pick the fellow up by his livery coat and shake it out of him.

Once the porter became convinced that the shaking would go on interminably, he suddenly realized he *could* reveal where Lord

Charles' set was located. On the first floor, number three, and would Lord Thorpe wish to be led there?

Roland would not, and jogged up the stairs and to the right. He found the set and gave the door a quiet and quick knock, as a porter might do. He stepped to the side of the door so no peering through the keyhole would give him away. It would not be well for Charles to suspect he was in the corridor and refuse to answer. He would break the door down if he had to, but he hoped that would not be necessary. On top of the trouble of it, such a thing would attract a crowd.

The door swung open and Roland stepped forward. He'd been sure he was at the right set, but a gentleman he did not know stood in the doorframe.

"Is this Lord Charles' set?" he asked.

"Yes, it is, but—"

Roland pushed past the fellow, assuming he was some drinking friend of Charles' come to while away the evening.

He looked round the room, but Charles was nowhere in sight. Then he heard the telltale whine of a dog and scratching on wood. He strode to the closed door where the sound emanated from and opened it.

There was Nelson, wagging his tail and hopping awkwardly on his three legs, his tongue drooping out of his mouth.

The relief of finding him came very near to overwhelming Roland entirely. All the terrible thoughts of how Nelson's disappearance might end in tragedy, the thoughts he'd worked hard to keep away, flooded through him. He blinked his watery eyes and swept Nelson into his arms.

"Sir, are you a relation of Lord Charles' aunt? Have you come to take the dog home to the lady? I'd be much obliged as he seems to wish to be gone. He bit me when I put his food in there."

"I do not know who you are," Roland said. "I am the Marquess of Thorpe, Lord Charles' brother, and this is not our aunt's dog. This is Lady Serenity Nicolet's dog, which I will speedily return to her. Where is my brother and why have you been left to do his bidding?"

The gentleman shuffled his feet. "My name is Michaels. As to how I came to be here, I got myself in a spot of trouble, cards, you know. My father has ordered me home and does not yet know I can't pay my bill here nor pay my way home. Lord Charles offered fifty pounds and, well, you see how it is."

"Where is he?"

"In *my* set," Michaels said, as if he could not imagine where else Charles would be. "He was afraid the dog would escape and grab him by the throat in the night." Michaels looked at Nelson. Nelson growled by way of answer. "I was afraid of it myself. I was planning to stay up all night on account of it."

"Where is *your* set?"

Michaels hooked his thumb to the left. "Number Four."

Roland walked toward the door. Nelson attempted to bite Michaels' arm as they passed by, but he was only able to rip his coat sleeve.

Roland knocked on number four. He heard his brother inside. "What is it now, Michaels? Just keep that door shut and he won't bother you."

Nelson growled.

"My god, have you let the damn thing out?"

The door swung open. It took Charles a moment to comprehend that his brother was standing in front of him with Nelson in his arms. "Thorpe?" he said, clearly thinking about what he might say to account for having the dog at The Albany.

Roland knew very well that they might go round in circles with excuses and lies. It was getting late though, and he was not particularly in the mood. Shifting Nelson so that he was supported in Roland's left hand, his right hand was free. He used it to punch Charles in the face.

As his brother lay sprawled on the carpet, Roland turned to leave. Michaels stood in the corridor, staring at his prone friend. "You might want to get him some ice for his jaw. Or not, whichever you prefer."

With that, Roland departed from The Albany.

CHAPTER NINETEEN

WHEN ROLAND HAD arrived back in the courtyard and untied his horse, he was not entirely certain how Nelson would feel about being taken anywhere on horseback. He should not have worried though. He put Nelson under his coat to secure him and the dog divided his time between wagging his tail, licking Thorpe's face with his eerily long tongue, and growling at the doors to The Albany. It was Spartacus who was perhaps more alarmed at this recent development. His horse's eyes were wide and he kept straining his neck to get a look behind him.

As much as he wished to hurry, Roland did not return to Grosvenor Square as fast as he had left it. He kept his horse to a calm walk. The last thing he needed at the moment was for Nelson to become frightened and leap out of his arms, thereby setting off a chase through London to get him back again. As well, the more time he had to compose himself the better. Nothing felt more fraught to him than a horse or dog in danger of harm, and the relief of finding Nelson alive and safe had really almost tipped him over the edge.

The slow and regular hoofbeats seemed to quiet the dog and finally, Nelson gave himself a little shake and yawned. A dog's shake and yawn was a sure sign that whatever had been troubling had been left behind.

Roland felt just the same. He could not say with any surety what Charles would do next, but he was not at all worried that he would attempt to meddle with his elder brother again in any near future. The punch to his jaw had been a long time coming, it had been delivered, and Charles had seemed shocked to receive it. He would just now be rubbing his jaw and attempting to explain to Michaels how it was that his elder brother had punched him in the face and taken his aunt's dog.

As he turned on to the square, he could see the lights of the duke's house blazing ahead of him. The doors swung open and a footman leaned out, looking forlornly down the street. The young man was on the verge of closing the doors again when he spotted Roland. Nelson gave a little bark. The footman dropped his hands from the doorknobs, stared at him, and then raced indoors.

SERENITY HAD BEEN dabbing at her eyes with her napkin while Valor talked about all the people who could be hanged for stealing dogs when Charlie burst into the room. "Nelson! He's outside! Lord Thorpe has got him!"

"Clever fellow," the duke said, throwing his napkin down.

Serenity was out of her seat like a shot. She was out the doors in a trice. There he was! Nelson was home. Lord Thorpe had just dismounted his horse with Nelson in his arms. He had found Nelson.

She threw herself at her beloved dog, which coincidentally meant she had thrown herself at Lord Thorpe too. He caught her and Nelson wagged his tail between them.

"Where did you find him?" Serenity whispered.

"My brother had him," Lord Thorpe answered.

"Lord Charles? I would not have thought…"

"Nor would I, until I did."

"What ho, Thorpe," the duke said jovially. "Returning as the conquering hero, eh?"

"I am sure not, Your Grace."

"Dispense with the modesty," the duke said. "My head pounds from the amount of weeping that has gone on in this house today—Nelson returned to us is better than any willow bark tonic my physician could give me."

"I am sorry that one of my own family should have caused such distress, Your Grace. I have just retrieved Nelson from The Albany."

"Why did Lord Charles do it, though?" Winsome asked.

"I expect he wished to raise himself in my estimation by returning a dog he stole in the first place," the duke said, shaking his head. "Second sons, nobody ever knows what to do with them."

"Is Lord Charles going to hang, Papa?" Valor asked with rather macabre delight.

"Never mind a hanging," the duke said. "Let us all go inside."

The duke ushered everyone into the hall, his daughters hovering round Nelson and petting him and saying all sorts of encouraging things to him. As Nelson was still in Lord Thorpe's arms, both man and dog were surrounded by feminine assurances.

"Listen here, girls," the duke said. "Nelson has just been through a very trying experience. We will not wish to overwhelm him with so many people. Two is all I think he'll be up for just now. Serenity, Thorpe, take Nelson into the drawing room and see that he's made calm. The rest of you, back into the dining room to eat that stale cake."

As Lord Stanford looked the littlest bit befuddled and wondering if he were to have to eat more stale cake, the duke said kindly, "Don't worry, Stanford, I'll open a bottle of the good claret to wash it down."

Serenity was very grateful for her father taking everyone in hand. Though, a little surprised that she was sent to the drawing room alone with Lord Thorpe.

The duke hustled them both toward that room. At the doors, he slapped Lord Thorpe on the back and said, "Take aim and fire, that's my advice."

He pushed them both in and shut the doors behind him.

Lord Thorpe set Nelson down on the carpet. The dog seemed delighted to be in a setting he knew so well. He promptly hopped on the sofa that he was not at all supposed to be on, seeming to know that nobody would scold him over it on account of his recent adventure.

Lord Thorpe suddenly took Serenity's hand. "Come with me," he said.

The feel of her hand in his was thrilling as she did not wear her gloves, and of course she would follow him anywhere at all.

He led her to the windows overlooking the square and pulled back the curtains. "It was just there, on a snowy night, that I looked out my window at the glories of a snowfall. It was there that I first saw Lady Serenity Nicolet. It was breathtaking."

Serenity felt the water make its reliable trip to her eyes. Such was the sentiment that there was not much of a chance of making it retreat.

"I think you know what I will say," Lord Thorpe said. "But before I do, I have a confession to make."

Serenity gripped his hand tighter. A confession? Surely not. Surely he could not have done anything that required a confession.

"I am not wholly the man you think you know."

Serenity felt as if her heart had stopped. She did not know what terrible secret Lord Thorpe harbored, but she was shocked that she had not sensed it. Of everyone in her family, she was the most sensitive. She could perceive things others could not. How had he hidden something from her? He could not have. She was very sure of who he was.

The silence in the room felt like a heavy thing. Finally, he said, "I'll just come out with it. I might seem like the emotionless and reserved lord, but the truth is, I have a rather sentimental temperament. I regularly ride to the park to shout into the wind to relieve my feelings. Not the sort of thing one might expect from a marquess."

Serenity could only be vastly relieved that no crime had been described. She found herself not at all opposed to hear of such passion. Shouting into the wind sounded rather romantic. It was poetic in some way. However, it did remind her that she had her own temperament to explain.

"You are shocked," Lord Thorpe said.

"I am not," Serenity said. "I am approving of the idea of shouting into the wind. It is just that I have to confess something myself. Shouting into the wind might be one thing, but I am quite another. I was planning to tell you all along. At the right time. The truth is, I weep over…most anything really. The sunrise, the sunset, anything beautiful, anything sad, anything that might turn out to be sad, sometimes just because a good cry is a good cry…"

"If you are not put off by my shouting into the wind, I am not put off by weeping," Lord Thorpe said.

"That is not the worst of it, though," Serenity whispered. "I have a box. A crypt. Of dead bees."

As she had thought it would, this did seem to take Lord Thorpe aback. "Bees?"

Serenity nodded and poured out the story of killing a bee through its sting when she'd been very young. "So now, I go looking for them," she said. "When I find one, I dry its poor little body in ash and put it in the crypt with the other dead bees."

As she said it, it sounded even worse than when she'd only thought about it. In truth, it sounded as if she was not in her right mind. She sounded macabre and deranged.

"And that's it? A box of dead bees?"

Serenity nodded. She was surprised when Lord Thorpe laughed. "We are a pair, then."

He leaned down and kissed her. His lips were firm and soft and perfect and she felt as if the bones in her body were melting as he held her upright. It was magnificent. He was magnificent. Tears streamed down Serenity's cheeks and he kissed them away.

Lord Thorpe pulled back. "This needs to be done properly.

Lady Serenity Nicolet, will you consent to wedding me?"

"Yes, I will," she whispered.

"I brought you something," Lord Thorpe said, reaching into his coat pocket, "which is rather more prescient than I had imagined."

He opened a small velvet box to reveal the most darling gold and pearl pin, fashioned as a bee. This was too hard on Serenity's feelings and she wept with gusto as he pinned it on her bodice.

There was a sudden banging on the doors. "What are you doing in there? You should leave the doors open!"

It was Valor, ever working to stop a proposal.

"Come away, Val," Serenity heard Winsome say.

Rather than do as she was told, Valor burst through the doors. "It's so dark in here! What are you doing in here? Why are you making Serenity cry?"

"Look, Valor, Lord Thorpe has given me a pin—it's a bee. You know how I love bees."

"Oh no," Valor muttered. "It's happened again."

"Has it?" the duke asked, coming in behind his youngest daughter.

"I have proposed and Lady Serenity has accepted," Lord Thorpe said. "With your permission, Your Grace."

"Yes, yes, I shoved you in here, didn't I? Your man and my man will work out the contract."

Once the duke had left his place in the dining room, it was inevitable that everybody else would follow him into the drawing room. There were congratulations all round and Lord Stanford in particular seemed approving of their being a point to the dreadful dinner he'd just suffered through.

Nelson got his own dose of attention and it was perhaps a toss-up on what was viewed most joyous—the duke unloading another one of his daughters, or his regaining his three-legged dog. Thomas brought in all sorts from the dining table, but for the stale cake that even Nelson would turn up his nose at, and set it on a platter for the dog to sample.

As was to be expected, only Valor was not delighted with the engagement. Rather than sulk about it, she seemed to turn herself to a more practical purpose. She took to following Verity around and listing all the reasons it would be terrible to get married. Having a gentleman staring at one in the night was prominently featured in her arguments.

"It's snowing!" Winsome cried from the windows.

This caused Nelson to go wild with joy, though he had not the first idea of what was going on. If a Nicolet was excited about something, then so was he.

Lord Thorpe leaned down and whispered in Serenity's ear. "We should go out in it, if your father will not stop us."

Serenity took him by the hand, passed by her father and kissed him on the cheek. "We are going out in the snow to rejoice in the glories of nature, Papa."

"Ah, she told you about the glories of nature, did she? Well! Best to know these things up front—it won't be the last time you hear about it!"

They hurried out the front doors and Serenity had not even stopped to have one of the footmen retrieve her pelisse. Instantly noting this deficiency, Lord Thorpe took off his coat and put it over her shoulders.

They raised their faces to the falling snow. "It's glorious," Lord Thorpe said.

"Entirely glorious," Serenity said. The wet snow mixed with the tears on her wet cheeks and she suspected she'd found a new cause for weeping—the happiness of her new situation. She was to be Serenity Garner, Marchioness of Thorpe. She was to wonder if he would stare at her in the night and privately hoped that he would.

She'd told him about the crypt of bees and he'd not been put off. In fact, she'd discovered that his temperament, his feelings, were more similar to her own than she could ever imagine. He turned to her and kissed her, right on the street, disregarding a carriage trundling by.

"Do you suppose we will have a highly charged household full of feelings running this way and that?" Serenity asked.

"I do suppose it. Though I do not suppose either of us will mind," he said, tracing his forefinger along her wet cheeks.

"No, we will not mind," Serenity said. "I suppose any children we may have will fly from a high to a low and back again."

"They will climb the Alps and tumble down and climb again."

"We will keep a supply of handkerchiefs in every room," Serenity said.

From the direction of the duke's house, a voice shouted, "Stop that!" Valor was hanging out the drawing room window. Winsome pulled her back inside.

They laughed at the picture and then held hands as they made their way around the square, taking in the beauty of the falling snow. Serenity was certain it was outrageous to hold hands; it would raise brows even if they were already married.

She did not care, though. After all, if anybody chose to be shocked they must live with it alone. Who would a complainer complain to? If they thought to go to her father, she imagined they'd regret the decision.

They talked about what was to come next. How quickly could they wed? Where ought they go for a wedding trip? What should they call each other? She, of course, would be Serenity. But there was always the question of him. They settled on Thorpe, rather than Roland. His given name was the same as her father's and she'd grown up hearing her aunt cry "Roland!" Therefore, Roland would be reserved for when his wife was very cross. As for him, Lady Thorpe might be used if *he* was very cross. They, neither of them, thought there would be many instances of anybody being very cross. Weeping, maybe, but not cross.

Thorpe said, "I do worry over Lady Valor, though."

Serenity nodded. "She is not at all happy that she is to lose the company of another sister."

"And a dog. I am assuming you will take Nelson, as he has seemed primarily your dog."

Serenity took a breath in. She had not considered that, as of course she must take Nelson. Nelson was accustomed to sleeping in her room and napping on her bed. When something unusual went on in the house, he would bark and run to her bedchamber. "Oh dear," she said.

"Say nothing to her. At least, not yet. I have an idea about it."

Serenity nodded. "What about your brother? What will you do about Lord Charles? He cannot be allowed to steal another person's dog."

"I punched him in the face."

Serenity would not, as a usual thing, approve of violence. But in defense of Nelson, well, she had already proposed to her father that she ought to have a club to beat off kidnappers. Now she would not need one, as Thorpe would be their protector. It gave her the shivers. "Goodness, you really are of a passionate nature," Serenity said.

"Yes, I am passionate," he said, pulling her close again to kiss her.

A carriage rolled by and they heard the distinct sounds of a gasp and a window slamming shut. Some matron returning home from a party or the theater had just been shocked to her shoes.

That was entirely too bad for the matron. Serenity was not at all shocked. She was rather encouraged, actually.

ROLAND HAD WALKED with his fiancée around the square and thought he might do it again, were it not for her beginning to shiver and her father standing at the door.

He would have kissed her again, had her father not been standing at the door. As he could not do that, he urged her to keep his coat on when she made a move to return it, bid her goodnight, and asked for permission to call in the morning.

That permission was speedily granted and one of the duke's

grooms handed him back his horse.

As he made his way back to his house, he mused over how everything had unfolded. Just hours ago, he'd set off for The Albany to discover if Nelson was there. Now he was an engaged man.

He thought Lady Serenity, or Serenity as he would now call her, had imagined he would be shocked over her crypt of bees. He'd not been particularly. Of course, it was unusual, there could be no denying it. However, he did not see anything wrong with unusual. The important thing was, he'd been honest. She'd been honest. There were no secrets between them and they were likely more suited to one another than they'd known.

It suddenly felt as if the ammunition that Charles had always fired against him had gone up in a puff of smoke. His brother could no longer threaten him with exposing his sentimental leanings. His future wife knew all about them and who else mattered?

One of his grooms took his horse and he bounded into the house. Not surprisingly, Quinn was waiting for him.

"I assume you've done it, else the duke will see you on a green in the morning."

"I have, and I assume you say so from looking out the windows," Roland said, laughing.

"Hanging out the windows, more like," Quinn said. "We saw you return with the dog, and then go inside and then…well, that walking round the square was rather daring from what I could see."

Roland nodded. "I told her of my real nature."

"I presume she took it well, then."

"Oh yes, she's even worse than I am. She has a box of dead bees. A bee stung her and died when she was young and she's felt bad about it ever since. Now she looks for dead bees, dries them in ash, and keeps them in a box. Apparently, she weeps over just about everything."

Roland could see very well that Quinn's mind was traveling

ahead in time, imagining a future with a Marquess and Marchioness with over-sensitive natures.

Rather than allow him to go on with it and frighten himself, Roland said, "I will write two letters before I retire. One to my father that his dreams of a wedding are finally coming true. The other to my brother, telling him to leave Town or else I will punch him again."

"You and Charles had a physical altercation?"

"Not much of one. I punched him, he landed on the floor. I took the dog and left."

"Well, it was a long time coming, I suppose," Quinn said thoughtfully. "Do you think he'll go?"

"I do. If he does not, he will be exposed as having kidnapped the Duke of Pelham's dog. The *ton* has strong feelings about that, considering it goes on rampant and the 1770 Act has not done much to curb it. One whisper of it and everybody in society will be thinking of their own dog or a friend's dog, and Charles would be roundly condemned. Add in that it was a poor three-legged dog that the duke was kind enough to take in, and I think he'll perceive how bad things could go for him."

Thorpe sat down and wrote out the letters. A short one to his father and a far longer one to his brother. He found himself entirely done with Charles' nonsense, pettiness, and discontent. He would not tolerate it longer, and Charles could test that idea at his peril.

After he'd finished the letters, he put some thought into Lady Valor's situation. After consulting with Quinn, and then with the duke the following day, he set a plan in motion.

CHAPTER TWENTY

THE FOLLOWING WEEK found it very convenient that Thorpe only lived two doors down from Serenity. He would walk over in the morning and then, at eleven o'clock, they would take Nelson and Havoc around the square. After that, they might disappear into the library pretending to look for a book or otherwise while away the afternoon. Thorpe was invariably invited to stay for dinner, and then of course, he would attend them in the drawing room afterward. Valor mentioned several times that it seemed like he didn't even have his own house to go to.

Not to be defeated by the youngest Nicolet, Roland had consulted with the duke, gained his agreement, made the necessary preparations, and then enacted his plan on one fine and brisk morning. It had taken some doing, but he'd found just the right approach. Now that everything was in place, the hired carriage with a mysterious coat of arms that in fact did not exist had been brought round to stop at the Duke of Pelham's residence.

The duke had been clever at arranging for his daughters, except for Lady Valor, to be elsewhere. He claimed they were to visit their maternal grandmother, the pious and reserved Lady Neville, who had relocated to Town for a month. The duke had explained that they never saw her, as she did not like the duke, but she did send his girls awful Christmas presents that were full of moral rectitude and modesty.

As the duke had predicted, everybody put up a fuss about it. What were they to say about receiving specially bound copies of *Sermons to Young Women*? Were they supposed to claim they'd read them? What if Lady Neville asked for their impressions of Mr. Fordyce's works? He only excused Valor from going, as she was deemed too young to face the stiff-lipped dragon and would crack under the interrogation.

After they had set off, the rest of his brood would discover they were only going to Lackington & Allen to wander the aisles of books for a few hours. They were sworn to secrecy to never reveal it to Valor, which they would all readily agree to once they were apprised of the plan.

Now, that plan was launched. One of the footmen showed Roland into the duke's drawing room, where he found Lady Valor and the housekeeper playing cards.

"Lady Valor," he said with a quick bow, "I am most relieved to find you at home."

Lady Valor, not particularly an admirer of him, narrowed her eyes. "Why?" she asked. "You're never looking for me. You're always looking for Serenity so you can steal her away from us. She's visiting our grandmother, but I didn't have to go because she's a dragon and I would crack under her questions. Maybe you should have gone and she could breathe fire all over you."

"Now, child," Mrs. Right said, patting her hand.

"She could, though," Lady Valor said. "Probably."

"I do not deny the charge of stealing away your sister," Roland said, "but in this case I most decidedly require your intervention. A certain Lord Westerven was at my club this very morning, joking about drowning the runt of his dog's latest litter. As you can imagine, I argued strongly against it. He could not be moved, though. Then I bet him at cards that if he lost, he must come and hear your views on the subject. It is my experience that you are not bashful of speaking your opinions in a forceful manner. I pray you can get through to him."

"Drowned!" Lady Valor cried, leaping from her chair. "Did

you win the bet?"

"I did, and Lord Westerven is even now outside. He is not happy about it, but he could not renege without embarrassing himself at the club."

As Roland had hoped, the expression of outrage on Lady Valor's face was sublime.

"Thomas!" she shouted, though the fellow was right there at the door, "I require my cloak!"

In just a few moments, the actor who had been hired to play the diabolical Lord Westerven was going to get an earful. He was the perfectly stern-looking older gentleman with delightfully pinched features. Anybody looking at him might really believe he'd drown the runt of the litter. They might believe he'd drown the entire litter. As it was, the fellow had been carefully instructed on his role.

Roland followed Lady Valor out of doors. She marched to the carriage and directed the groom to open the door.

The young fellow did so with alacrity, as what else was he to do? He was an actor too, as was the coachman up on the box and they all knew precisely how this was meant to unfold.

Valor stared into the carriage at the old gentleman with a wood box beside him. The alleged Lord Westerven looked derisively at her and said, "What is this? I imagined I was to hear from some seasoned matron. How old are you?"

"Never mind how old I am, *sir*. I am old enough to know a villain when I see one. Lord Thorpe has told me of your shameful joking about drowning a poor defenseless pup."

"I wasn't joking, though," Lord Westerven said. "I will direct my coachman to make a small detour to the Thames and be done with the undersized creature."

"Oh no, you will not!" Lady Valor said, climbing into the carriage. She picked up the umbrella lying on the seat and beat Lord Westerven around the head with it.

This was an unexpected development. Roland had not warned any of the actors of a physical attack. He jumped in after her and wrested the umbrella from her hands. "Lady Valor, I am certain we can resolve this matter without undue violence."

"We should throw *him* in the Thames," she said, glaring at Lord Westerven.

"For heaven's sake, child, what do you expect me to do with this weak and substandard specimen?"

Lord Westerven looked into the box to draw Lady Valor's eye there, rather than where it was, which was looking around for another implement to beat him with.

Valor peered in. "Weak and substandard? I must believe you are near blind, sir. You should be deeply ashamed of yourself."

"Well I'm not. I've got a right to do what I want with a creature that belongs to me, and no impertinent little miss will tell me otherwise. Thorpe, I've held up my end of the bet, and now I must be off. Get this young person out of my carriage."

Valor looked toward Lord Thorpe with tears welling in her eyes, no doubt considering the fate of the tiny pug looking up from the bottom of the box.

"See here, Westerven," Roland said sternly, "I won't have it. We will take your dog from you and you will say nothing about it. Unless, of course, you would like to meet me on a green at dawn tomorrow to settle the matter."

Roland gave that challenge a tone of deadly threat. It was important that Lady Valor be convinced that he'd shoot Lord Westerven to pieces if he did not hand over the dog.

"Take it if you like, it will save me a trip. Don't expect it to amount to much though, I doubt it'll survive the night."

Roland picked up the box, helped Lady Valor down to the road, and shut the carriage door. To the coachman, he said, "Be off with you."

He strode inside with the box. He carried it into the drawing room with Lady Valor close on his heels. The pup did indeed look exceedingly small, but that was due to the breed. In fact, he was a rather roly-poly eight-week-old pug with not a thing wrong with him.

"Is it true that he might not survive the night? What should we do?"

"Send for blankets to keep him warm. Warmth, food, drink, and attention. That is always what's required to keep a young dog going."

He picked up the pup, who was really very sturdy, and placed him in Valor's arms.

Mrs. Right, who well knew of the plan from the duke, said, "There now, I know you will take good care of him, Poppet."

As Lady Valor scratched under the pug's chin, she said, "We'll need the box put in my room. He'll need to stay with me in the night. That way, I can check on him if he cries." Lady Valor paused. Then she said, "And he could make me feel better when I have a nightmare about Lord Westerven and the Thames. I will definitely have nightmares about him. Probably forever."

And that was how Sir Galahad, as he would be named, slipped into the house, allowing Serenity and Nelson to slip out of it.

THE WEDDING BREAKFAST was held in the duke's house, though Serenity did not allow the duke to hire performers from Astley's Circus like he had for Felicity's breakfast. Lady Marchfield was very appreciative of it, since during that particular breakfast she'd been knocked off her chair by an acrobat, doused with water when the fire-eater set curtains ablaze, and had her ankle grabbed by a fellow walking on his hands.

By comparison, Serenity's breakfast was positively sedate. That was probably for the best, as the couple were in a high state of feelings after the vows were spoken and any unnecessary excitement might have sent them both over the edge. It was only a few family and friends and there had been no cause to even think about inviting Lord Charles, as he had hightailed it to the continent with nary a look behind him.

The wedding had been done through a special license and as nobody was eager to rise early, it was held in the afternoon in the duke's drawing room. The curate from the Grosvenor church was brought in to officiate, as the duke thought it might soothe any lingering ideas the fellow might have about reports that his housekeeper had dealings with the devil. While the celebration that followed was called a breakfast, it was rather more an early dinner, which suited everybody.

Afterward, Nelson and Sir Galahad, as the pug pup had been named, said their adieus. It was done in the usual dog manner of sniffing unmentionables, so it was not very prettily done. Valor was in much better spirits as she was wholly consumed with Sir Galahad and feeling exceedingly heroic over saving him from a tragic death in the Thames. Her recounting of her encounter with the evil Lord Westerven had grown by the hour. She'd been overheard at the dining table informing the curate that she'd been forced to retrieve her father's pistols to make Westerven give up the poor little mite. As she said, "I was prepared to put several holes in the gentleman." One could not say if that helped the curate's ideas regarding the state of the duke's household.

Serenity, her newly-acquired husband, and Nelson walked the two doors down to the marquess' house amidst cheering and good luck. He swept her up and carried her over the threshold into his house. Her house too, now.

She giggled over it, as the carrying over the threshold might guard her from evil spirits lurking at the door, and it might also indicate her girlish reluctance over the wedding night and subsequent giving up of her virtue. It was rather ridiculous, as she was ready to *throw* her virtue at Thorpe if necessary.

Her married sisters had spared no detail from her regarding what could be expected, though they all concluded with the same piece of advice—do not think ahead, simply allow things to naturally take their course.

Quinn had admitted them to the house and made arrangements for their privacy. Most of the staff had been sent below stairs and given free rein of the wine cellar. The morrow would be time enough to pay homage to their new mistress. He'd arranged things upstairs to account for every convenience the couple might want—trays of cheeses and fruits, rolls, cold meats, bottles of hock, and a fine champagne in a bucket of ice chips. Then, Quinn took Havoc and Nelson, who were thrilled to be reunited, below stairs with him.

Serenity supposed she ought to be nervous to do what she had never done. She had not really thought about doing it, at least not all of it, until her sisters had spelled it out. She found herself not too nervous though. Thorpe felt like safety and she trusted him to lead the way.

And so he did. She supposed it would not surprise anybody that the feelings between them were powerful, almost overpowering, as they were both capable of feeling things more deeply than most. Feelings brought passion, and there was passion to spare between them. If there was happy weeping too, nobody but them would ever know it.

Hours later, as the sun set over the square, they lounged on the window seat together with only a sheet wrapped round them. They admired nature's final display of the day and thought about what the sunrise would bring.

Thorpe said, "This is where it all began, right where we sit now. It was snowing and I was just here, looking out the window. And you were down there in the snow, looking more glorious than any woman ever has."

The marquess did not appear at all alarmed when his bride wept buckets over it. He might have done some rapid blinking himself.

On the morrow, they would depart for Scotland. Thorpe owned a rather well-situated fishing lodge on a river there and they would stay a month. They had set the time of departure for eleven, and the duke and her sisters would be there to wave them off. Life had become a pleasant dream and they fell asleep dreaming together.

When they woke would be time enough for Thorpe to wholly take in that Serenity did not, as yet, have a lady's maid. He would have to do her buttons and help with her hair. She did not know if he'd be any good at it, but she was certain he would not mind it. He'd certainly not minded undoing them, after all.

MRS. RIGHT WAS well satisfied with how the season had shaped up. There had been some hiccups, as there always seemed to be. But it had all come right. At least, she understood that things had run their proper course. She could not help sympathizing with Valor over the emptying of sisters from the house. Now, they would return to the Dales with only Winsome, Verity, and Valor. All too soon, Verity would take her place in society and then she would be down to two. She could not feel it any more deeply than if she'd borne these girls herself.

The duke had done a terrific job of cheering her the night before. He'd ordered a case of champagne for the staff and they'd made very merry below stairs. Then, after the girls retired, she'd sat with the duke in the drawing room, each with their brandy. He tried to cheer himself up too, though he always hid his dismay at losing another daughter. They both speculated that his long-dead duchess would be mightily impressed that he'd settled four of the girls so admirably.

Now the sun was well up and they'd all donned coats and stood outside, ready to wave off Serenity and Lord Thorpe. They were off to Scotland to a fishing lodge of some sort for their wedding trip. It would not be Mrs. Right's idea of a good time, but Serenity had seemed pleased enough with the scheme.

"They'll be making quite the journey," the duke said. "I hope they choose well-appointed inns on the way, you know how some of them are run by rather nervous innkeepers."

Mrs. Right smiled at the idea. And then her smile dropped and she felt her heart begin to pound. The carriage springs. She'd entirely forgotten about it. Once she'd absolved herself of any fault for being mistaken about Lord Thorpe, she'd not given it another thought.

What was she to do? How was she to stop them?

"There they are!" the duke said.

Mrs. Right stared as trunks were loaded and the husband and wife came out their doors. She felt paralyzed. It was as if she'd been struck by lightning. She clung to her original idea that any coachman worth his salt would regularly crawl under his carriage and have a look at the springs and bolts.

Certainly, he would have.

She watched the scene as if time had slowed. Serenity in her pretty travelling cloak of brown velvet. Lord Thorpe looking every bit the marquess in his greatcoat with too many layers of capes to count. Serenity gave them all a little wave as Lord Thorpe put aside the groom and helped his bride into the carriage himself.

Mrs. Right squinted. The trunks were loaded, the people were loaded and the carriage appeared perfectly fine. She let out a breath she had not even known she'd been holding.

The carriage set off. The coachman had the horses at a slow walk for the bon voyage. He would drive right by the duke's house so they might shout their good wishes. Serenity hung out the window and Mrs. Right could not remember when she'd seen her girl look so happy.

As the carriage slowly made its way past the duke's house there was a sudden shudder of the coach, the back half of it sunk to the ground, and the groom did a slow slide off the hide rumble.

Mrs. Right staggered. There was a moment of absolute silence before everyone sprang into action. The coachman jumped down from his box, the groom scrambled to his feet, and Lord Thorpe carried Serenity out and gently set her down on the street.

Lord Thorpe's butler ran out as he must have been watching from his window, that fellow keeping the house open and acting as governess to Nelson and Havoc.

The coachman had flung himself on the ground to peer underneath the carriage as Mrs. Right casually stepped behind the duke.

"It's the springs, my lord," the coachman said. "They've been tampered with, it looks like someone has loosened the bolts and taken a saw to the springs."

"Sabotage!" the lord's butler said. "Do you suppose—"

"The bag of tools discovered next to Lord Luddington's wall," Lord Thorpe said.

"Do you think it was your brother?" the duke asked.

Lord Thorpe seemed to consider it. "It might have been. I cannot imagine who else would have done it."

Mrs. Right was rather torn. On the one hand, it was not ideal that Lord Thorpe's brother was blamed for the damaged springs. On the other hand, it would be even less ideal if it were discovered that she'd crept over there under cover of darkness and done it herself.

"I know what we'll do," the duke said. "You'll take one of my carriages and I'll have yours fixed up. On the way back from Scotland you can detour to the Dales, and we can exchange again."

This was thought a genius idea all round. As everybody did seem so happy about it, Mrs. Right comforted herself that she might have been on the verge of admitting her crime, but now it seemed too late. After all, she might have.

Horses were unhitched, the broken carriage pulled away by all the footmen from both houses, one of the duke's carriages hitched up, and the couple were finally on their way.

Mrs. Right wildly waved, determined to add this interlude to more water under the bridge.

THE COUPLE TOOK their time making their way north and it was a full six days before they reached Mariton Lodge on the River Carron. As they had been heading north along the usual routes, it was hardly surprising that they did stop at some of the inns where the duke had made his mark.

However, Serenity soothed the innkeepers by pointing out that they would not ask for anything from the kitchens that they'd just invented, did not bring the duke, and did not bring the footmen who liked to live like lords on a grand tour.

They finally did arrive and Serenity had been rather taken aback by their destination. She'd not had any firm ideas of what a fishing lodge might look like, but she had imagined something very modest where they might cook their own food in the fireplace.

She supposed that was never going to be a duke's idea of a lodge. The place was exceedingly large and well appointed, and housed a bevy of staff. Those staff were rather grim-faced when they arrived, though they'd had notice of it. At least, they were grim-faced to her. They rather doted on Thorpe.

He finally explained that they would be prejudiced against her on account of her being a lady from London. They imagined she would think herself above them and a Scot did not believe they were below anybody at all.

It was always Serenity's nature to be kind and courteous, but once apprised of that idea she redoubled her efforts. Any request she made, even for just a tea tray, she spoke of as an outrageous favor. They did finally warm to her once they were convinced she was not going to swan around the place acting like she was better than them.

As well, they were a discreet group of people and gave Thorpe and Serenity plenty of privacy. That privacy was well taken advantage of. Early nights and late mornings in the best suite of rooms that overlooked the river became the schedule, and so dinner was early and breakfast late to accommodate the couple.

The staff of the house also did not seem to find anything amiss in the master and mistress wet-eyed over sunrise, sunset, the mist rolling in on the river, the local otters playing in the river, or really nothing at all. They had been used to the marquess' rather sentimental temperament and were approving of him bringing a bride who was even more sentimental. It was a deal better than the nose-up London lady they had feared. They could meet weeping in all equanimity, it was anybody forever pointing out their rank that would have set them off in a revolt.

Far in the future, their children would race through those corridors and delight in the local otter pair and defeat the staff with their good-heartedness. For now, though, a month had gone by very much faster than they'd imagined. Thorpe sent a letter to the duke informing him that they were delayed and would stay another fortnight. After that, they really did need to go. The Scots were not shy about hinting that they'd had enough for one season and looked forward to minding an empty house where nobody needed a tea tray.

A stop of some weeks was made in the Dales so that Thorpe and the duke could switch their carriages. It was an enlightening time for the marquess and he got a clearer picture of how the family became so original in their views. The lone individual in the vicinity of the estate that seemed to disapprove of their modes of living was the vicar, but as he owed the duke his living, his protests were rather half-hearted. They were their own kingdom, and the duke ruled as absolute king. Unless challenged by one of his daughters, as he could not hold up against them very well at all.

Lady Valor did begrudgingly allow them to leave the house at the end of the visit, though that was only because she was so taken up with Sir Galahad. The pup had grown while they were gone, but not by much. He was a pug after all. He was roly-poly and full of fun, though the duke commented that he looked as if he'd taken a hard run at a closed door and hit it face first. Lady Valor ignored that comment on Sir Galahad's scrunched features, and congratulated herself on the pup's survival, for as she said: "He really was on the brink of death. I nursed him back to health."

When Serenity and Thorpe arrived to Mariton Hall nobody could have greeted them more warmly than the Duke of Mariton. He did not keep it a secret that he'd waited for this day for years. He was a rather jolly fellow, and so he was willing to admit that his new daughter-in-law had been worth the wait.

The couple made a pilgrimage to the beehives to carry on the tradition of telling the bees of a wedding. There, Serenity was entirely relieved to note the slatted skeps. It might be imagined that a couple going to a hive to tell the bees of their union would make short work of it. "Dear bees, we are wed, we ask for your blessing and thank you to spread the news." There would not be much to be said beyond that, as the bees would not hold up their end of the conversation.

However, it was not to be supposed that this momentous meeting would be done in such an offhand manner by Serenity, who had been thinking of the bees since she was six years old. Her apology went on long, she eventually wept, then Roland went wet-eyed on account of his bride weeping, and then a groom ran across the field to discover what was wrong. Considering the disposition of the marquess and his bride, the poor fellow had assumed they'd been attacked by footpads or otherwise experienced a terrorizing event. He was sent away scratching his head after he was informed by the new marchioness that they were paying their respect to the bees.

Over the next months, Roland would have a proper crypt built for any dead bees turning up in the gardens. It was a large stone edifice with an enormous bee, fashioned from iron, plated in gold, and suspended over the doorway. Inside was a small fireplace where ash might be produced to dry out a dead bee and there were shelves where any bee might comfortably experience eternity. Serenity's box of already long-dead bees, which she had carefully carried from London to Scotland to the Dales and finally to Suffolk, was placed in it with solemnity.

Roland's father found himself befuddled by the whole palaver, but he'd demanded his son wed, and his son had wed. He'd never thought to put any stipulations on it against a strange affection for bees. In any case, he grew very comfortable with Serenity's brand of sentimentality and care. Especially when he grew older and she saw to his every comfort and read to him at night.

The marquess and his lady would go on to become exceedingly doting parents, but perhaps not very steady when steadiness was called for. Any time one of their children was ill enough for the doctor to be called, the two distraught parents spent most of their time pacing, wringing their hands, and weeping. Their very no-nonsense nurse had once been so exasperated she'd said, "For the love of all that's holy, stop planning funerals over head colds." That practical woman had presumed she'd be dismissed on the spot, but both the marquess and his marchioness found her scolding rather comforting.

The children Serenity brought into the world were of varying temperaments. The eldest, a girl, was not at all like her mother and father and was forever sighing over whatever they were wet-eyed over. She'd been named Margaret, though they would call her Daisy. Their son, Roland, was a copy of his father—a strapping lad with a sensitive nature who would do right by all the world.

Daisy and Roland, though so very different in their temperaments, would get on well. She would act as a bracing starch when it was needed, and he would act as a calm salve when it was needed. What they both had very much in common was their adoration of Dales ponies. Serenity's Jupiter and a lovely Dales stallion named Winter's Night had produced two fine specimens for them, named Sixes and Sevens.

Quinn would go on to become a steadying force on the premises. When the household was reaching an uncomfortable pitch, he might suggest deep breaths and chamomile tea. He would remind the couple that they often set each other off—one would be struck, which would strike the other.

They were just as sentimental regarding various animals on the estate, which seemed to increase their number with regularity. Somehow, injured or otherwise not perfect specimens were forever making their way there. Cats and dogs had the run of the house, horses were forever being fussed over. Havoc and Nelson made themselves very comfortable on the estate, roaming it at will. Havoc got in the habit of shortening his stride to allow his little friend to keep up with him. They were often to be found in the small wood, as locating a fallen branch and running with it to keep it away from the other became a favorite pastime.

Charles eventually did what Thorpe had predicted he would do—he'd spent some months on the continent and then returned as if nothing at all had occurred. His life, and his attitudes, were not to go on as they always had, though. Upon returning to Town, Charles was introduced to a certain Lady Mary Helderburton. His first impression of the lady had been as if he'd been hit on the head with a pile of bricks. For the first time in his life, Charles put another person on earth ahead of himself.

As Lady Mary was both practical and genial and not willing to contend with nonsense, Charles' habit of complaining over being the second son was speedily stopped by that lady. As he talked about it less, he began to think about it less. Over time, Charles and his brother would develop a cordiality of sorts. They would never be the best of friends, but Charles gave up his self-pity and bitterness in order to have Lady Mary by his side.

All that was to be, but for now, the couple must make plans to attend the next London season. Verity would take her place amongst the *ton* and they would be on hand to assist. They would be on hand very close by, too, as they were only two doors down on the square.

It was to be supposed that Verity would need all the assistance she could muster. She'd been in the habit of claiming to know things she certainly did not. A certain intellectual, Henry Foster, Baron Wembly, and esteemed member of the Royal Society, was poised to catch her out.

The End

About the Author

By the time I was eleven, my Irish Nana and I had formed a book club of sorts. On a timetable only known to herself, Nana would grab her blackthorn walking stick and steam down to the local Woolworth's. There, she would buy the latest Barbara Cartland romance, hurry home to read it accompanied by viciously strong wine, (Wild Irish Rose, if you're wondering) and then pass the book on to me. Though I was not particularly interested in real boys yet, I was *very* interested in the gentlemen in those stories—daring, bold, and often enraging and unaccountable. After my Barbara Cartland phase, I went on to Georgette Heyer, Jane Austen and so many other gifted authors blessed with the ability to bring the Georgian and Regency eras to life.

I would like nothing more than to time travel back to the Regency (and time travel back to my twenties as long as we're going somewhere) to take my chances at a ball. Who would take the first? Who would escort me into supper? What sort of meaningful looks would be exchanged? I would hope, having made the trip, to encounter a gentleman who would give me a very hard time. He ought to be vexatious in the extreme, and *worth* every vexation, to make the journey worthwhile.

I most likely won't be able to work out the time travel gambit, so I will content myself with writing stories of adventure and romance in my beloved time period. There are lives to be created, marvelous gowns to wear, jewels to don, instant attractions that inevitably come with a difficulty, and hearts to break before putting them back together again. In traditional Regency fashion, my stories are clean—the action happens in a drawing room, rather than a bedroom.

As I muse over what will happen next to my H and h, and

wish I were there with them, I will occasionally remind myself that it's also nice to have a microwave, Netflix, cheese popcorn, and steaming hot showers.

Come see me on Facebook! @KateArcherAuthor